HAUNTED TAYLORS

HAUNTED TAYLORS

SHAWN A. JENKINS

HAUNTED TAYLORS

iUniverse books may be ordered through booksellers or by contacting:

iUniverse
1663 Liberty Drive
Bloomington, IN 47403
www.iuniverse.com
1-800-Authors (1-800-288-4677)

ISBN: 978-1-4917-9635-1 (sc)
ISBN: 978-1-4917-9638-2 (e)

Print information available on the last page.

iUniverse rev. date: 08/10/2016

For my Mother…Doris Ilene Jenkins.

CONTENTS

A Letter to my Dear Friend ix

Foreword xiii

Chapter 1 1

Chapter 2 9

Chapter 3 16

Chapter 4 23

Chapter 5 32

Chapter 6 37

Chapter 7 42

Chapter 8 46

Chapter 9 51

Chapter 10 63

Chapter 11 66

Chapter 12 73

Chapter 13 82

Chapter 14 86

Chapter 15 99

Chapter 16 107

Chapter 17 113

Chapter 18 117

Chapter 19 122

Chapter 20 133

Chapter 21 137

Chapter 22 140

Chapter 23 146

Chapter 24 149

Chapter 25 157

Chapter 26 164

Chapter 27 169

Chapter 28 174

Chapter 29 176

Chapter 30 180

Chapter 31 185

Chapter 32 190

Chapter 33 199

Chapter 34 206

Chapter 35 210

Chapter 36 216

Chapter 37 218

Chapter 38 223

Chapter 39 226

Chapter 40 231

Chapter 41 235

Chapter 42 242

Chapter 43 245

Chapter 44 248

Chapter 45 252

Chapter 46 259

Chapter 47 265

Chapter 48 274

Chapter 49 280

Chapter 50 286

Chapter 51 288

Chapter 52 295

A LETTER TO MY DEAR FRIEND

The first time I met Stacia Taylor and her two grandkids I saw three persons that were as possibly typical as typical could be. Stacia was a hard working woman who had overcome many obstacles in her life. Her grandchildren, Sidney and Devon, I must admit, were two of the most well behaved young people I had seen in a long time, or in this particular era of our society.

When I was first approached about the Taylor's situation, I was at the outset, as one would believe, skeptical. The look of absolute desperation upon Stacia's face frightened me to the point where I wanted nothing to do with her. At 73 years old, I have had the not so welcomed privilege of hearing over the top, outlandish "fish tales." But there was Stacia, a woman that not only had nowhere else to turn, but was also suffering both physically and emotionally to the point where there were even murmurs of sending her away to some "special" hospital. I knew full well I couldn't have allowed that to take place.

I have at oft times been elicited by the younger members of my parish to view some of the cinema of today's film culture. However, what most of them do not seem to realize is that I not only have no interest whatsoever in movies, but I also haven't been to see a movie since 1982. With that being said, upon the Taylors' incident, I approached one of my members about a certain film, which will remain nameless, on such a matter as the Taylors were experiencing. Yes, it is Hollywood, but even an old miser like myself is at times forced to relegate to the undercrawlings of a certain territory in order to establish, if you will, a psychological understanding of sorts.

I remind you, I was not privy to the happenings that occurred after the preliminary attacks, so the Taylors' conduct after the fact will always be beyond me. But I am a firm believer in what I can and cannot see. That is one of the requirements of being a minister. It's called faith, my friend.

Have I myself experienced such ramblings personally? I'd rather not say, but I have come across those individuals who have at one point or another touched an alternate reality, but not like this case.

Is that what took place with the Taylors? It's hard to say. But I do believe that they themselves believed in what occurred. I have no right whatsoever in doubting any of them. No right.

I felt the worst for the grandchildren, they were young and unsuspecting. At first glance, at what was taking place, I felt that I should have at least contacted someone of authority just to make sure they were safe and sound. I've seen far too many tragic cases in my time of young ones being manipulated by their parents' psychological warfare's. But with Devon and Sidney, there was something completely out of sync. They, much like their grandmother, were actually falling down the same dark tunnel.

I remind you, I am not an exorcist. Do I believe in such rubbish? Perhaps at one time in our world's history, but with modern medicine and techniques, such tomfoolery can be rationally explained away. However, when I first ventured into that house, I knew right off the bat that there was something undeniably immoral.

I became aware of the house's backstory, as well as the person that once lived and died there. Such a history should only be locked away in the darkest regions of humanities soul. But as ugly and tormented as that house felt, I unfortunately realized that it was all the Taylors had left in the world, besides themselves.

Therefore, it was never about Husk Drive, it was always about Stacia, Sidney and Devon, three poor souls that longed only to be left alone to live their lives in peace. And at the end of the day, that is the longing of the human spirit. It's not about houses, supernatural beings or lack of money, but harmony in our lives.

I write this piece not only for you, my dearest friend, but also for myself. I knew the Taylors, and I knew of their plight. Yes, evil was afoot in their lives. I am certain of one thing, God is real, the Devil is real, and Stacia, Devon and Sidney were not delusional. What they encountered, malign as it could be, was as real as the hand that I am using to write this letter. Please do not ask me if I believe in evil...I just said that the Devil is real. I believe that fact from a personal standpoint.

And as I said before, I'd rather not elaborate upon my own personal experience at this course and time.

From what was recollected to me, for the Taylors, the ordeal inside that house lasted exactly 33 days. And then...everything for the Taylors came to an end.

Sincerely yours, Reverend Frederick Freehoff.

FOREWORD

Patrick: "Okay, okay, let's hurry and film this before we run out of tape."

Dee: "You act like we've been doing this all day long. We've only been at it for three hours."

Patrick: "I know that, but it's almost six, and I wanna hurry and get something to eat before the sun goes down.

Dee: "Oh, sorry, I forgot, big people are like vampires, they have to eat before they turn into stone."

Patrick: "Keep talking like that and I'll forget you're my fiancé."

Dee: "Knowing you, you probably forgot that two days after you proposed."

Patrick: "That's why I fell in love with you, that blunt, yet, compassionate humor."

Dee: "Okay, we're rolling. So, the question at hand is, do you, Patrick Rollins, believe in ghosts?"

Patrick: "Well, in order to believe in ghosts, one first must have a belief in a human soul. I may not practice my religion, but I do have this belief that we all have what most cultures call a soul. Now, in saying that, I believe that when a person dies, various happenings occur. Either their soul moves on, or it stays behind.

Dee: "Setting aside for a moment where a soul moves on to, why do you believe that some souls stay behind?"

Patrick: "It could be for a variety of reasons. Unfinished business. Anger. Or they may not be conscious that they're actually dead. In some religions they call that purgatory."

Dee: "So that's why we have ghosts in this world?"

Patrick: "You could say that. A spirit is a very peculiar entity. It exists between our living world and the world of the unseen. It experiences things both physically and emotionally that our human minds cannot even begin to fathom."

Dee: "So, let me ask you, how many ghosts or ghostlike occurrences have you experienced in your years of paranormal investigating?"

Patrick: "Is that supposed to be a trick question?"

Dee: "Honey, we have to document this in order to remain both relevant and factual. You don't want to apply to the institute and have everyone there believe a lie, do you? How else do you separate yourself from all the other paranormal investigators out there in this great big world?"

Patrick: "Okay, okay. Since both I and my team have been investigating paranormal happenings, I've encountered seventeen supernatural occurrences. Most notably at the Sutton Manor in Cincinnati."

Dee: "And what exactly took place there?"

Patrick: "We recorded about ten hours of raw footage of a chair levitating in mid-air. Pretty startling stuff."

Dee: "Oh really?"

Patrick: "C'mon, Dee."

Dee: "I'm only being impartial, dear."

Patrick: "It was pretty startling considering all those people that were murdered inside that house years ago. I'm surprised that's all we saw."

Dee: "Okay, here's the million dollar question. Have you ever seen a ghost?"

Patrick: "Uh…not yet. But Scott, our mic guy, said that he saw a woman dressed in a nightgown walking from the kitchen to the dining room."

Dee: "So?"

Patrick: "Not only was the woman glowing, but she had already been dead for seventy-two years."

Dee: "And where did this occurrence take place?"

Patrick: "This happened in Toledo about two years ago."

Dee: "I think it's amazing how the only ghosts people ever see are white women and girls dressed in white nightgowns. It's like all white females wear the same thing to bed right before they die. You hardly ever see any minority ghosts anywhere."

Patrick: "Are you gonna be serious, or you gonna clown me?"

Dee: "Sorry, go right ahead."

Patrick: "As I was saying, Scott actually approached this apparition."

Dee: "And what exactly took place?"

Patrick: "Well, according to Scott, the spirit stared at him before smiling and floating back into the kitchen and out of sight."

Dee: "Okay, cut. That's not what Scott told me. He said that the woman just vanished right there in the dining room."

Patrick: "You and I know that, but the university doesn't. We have to keep this interview lively. If we left it all up to Scott then he would've said that the woman screwed his brains out right there on the floor."

Dee: "Knowing him, I'm quite sure that's what he wanted."

Patrick: "Let's wrap for today. We'll do some editing in the morning."

Dee: "Do you honestly believe the university will fund us this time? I mean, after all, we do have raw footage."

Patrick: "Honey, your guess is as good as mine. Hell, if we don't come up with something soon, we're as good as dead ourselves."

Dee: "That's a great way of putting it."

Patrick: "It's the truth. You wanna be married at the Locklund Resort, or White Castle?"

Dee: "Perhaps we can say that we visited an old castle in England and that King Arthur's ghost threatened to behead us with Excalibur. Do you think that'll grab their attention?"

Patrick: "Keep it up; White Castle is looking more and more appeasing."

CHAPTER 1

"**W**atch John drop him on his head!" Devon hollered while sprawled out on the living room floor.

Sidney, rolling her eyes at her brother's jubilant rant, continued to feverishly punch away at her phone while Stacia, seated on the adjacent couch from her granddaughter, studied the words that were being texted back to her from her longtime friend.

She heard every word Devon was yelling at the television, including the curse words that the boy knew full well he wasn't supposed to be uttering, but to Stacia, the words might as well have been sign language because she was in her own world.

Every so often, she would glance up at the TV and watch as John Cena would bounce off the ring ropes onto his opponent, or watch as Sidney's eyes would light up every time a response she liked came across her phone's screen. Stacia, too, longed for the same kind of reply, or any reply at all. It had been well over five whole minutes and sitting there on the couch all crunched up like a caged beast didn't bode well for the woman that only saw her waiting time as an unbearable nuisance that she could have done without.

After so much glancing at the television Stacia decided that a cigarette would be in order. Smoking was always the one stress reliever, among many, that seemed to grant her a sense of stability in an otherwise staggering situation.

The very second she lit the tip of her Marlboro, her phone right then began to ring. Like she was in a race, Stacia pushed a button and breathlessly answered, "Hello!"

But the individual on the other end was only collecting for the Salvation Army. Stacia saw fit to not only roll her eyes but also push the off button as well.

"Holy crap, here comes the Big Show!" Devon screamed out in awe.

Upon any other instance, Stacia would have put a well ordered clamp down on the boy's euphoric Monday night stimulation, but on that evening, she could have honestly cared less. It was a text, and only a text, that seized her every emotion.

She puffed on her cigarette that was nearly half done before shaking the phone just to make sure it was still working.

After about nearly five minutes, it happened, and without any warning whatsoever, something hard and loud began pounding at the front door. Stacia's phone dropped to the floor before she jumped up and ran to the door.

Both Sidney and Devon stopped what they were doing at that instant to see what was happening. Stacia looked out the peephole before turning to Sidney and screaming, "Go get the gun!"

But Sidney was stuck in place on the couch she was seated on. Stacia pressed her body up against the door as hard as she could while the individual on the other end kicked at it with such a force that she could actually feel the wood pulsate against her backside.

A drenching sweat saturated Stacia's entire body as she used all of her might to keep the door from being pushed down on her.

Still, both Devon and Sidney sat still and petrified; it looked as if someone had hit the pause button on their lives, because neither would move a single muscle.

Staica tried and tried; the intruders on the other end were as strong as bulls and the door itself was about as sturdy as straw. Her hands were too sweaty to maintain a solid grip on the door.

"Somebody help us!" Stacia hollered her lungs out before the door hit her right in the face, sending Stacia flying to the floor.

"Get the fuck down on the floor, now!" One of the four black ski-masked invaders commanded as he waived his .38 in the air. "Close the door, man!" He ordered one of his comrades before running over and snatching the phone from out of Sidney's hand. "Get down on the floor!" He yelled as he pointed his gun at her face.

The child did as ordered, shaking hysterically on the way down.

"Please don't hurt my babies!" Stacia desperately cried as she attempted to get back to her feet.

"Bitch, get on the fuckin' floor!" Another one of the gunmen screamed, shoving Stacia back down.

"Get the little nigga and bring him over here!" The largest of the four ordered.

One of the other masked men did as he was told and yanked Devon by the arm, kicking and screaming to his grandmother.

Stacia quickly took hold of the boy and pulled him close to her bosom. Meanwhile, the larger masked man stood back. Stacia watched as the supposed leader waved his shotgun in the air and meandered about the small living room, appearing as though he were lost within the small space.

"Bring your ass over here!" He roared at Sidney as he snatched her up by her left arm. "Where is it?" He asked one of his subordinates.

"I think it's hidden in here somewhere, man!" One of the other men pointed to the China closet.

The leader pushed aside Sidney and joined the other three in the search. Stacia looked over at Sidney and stretched out her arms for her to come and join both her and Devon, but the girl wouldn't budge, she held herself while pulling down the bottom half of her long, white undershirt over her knocking knees.

Crying and shaking, Stacia pleaded, "Please, just take what you want and leave!"

But it was as if all four men hadn't heard a single word, as they tore apart the living room like rampaging beasts, tossing pictures, the coffee table and even the plasma TV onto the floor.

All Stacia could do was helplessly watch as her meager home was taken apart, piece by piece by the thugs that just barreled their way in, as though it was their house to begin with.

Every painstaking moment for Stacia was unfortunately set in slow motion in her frazzled mind. Her eyes shifted from one end of the living room to the other.

All four men reeked of weed and liquor as they haphazardly waved their weapons in the air like they were on a battlefield.

"Find it, nigga, so we can get outta here!" The leader of the pack roared as he shoved one of the other thugs into motion.

"What are you looking for?" Stacia yelled, still holding tight to Devon.

Stomping his way towards her with his gun pointed at Stacia's sweat soaked face, the leader furiously screamed, "Don't fuck with me, bitch! Where the fuck is it?"

"Where is what?" Stacia slobbered.

"The fuckin' money," he nearly hit her with the gun.

"I don't have any money!"

"This bitch is fuckin' lyin'!"

"I'm not lying!"

"C'mon, man, maybe it's in the bedrooms or something!" One of the other men urged while taking off for the nearby hallway.

"Grab these niggas and c'mon!" the leader barked before heading down the dimly lit corridor.

The other two men did as commanded and grabbed Stacia, Devon and Sidney along on the frenzied search.

Sidney was tossed into a corner while Stacia and Devon, still holding each other, watched in horror as the kids' bedroom and all its contents were thrown about in reckless abandon.

Both beds, that were placed side by side, were flung over. Their closet door was swung wide open. One by one, articles of clothing and shoes were pitched out and onto the floor. Posters of John Cena and Kanye West were ripped down from off the wall, along with a stereo that was picked up and hurled against the wall.

"Ain't nothin' in here, man!" One of the four called out.

"Try the bathroom, and then the other room!"

Once again, all three victims were yanked out of one room and into another. The bathroom was the next location on the tour, and just like the children's room, it, too, was ransacked, bit by bit.

The leader, who was built like a tank, nearly ripped the toilet from out of the floor in his ravenous pursuit to secure his aforementioned plunder.

"Bring their asses in here!"

From the wrecked bathroom, to Stacia's bedroom was the next stop. Like before, all the victims were told to sit down. As in previous rooms in the house, Stacia's bedroom was trashed beyond recognition. Powerless eyes viewed the carnage, looking as if they were watching a horror movie they couldn't shut off.

"Bring her little ass over here!" The leader hollered.

"No, no, stoppit!" Sidney squealed as one of the invaders pulled her by her hair over to where her grandmother and brother were standing.

Stacia stretched out her arms in desperation, only to be pushed back into a wall next to her bed. "Just take whatever you want and go!" She urged.

"Bitch, you know what I want!" The leader angrily remarked.

"No I don't!"

"Fuck this place up so we can get outta here, man!"

Stacia's oak dresser, as well as the drawers inside was turned over onto the floor. Earrings, necklaces and other various feminine items were strewn all over. For Stacia, it was like watching her entire life end right before her watery eyes.

Right above where the dresser once stood were pictures of both of her grandchildren, as well as an older black gentleman. Stacia watched in stunned repulsion as the precious valuables were smashed into pieces, one by one.

"Stop that!" She screamed with wrath. "You all stop breaking those pictures!"

But it seemed that all Stacia's angry voice did was add more fuel to the already intoxicated leader's fire.

"Who the fuck is you yellin' at, bitch?" He asked with a somewhat surprised tone as he approached her face with his shotgun.

"Stop throwing those pictures! You don't have to do that!"

"Grandma, please, don't yell at him!" Sidney begged.

"You need to listen to your girl over there!"

"And you need to get outta here!"

"What the fuck?" The leader fired back before striking Stacia in the jaw with the butt of his shotgun, sending her crashing to the floor.

Both Sidney and Devon screamed out in terror as they watched their grandmother fall flat on her face. Blood drizzled from her mouth; she could see two of her own teeth lying in front of her on the floor.

The pain from the blow should have sent Stacia reeling into nauseating agony, but her entire face at that point was already numb.

"Dumb bitch," the leader roared as he began to mercilessly beat Stacia's legs with his gun.

With every shred of hateful energy the man supposedly had locked up inside of him, he pummeled the woman like she was an unruly animal.

"Where the fuck is the money?" He kept on viciously screaming over and over.

The three remaining thugs stood by the two wailing grandchildren and looked on in still, speechless wonder, watching their leader take the robbery to a place they themselves probably never saw it going.

"I gotcha now," the raging leader panted heavily before ceasing his whipping tirade and pointing his gun directly to the back of Stacia's neck. "Bitch, I'm a mother fuckin' rida! You fuckin' wit' a rida!"

Stacia could feel the cold barrel of the weapon pierce her neck; she could hear the chilling fury in his voice that sounded like something from out of a nightmare. He just didn't sound human, he was something else completely.

Stacia held on with every fiber in her being. The woman could actually hear the man's finger tickle the trigger.

It was at that very instant in time that Stacia, rather than see her own life flash before her eyes, saw that of her grandchildren's. With one pull of the trigger, their existence would be left up to whatever fate the world saw fit to lay upon them.

Stacia was crying, she hadn't stopped since the invasion began, but just the knowing that Devon and Sidney would be without anyone caused her to grit her teeth as hard as she could while holding back the urine that wanted to spray out so urgently. All it would take was one pull of the trigger.

"C'mon, man, I think I hear the cops comin' this way!" One of the other intruders cautiously warned.

The leader stood there behind Stacia, seemingly ignoring his comrade while keeping his finger locked on the trigger. Stacia continued to hold on as though she were falling down a thousand feet.

"C'mon, man…we need to bail before five-0 gets here!" The man eagerly persisted.

The leader, with his gun still pointed against Stacia's neck asked, "Is the cops really comin'?"

"I hear 'em around the corner, man!"

A whole minute passed by before the leader eventually said, "Cool…we can come back anytime. Ya'll come on!"

One by one, all four individuals darted out of the bedroom. The very second the front door could be heard slamming shut, Stacia jumped up from off the floor and rushed over to her grandchildren.

The three, on the floor, held each other as tight as they all could while shaking and drowning in their own tears. The fact that Stacia's jaw was broken, and her legs were in excruciating pain was the furthest thing from her mind; she had her babies, safe and sound.

Stacia had at last hit the ground…face first.

CHAPTER 2

W ith a dimly lit cigarette dangling in between her lips and a tiny radio seated right next to her, Stacia sat at the small kitchen table as emotionless and composed as she had possibly ever been before in her forty-three years.

For the past three hours she had heard over and over again the news reports on the radio about her invasion. How reporters were not able to get an interview with the victims, police vowing to find the perpetrators and how traumatizing it must have been for the ones involved.

The more the news recounted the incident the number Stacia seemed to become. She couldn't move a single muscle there in the quiet kitchen. The bright morning sunshine seeped its way through the backdoor window, causing its luminescent glow to penetrate just about every corner of the dreary looking kitchen.

It had been exactly thirteen hours removed from the attack, but to Stacia, thirteen hours might as well have been thirteen seconds ago, because every hateful word, and every painful blow to her legs was as fresh and new as if it were happening all over again at that very moment.

Stacia was in pain, but there was nothing on earth as agonizing as watching the children cry and scream all night long. She could still see the looks on their faces as they were being snatched from one room to the other in the violent rampage. The shrill screams rang in her head like scraping steel. Yes, Stacia was in pain, but at that moment in the morning, she would have rather have been dead than to recollect upon her grandchildren's torture.

Stacia's long, black hair was tied up in the back in a ponytail. She had kept on the same clothes from the last evening, a pair of sweatpants, socks and a blue T-shirt that read, *Number One Granny.*

Her brown toned arms felt as heavy as cinder blocks; even if she wanted to reach over and cut off the radio, it would have been virtually impossible for her to do so.

Her brown, bloodshot eyes were glazed over and far off; she hadn't slept all night long, and she was about two seconds away from passing out right there on the table in front of her.

From out of nowhere, an older, brawny, black man came into the kitchen sighing, "I got the front door fixed up again, but the lock—

Stacia all of the sudden noticed that he had stopped talking. Ever so gradually, she lifted her head and watched as the man stood against the stove with his arms folded and a downcast face that reached the floor.

Stacia could sense just by his subtle body language that he wanted to talk, but whatever he expected her to say would be a flat out disappointment. Her words were lodged so deep down inside of her that all that would possibly come out would be gibberish.

"Are you even listening to that thing?" He pointed with his head at the radio.

Opening her eyes a bit more, Stacia replied, "Oh…I wasn't even paying any attention to that nonsense."

Lifting his self away from the stove, the man began towards Stacia saying, "I can tell that. Like I said a moment ago, I got the door back on its hinges, but the latch needs to be replaced."

"Okay." Stacia soberly answered while trying to keep her drowsy eyes open.

"You been to sleep yet, girl?" He asked while scratching at his mustache.

Chuckling lazily, Stacia said, "I'm tired, but I don't have the strength to sleep, if you can figure that out."

"I've been there a time or two." The man grinned somewhat. "Why did you send the kids to school today?"

Dropping her shoulders, Stacia shook her head, "I dunno, on one hand I wanted them to stay home, but on the other hand...I didn't want them to be around here all day long, either. Just too much to take."

"They'll have to come home eventually."

Slouching in her seat, Stacia sighed, "I know, I know. I'm just not thinking right."

Seconds later Stacia felt the strong, yet consoling hands of the man rub her aching neck and shoulders.

"Did you call off from work today?" The man asked softly in Stacia's ear.

Closing her eyes, she responded, "Yeah. Max said that I can take off the rest of the week if I needed to, but I'll go back tomorrow."

Breathing heavily, the man said, "So tell me, what exactly happened here?"

Stacia opened her lazy eyes and dragged out, "We were sitting in the living room. I was actually waiting for you to respond to my text."

Grunting from the belly, the man said, "Sorry about that, one of my nephews was calling me at the same time I was talking to you."

"Anyways, me and the kids were just minding our business, when all of the sudden someone starts kicking at the door, and then...

Stacia caught herself in mid-sentence. The sensation of throwing up seized her to the point where going any further with her explanation caused her to brace herself.

"What time did the cops roll around?"

Twisting her lips, Stacia moaned, "You know how long it takes those fools to get their asses here to this neighborhood." Stacia then put her head in her hands and mumbled, "They kept asking for money."

"What money?"

"The money, Dixon," she lifted her head.

"Oh…that money," Dixon slowly uttered. "How the hell did they know about that money?"

"Beats the shit outta me," Stacia tossed up her hands before shooting up out of her seat.

Walking towards Stacia, Dixon, with his head lowered to where only his eyes could be seen, murmured under his breath, "You know what the money was for, don't you?"

"Dixon, don't start that up again." Stacia groaned while rolling her eyes.

"Start what up again?"

"That money bullshit, I don't wanna hear it!"

"You don't wanna hear it, huh?"

"No I don't, so let's just close the damn subject!"

"You need to hear this!" Dixon strongly stated. "Last year, your damn car got stolen right in front of this place. Five months ago, the kids got jumped while playing down at the park. Last month, someone did a drive by and shot up the front window. And then, last night. What the hell is it gonna take for you to finally wake up and realize that this fuckin' neighborhood is gonna be the death of you three?"

"That money is for the kids' college."

"College," Dixon questioned amazed. "What good is college if both of those kids are too dead to attend? We've been over this ten thousand times!"

Stacia closed her hazy eyes and said, "I just can't squander that money away just like that."

"You're not squandering anything, you're trying to survive!" Dixon passionately yelled. "You owe it to those babies, and yourself!"

Without even looking at the man, Stacia could feel every word that Dixon spoke soak into every pore in her body. The subject itself was age old, but just recalling all of the past incidents that occurred at the house only caused a bitter stir to rumble inside her already queasy stomach.

Unable to look at the man any longer, Stacia limped herself into the living room to find the plasma TV on the floor, as well as various other items such as two lamps and the coffee table that was flipped upside down.

Once she was through scanning the wrecked living area, Stacia ventured down the hallway and into her own bedroom. She stopped right at the threshold; it was as though something were blocking her further progression.

From where she was standing was enough to break her into a million pieces. Her bed, dresser and everything else that mattered was demolished. But the one that thing that seemed to inflict the most misery upon her was the picture of her grandchildren that was broken apart. Stacia stepped over mountains of clothes just to get at the frame.

Ignoring her aching legs, Stacia knelt down, and with quivering hands picked up the shattered pieces of the photo. She had plenty of pictures of the children, but that particular one was the most valuable to her. The invaders even managed somehow to rip the photo into shreds; all that was left were bits that were too small to be taped and repaired.

All Stacia could do was drop the pieces back to the floor and look back at Dixon with watery eyes. For her, it wasn't so much the look of the bedroom or the house itself that shocked Stacia as much as it was the feeling. The four intruders left an ugly, permanent print on the house.

The entire home felt dreadful, like it had been raped. She could still hear the voices screaming and yelling. Stacia could see her babies being tossed and dragged from one end of the room to the other.

Dixon proceeded to take Stacia into his arms, but Stacia managed to slip away before he could even put a single hand on her.

Stacia began to wander the bedroom, talking to herself along the way. "I was sitting in the kitchen thinking. I'm forty-three years old. I've worked all my life, and…this is how life repays me? I can't get a raise at my job after two years, but I can get four black ass motherfuckers comin' in and trashing my fucking house?" Stacia angrily screamed.

Once again, Dixon tried to embrace the woman while saying, "Come here, girl and settle down."

But Stacia kept on evading the man as she continued to ramble on as a loud vehicle outside played its music for the whole neighborhood to hear. "I have to sit back and listen to that fuckin' shit every day and night? I hate this fucking shit! I hate it to hell! I hate it, I hate it, I hate it!"

Stacia stomped and hollered while picking up clothes and tossing them in all directions. "I hate these ghetto motherfuckers! I hate all their fucking asses! I hate them all!"

Stacia kicked, tossed and cursed until tears flooded from her eyes, and blood started to froth from out of her mouth.

Dixon forcefully grabbed Stacia by the arms as she continued to fight and scream. Stacia tried to free herself from whomever it was that had her restrained. It was blind fury that was pushing her along, and she was as resilient as the one holding her down.

Dixon then snatched Stacia by the neck before pressing his lips against hers and forcing her against him as hard as he could.

"Stoppit," she hollered.

But Dixon would not pull back. Stacia kept on fighting and trying to shove the man away until fate eventually set its way on in.

Stacia's tight lips began to loosen, allowing her tongue to come out of her mouth and into Dixon's. Her physical resistance soon yielded, as did her crying.

Dixon squeezed all over Stacia's ass while taking his lips away from hers and placing them on her neck. Stacia whimpered and moaned while kissing all over the man's greying hair.

Dixon then pulled off Stacia's t-shirt and sucked all over her bare breasts. Stacia cried out in bliss while rubbing all over his head.

Dixon laid Stacia down onto the pile of clothes that were on the floor before pulling down her sweatpants and pink panties and bowing his head in between her quivering legs.

Stacia closed her eyes and clinched her fists before screaming out the name of "God" and shoving the man's head deeper into her snatch.

"My tongue…is bleeding." Stacia faintly whimpered as she felt Dixon's tongue play with her ultra-sensitive clit.

CHAPTER 3

T he house reeked of cigarette smoke from one end to the other. From the time she and Dixon had finished their business, up until the man left she had emptied at least two and a half packs of smokes.

Clothed in a pair of faded blue jeans and a tank top shirt, Stacia did exactly what she had been doing all day long, wandering the house back and forth.

She wasn't concerned about going back to work the next day, and the incident, while still fresh in her mind, was beginning to lose it potent sting after so many hours removed. She was hard pressed about the children. They would be home from school in only a matter of minutes, and the house was still a brazen mess.

Their weeping and yelling from the night before was beginning to give her a headache; not so much that she hated to hear them cry, but just knowing that they were only mere feet away from death.

As soon as she was done gawking at her own bedroom, Stacia turned around to see the children's' room which was located on the other end of the hallway. The woman, with a cigarette in between her lips, stood at the threshold and looked in at the wrecked bedroom.

From where Stacia was standing she could see Devon and Sidney being restrained in a corner while watching their room being ransacked.

Stacia's legs wobbled. The room itself was a cramped area; just having two beds inside of it only seemed to take up all the more room, but somehow the kids always seemed to find a way to carve out whatever space they needed in order to breathe.

Before Stacia could step any further, on the floor, all crumpled up, was Devon's beloved poster of John Cena. Right then and there the woman began to cry like a baby before she carefully laid the poster back down onto the floor and out of sight.

The very second Stacia got back up, out of the corner of her right eye she spotted a tiny hole next to where Sidney's bed once sat. Wiping her eyes, Stacia strolled over and bitterly examined the crevice where a stray bullet shot through just missing the little girl by scant inches.

Once more, just the thought of knowing that one of her babies was near death not only caused Stacia's tears to erupt, but also a swell of rage and contempt to boil over.

She truly hated her environment, so much so that just talking to her neighbors was a burden. Nothing about the community in which the Taylors lived gave Stacia one morsel of solace. Just knowing that she was only a few feet away from a mother who had a different man around her children every weekend caused Stacia to roll her eyes in repulsion. Clear on the other side of the street was a drug house that everyone else in the neighborhood wouldn't even dare look at twice for fear that one false eyeball could very well raise an unwanted suspicion amongst the residents of the trashy home.

Yes, it was outright hatred that overwhelmed Stacia, so much so that the tears she was crying caused her to not see straight. She detested every loathsome, disheveled house on the block. Every low pants riding thug that bounced by down the sidewalk. And even more, the booming cars that rather than just pass by on their way to the main road, would instead sit and talk with someone they happened to know while blasting their vile music for the world to hear.

It was disgust that propelled Stacia along; Dixon's speech earlier in the day was the spark, the bullet holes in the wall and the cramped living space in which all three had to exist was the fuse, but what took place last evening was the eventual explosion. Stacia already had plans for the money she had stashed away, but for the time being those plans would have to be shoved aside. She at last realized that she needed her hatred to inspire her further along. It wasn't what she wanted, but then again, there were a lot of things Stacia Taylor didn't want, but she ended up with all the same.

Stacia left the wall and went for her bedroom. Removing clothes away from a particular part of the floor, she knelt down and slid back a sliver of carpet to reveal a small hatch. Stacia lifted open the hatch, reached into a hole and pulled out a shoebox. Within the box was wrapped wads of hundred dollar bills. Stacia eyed each and every wad while still holding onto the irate bitterness that she needed.

The instant she heard the rattling at the front door, Stacia immediately stuffed the bills back into the box before stuffing the box itself back into the hole in the floor.

"Grandma…are you here!" Sidney called out in a nervous stutter.

Stacia, crippled legs and all, sprinted out of the bedroom to find both Sidney and Devon, clothed in their white shirts and navy blue slack school uniforms, standing by the door, appearing as if they were too afraid to step any further.

Fixing her hair and cleaning her face, Stacia grew out a forced smile before looking at the little girl and asking, "Didn't you see my car out there, honey?"

Sidney, with her pony tail and flushed face just tossed her book bag to the floor before dropping her skinny self down onto the couch.

Sighing, Stacia questioned, "Well, how was school today?"

"It was fine," Devon replied while taking off his glasses and cleaning them with his own spit, "everyone asked how we was doing."

"No, it wasn't fine." Sidney jumped in. "Everybody kept on looking at us all strange and asking us if there was anything they could do for us. I hate going to school." She pouted.

Cracking a tired grin and planting herself down next to Sidney, Stacia remarked, "It's not school you hate, honey, its everyone in your face all at once." Stacia then breathed out saying, "I hate that I sent you two to school today. But I just didn't think it would be…

Stacia had to catch herself in mid-sentence just to keep from bawling in front of the kids. She then pulled Sidney close to her before motioning for Devon to come and join them on the couch.

Sighing as heavy as she could, Stacia said, "Look…I know what happened last night was scary. And I am sorry for sending you both to school today. But…last night will hopefully be the last time that ever happens again."

Sidney looked up at her grandmother and asked, "Are you gonna get a gun?"

Chuckling mildly, Stacia remarked, "No, baby, we're moving to another house."

Right then, it was as if someone had set off a series of fireworks inside the living room because both Sidney and Devon's faces lit up with such animated jubilance at the same time.

"Are we gonna move to where Rodrigo lives at?" Devon smiled from ear to ear.

"Can we move to Dawson Hills, please?" Sidney begged. "They have all those really pretty houses over there?"

Amused by the children's excitement, Stacia patiently stepped in. "Hold on, just hold on. We're gonna find a place that I can afford, and one that is safe. Safer than this neighborhood," she grimaced.

"Can we move somewhere where they won't beat me and Sid up anymore, Grandma?"

Stacia caressed the boy's face before saying, "I sure hope, son. Somewhere we don't have to worry about the wrong kind of element bothering us."

Without warning, Sidney began to cry. Stacia lifted the girl's head up, and with a worried look on her face she asked, "Sweetheart, what's the matter?"

At first, it appeared as though she couldn't even open her mouth to speak, but after so many minutes of breathtaking weeping, Sidney finally replied, "I'm sorry…I was too scared to call the police last night."

It was happening, the moment in time that Stacia dreaded more than anything else. All she could do at that point was grab Sidney and hold her until she stopped crying, while trying to keep herself from unloading all over again.

"Stop that, little girl." Stacia clenched her body. "You didn't do anything wrong. We all were scared last night. You have nothing in this world to be sorry for. You hear me?"

Sidney only shook her head yes while being coddled inside her grandmother's bosom. Stacia wanted to hold her for as long as she could and never let go, but she soon realized that words were as potent as physical intimacy.

Pulling away from Sidney, Stacia grinned at the girl and asked, "Besides, you're only nine years old. What makes you think you could've done something?"

"I bet if I was big like the Big Show then I could've beat them up!" Devon pumped his tiny fists.

Laughing at the boy, Stacia said, "I bet you could have, too, baby. One day maybe, one day. But you're only seven; you've got a long way to go still."

"Where are we moving to?" Sidney wiped her eyes.

Getting up from off the couch, Stacia said, "I don't yet, I still have to do a lot of looking."

"Can we still go to the same school?"

Stacia stood and pondered for a moment. The questions were coming so rapid fire that she was finding it hard to catch them all at once. Not one time during the day had Stacia even considered where in the city they would possibly end up.

Shaking it all off like dust, Stacia turned back to the kids and said, "Look, we'll cross that bridge when we come to it. Right now, I want you both to go into your room and pack up your clothes; we're going to stay in a hotel for a few days."

"Why can't we stay with Dixon, Grandma?" Devon batted his eyelashes.

Stacia, looking as if she were caught completely off balance, stood and stared down at the child for a few seconds before eventually coming to and responding, "Because…Dixon has other things to do right now."

"Well, can I get another John Cena poster since mine is all torn up?"

"Yeah, baby…we'll see what we can do." Stacia muttered under her breath.

Without another word, both children shot up from off the couch and raced down the hallway. Stacia couldn't even watch them any longer. All she could hear from the living room was the clatter of drawers being opened and two children rummaging about like they were opening gifts on Christmas morning.

The very second Stacia found the strength to move, she took both a cigarette and her lighter out of her pants pocket before going to the front door and lighting up.

With menacing, red eyes, Stacia smoked along while viewing her ragged neighborhood from one end of the street to the other. Not one speck of the community pleased her.

Directly across the street, a young, hefty black woman came out of her house yelling and screaming at her three children like they were cattle that needed prodding.

Stacia only eyeballed the surly woman like her very presence in the world was a pox upon humanity. Curlers and flip flops with her large breasts nearly falling out of her shirt for all to see.

The instant the woman looked up and saw Stacia she smiled and shouted as loud as she could, "Hey, girl, how ya'll doin'?"

Without parting her lips, Stacia dashed her cigarette out on the pavement before twisting her scornful lips and going back inside her house, slamming the door shut as hard as she could behind her.

CHAPTER 4

The following morning caught Stacia sitting inside her car staring straight ahead at the massive building where she worked.

All she could think of was Devon and Sidney and their ordeal at school the day before, having to be ogled and coddled like poor, little victims. Stacia knew full well what she was in store for the second she stepped inside, and she was also aware that sitting and sulking over the situation wasn't going to lighten her load any more.

Ever so gradually she pulled the keys out of the ignition, got out of her 2008 grey Saturn and dragged herself towards the building like her two feet were made of solid brick.

It was a cloudy, but warm morning, which was why she kept her light jacket unzipped. Her loose fitting jeans and sweatshirt were beginning to stick to her skin. The closer she drew to the building the more Stacia began to realize that perhaps going back to work so soon wasn't a good idea, no matter how many more vacation days she had left.

"Excuse me, Ms. Taylor!" A female voice shouted from behind.

Stacia stopped dead in the middle of the parking lot and spun around to see a plump, middle-aged white woman running towards her. Stacia didn't recognize the woman, and the closer she drew the more she wanted to race back to her car and drive away.

The woman was dressed in a tan suit jacket and matching slacks. Stacia right off the bat could feel the sweat encapsulate her body like someone had rubbed her down with a wet rag.

Huffing and puffing, the woman said, "Good morning, Ms. Taylor."

"Good morning." Stacia uneasily mumbled.

With a smile, the woman continued, "Sorry I had to call out your name like that, I wanted to catch you before you got inside."

Eyeing her from head to toe, Stacia asked, "What do you need?"

"My name is Detective Paulson. I'm investigating the robbery that took place at your home. I dropped by your place yesterday, but no one answered the door."

Nervously, Stacia glanced at two workers that were entering the building before turning her attention back to Paulson and saying, "Yeah…I kinda had other things going on yesterday."

"I completely understand. I'll only be a moment."

It was a moment that Stacia could have done without. She didn't want to recall any part of the incident, just having it thrown back in her face, at work of all places, seemed demeaning at that point.

"Ms. Taylor, I just wanted to ask about the assailants themselves. You mentioned in your statement that it was four men, correct?"

"Yeah," Stacia muttered.

"I see." Paulson shook her head while scribbling in a note pad. "Now, you said that they were masked. Did you notice anything distinctive about the assailants? Anything that stood out the most?"

Agitated, Stacia began to fidget in place while saying, "Look, I told the police everything I needed to. You have to understand, everything from that night was a blur. It all happened so fast."

Appearing compassionate, Paulson slipped her pen and pad back into her jacket pocket and said, "I totally understand, Ms. Taylor, but we have reason to believe that the assailants may have struck in other places in the city. From what you were able to describe to police the other night, they sounded awfully familiar. There was a similar incident that occurred back in December on the west side of town—

"Yes, I'm familiar with that story, but I have to go to work now." Stacia impatiently interrupted. "And please, I'd appreciate it if you wouldn't come by my job again. If you have any more questions for me, you all have my phone number."

And just like that, Stacia turned and left Detective Paulson in the parking lot where she found her. She didn't even take a second to turn around and look at the woman one last time.

From the parking lot, Stacia used her security badge to let herself into the building. Once inside, she was met by two male guards who wanded her from top to bottom before allowing her to proceed any further.

"How you doing, Stacia," one of the guards casually asked.

Without even looking at the man, Stacia just replied, "Good, good."

Stacia then stepped through two, large doors on her way out into an open and loud area filled with roaring machines. Forklifts ripped back and forth across the floor while people worked diligently to load trucks with whatever boxes and supplies they needed.

As she walked along, with her eyes stuck to the floor beneath her, Stacia could sense faces beaming at her; she didn't even have to look up, it was as apparent as the air that she was breathing.

"Hey, Miss Stacia, how you doin'," a young, white man passionately cooed from his loading station.

Stacia glanced at the grinning fellow and gave a brief wave before seeing the office that was located up a flight of steel stairs.

Like a cat, the woman leapt up the steps and opened the office door to see one heavyset, older, grey bearded white man seated behind a desk, and a white woman sitting on the other side.

"I'll talk to you later, Jane." The man said.

Jane got up from her seat and handed Stacia a polite smile before exiting the office. Once the door was closed, Stacia dropped her tired body down into the already warm seat and exhaled all the stress of the morning out like hot steam.

For moments there settled a calm quiet in the small office. Every so often the phone that sat on the desk would ring, but neither individual seemed to care enough to answer the thing.

Holding a pen in his hand, the man looked up and quietly asked, "How are you and the kids?"

Stacia lifted her heavy head and replied, "We're doing okay, I guess."

Once more, a prevailing silence took place inside the office. All that could be heard was the overbearing racket of forklifts and ringing bells from outside in the warehouse area.

"What did they do to your face?" He pointed at Stacia.

Rubbing her chin, Stacia said, "One of the bastards hit me with his gun."

"Did they hurt the kids?"

"No, they're fine," Stacia scrounged about in her seat.

"You know that a lot of people around here are worried about you."

"I know, I wish I had stayed home today again."

"I told you to take as much time as you needed to."

"I know, Max, but I just couldn't stay in that fucking place anymore. I feel like a prisoner in that house… in that neighborhood. Me and the kids stayed at a hotel last night, and that's probably where we'll end up staying until we find another place."

Max suddenly sat up in his chair and asked with a blushing face, "You mean to say that after all this time, you're finally gonna move?"

Cracking a grin, Stacia huffed, "Yes, Max, I'm gonna look for another place."

"You know you should've done that when the drive-by happened."

"I know, I know." Stacia urged. "But…I had other plans for my money."

"Stacia, you're damn lucky to even be alive right now, you and the kids. Where do you plan on moving to?"

"I don't know, I haven't had a chance to think that far ahead."

Shrugging his hefty shoulders, Max suggested, "Why not Clinton Hills, or down on the south end around Highbank?"

Opening her eyes as wide as she could, Stacia exclaimed, "Do you know how much houses out there cost? I work on a loading dock, not Wall Street."

"All I'm saying is that Lane has a lot of nice places, way better than where you guys live right now."

"I need something that I can afford on my budget. I got a car note, the kids' tuition and I'll have to make mortgage payments because I am not going back to section eight again; I'll hang myself before that happens." Stacia strongly stated.

"Hold on, no one said you had to go back to section eight, I'm just saying that you have plenty of options on the table. Not every neighborhood in this city is ghetto."

Turning her head away, Stacia lamented, "Yeah I know. I just feel like it's all been taken out of my hands. I had so many plans for us three, now…now those plans are fucked."

"They don't have to be. It could be worse."

"How so," Stacia stared hard at the man.

"You could live up in Addington."

"Oh, good God," Stacia rolled her eyes while laughing out loud. "You just love giving me good news, don't you?"

"That's what I'm here for, sis," Max laughed back.

As soon as Stacia caught her breath, her body was suddenly overcome with a sensation of subtle relief. Just joking and talking about moving to another place seemed to grant the woman a brief and much needed respite from the chains she had been shackled to ever since the incident took place.

"I told the kids that I would look for a place tonight when I got home."

"Good girl." Max said. "In the meantime, take it easy around here. For the first time in months we have a full crew today."

"Oh really," Stacia lit up. "What happened, did you tell them that if they showed up they would get free pizza for lunch?"

"Don't ask me, all I know is that with a full crew we may actually get out of here before five this evening." Max said as he got up from out of his seat and handed Stacia the daily duty roster.

Stacia took the clipboard and discussed a few more matters with the man before leaving the office and heading downstairs to her main work area where at least thirty people were hard at work packing boxes, scooting them across the floor on pallet jacks or loading them onto trucks.

Some of the people greeted her with kind smiles and warm embraces, while others just carefully glanced at her, either too embarrassed to say anything or just plain too busy and indifferent to even give a second notice. Nonetheless, Stacia stayed her course, handing out specific orders to those working under her.

The second she put on her thermal hat, Stacia went about the diligent process of packing as many boxes as she could before sending them down the assembly line for the next process to follow.

The tedious detail went on for hours. From time to time the monotony was broken up by the chatter amongst co-workers, provided they paid attention to their work along the way.

Mindless rants involving spouses, boyfriends, girlfriends, kids and the such were common banter for the workers. It managed to keep each person on their toes. In times past, for

Stacia, the daily rattling's were just another day in her weekly routine, but on that particular morning, she needed every bit of coarse, non-job related dialogue that she could stand just to keep her mind off of home. Home was exactly where the pain existed, and for the very first time, work was the liberation that was relished with zeal.

"Hey, Stacia, we missed you yesterday." The young, white fellow smiled behind her.

Wrapping a box up, Stacia turned around with a blasé, sly smirk on her face and looked the young man up and down.

He wore a Cincinnati Bengals ball cap, a white undershirt and a pair of baggy sweatpants. His brand new pair of Nike's and the gold chain around his neck suggested to Stacia that he was in the mood for impressing. But nonetheless, Stacia held on to her smirk as if she were supposed to be amused by the character.

"We missed you yesterday, beautiful." He slinked his way over to her end of the assembly line.

"Oh really," Stacia batted her eyelashes. "And just what about me did you miss, Jeremy?"

Jeremy stood and scanned his supervisor from top to bottom with drooling eyes before saying, "Everything and more, sexy." "Boy, if you don't come over here and get these boxes I'm gonna wrap your Vanilla Ice ass up in one!" A fat, black woman irately yelled.

Stacia, along with a few others, laughed at Jeremy before her attention was all of the sudden distracted by an old, white woman that was losing boxes left and right from her end of the line.

Stacia dropped what she was doing and ran over to aid the woman. One by one she helped the elderly lady pick up her stack of boxes from off the floor before staring at her and asking, "Are you new here?"

At first the woman didn't reply. She just steadily reached down and scooped as many boxes as she could fit in her frail arms. Stacia continued to stare down the woman with an odd curiosity that wouldn't let go.

She was a fragile, white haired woman who looked as though she belonged in a nursing home rather than a warehouse lifting fifty pound boxes in an eight and a half hour day.

Stacia eyed the liver spots that covered her arms before taking the box she had in her hands and placing it down on the conveyor belt.

"Honey, what's your name?" Stacia looked hard at the woman.

With a shivering jaw, the lady answered, "My name is Judy, ma'am."

Blushing, Stacia said, "You don't have to call me ma'am, I ain't that old." Stacia then squeezed her eyes and asked, "Sweetheart, are you sure you can handle this?"

Judy shook her head yes before smiling, "I may be old, but I can still move with the best of them."

Stacia only handed the woman a compulsory smile, as to say she was amused with the sweet, old thing before saying, "Well," she sighed while gazing around the area, "I can't have you lifting heavy boxes, you'll hurt yourself. But, we could possibly have you do some janitorial work, if you want. I mean, it may not be what you signed up to do, but it's not as hard as lifting boxes, either."

Judy only frowned before lowering her head and taking off her work gloves. Stacia felt bad for the woman, but as sorry as she felt for Judy, she was wise enough to realize that the woman had no business even being inside a warehouse, let alone working on an assembly line.

Once Stacia situated Judy with a broom and dust pan she quickly went over to Max who was herding along his own group of workers. She approached the busy man and pointed, "How long has that woman been here? I've never seen her before."

Max stopped what he was doing and stared over at Judy who was steadily sweeping the floor with her extra-long broom.

"Uh…I don't know for sure. I don't remember seeing her much."

Frowning, Stacia said, "She looks like she's ninety-nine years old."

Max only giggled before saying, "Perhaps she is. I'll check the roster later and find out what temp agency she's with."

Stacia walked away from the man and carried herself back to her group, all the while keeping a vigilant eye on the elderly woman slowly pushing her broom up and down the floor.

Not once did Judy take her eyes off of the floor upon which she was working.

CHAPTER 5

That evening, inside the hotel room, Stacia sat at the desk while scrolling through various houses that were pictured on her laptop computer.

The children were in the room along with her watching television and doing their homework. Stacia was aware of their presence, but she had an ardent duty to undertake. She had been at it ever since picking the kids up from their afterschool program.

Page after page and house after house; searching for the right school districts, the proper community, distance, local shops, the commute from the house to work, nothing was overlooked or simply glanced at. Stacia made extra sure to study each residence with meticulous precision.

"Grandma, I'm starting to get hungry." Devon whined, standing behind Stacia and rubbing his belly.

"Okay, baby." Stacia replied in a far off tone without even taking her face away from the computer screen.

"Grandma, can we have pizza tonight, please?" Sidney soon chimed in. "I don't want any more of that lasagna we had last night, it gave me a stomach ache."

Stacia could hear chatter linger behind her, but after so much of it came at her all at once, she eventually managed to tune it out, much like turning off a radio.

Stacia scrolled down several more pages before knocks at the door interrupted her all-consuming concentration.

"I'll get it!" Devon excitedly panted.

"No you won't!" Stacia jumped up from her seat before going to the door and opening to see Dixon standing on the other end with three pizza boxes in his large arms.

"Dixon!" Sidney and Devon leaped for joy.

Stacia kissed the man on the lips before stepping aside and letting him and his dinner in. She stood back and watched as Dixon interacted with the children like he himself were young all over again.

There were times when she would just step away and look on at the three with the kind of fondness that she herself savored.

Walking towards the three, Stacia said, "You must've read their minds, because all they could talk about was pizza."

"I've been craving it myself for the past few days." Dixon said while gnawing away at a piece.

Stacia sat down on one of the beds before helping herself to several slices. For at least a half an hour, all four individuals ate, watched television and carried on about their day. Once more, Stacia found herself in a familiar, warm place, far from the cage of two nights earlier.

Once she was done eating, Stacia got up and went back to her laptop. Dixon stepped up behind her and asked with pizza breath, "You found anything yet?"

"Grandma is gonna get us a mansion!" Devon eagerly exclaimed.

"No she's not!" Sidney scolded her brother.

"That's enough, you two." Stacia stepped in. "If there is one thing about this house hunting that I'm concerned about is how far it'll be from their school." Stacia said to Dixon.

"Can't you move them to another school?"

With her face stuck to the computer screen, Stacia responded, "You know how hard and long I fought just to get those two onto the waiting list for that school, Dixon. It's a good school. The teachers there are really good, and I love their afterschool program. Nope, no matter where in Lane we move, they're going to that school no matter what."

"On Friday they got free popcorn day for everybody!" Devon explained.

"They have, not", 'they got, baby.' Stacia corrected the child before she got up out of her seat and escorted both herself and Dixon out of the room and onto the hotel's balcony.

The second Stacia shut the door behind her, she went around Dixon and leaned up against the balcony's railing before folding her arms and saying, "I got a visit from some detective today at work."

Frowning, Dixon asked, "What the hell was a detective doing there?"

"I wasn't at home, so she decided to stop by there."

"What did she want?"

"She said that she may have a lead on the bastards that attacked us the other night. Apparently they did the same thing some months ago."

Appearing absolutely enraged, Dixon growled, "Man, when I find these motherfuckers, I'm gonna blow their fuckin' heads off! Each one!"

Sighing, Stacia said, "What good is that gonna do anyone, Dixon? I'm sure they got some boys of their own that'll come back after you. You see? This is what's got me so on edge. All this thug shit. You and I both came up being surrounded by this life. Is that all we black folks know? How to kill each other?"

Dixon calmed his furious body enough to where he could slump his hulking back against the stone wall. While Stacia remained perched against the balcony's railing, glancing down at the parking lot.

"But they almost killed you three!"

"But they didn't. And that's what matters the most." Stacia defiantly remarked before wiping strands of hair away from her eyes. "The kids asked me why we can't come and stay at your place."

Dixon stood straight up at that instant and asked wide-eyed, "What did you tell them?"

"I didn't say anything; I just let the matter go."

Handing Stacia a nervous grin, the man tossed up his hands and said, "Look, I just got—

"We're getting too old for this, brotha." Stacia interposed herself. "Those babies in there love you to death, Dixon. As far as their concerned, you're their grandfather. They don't know anything else. There was this old woman at work today. She looked like she could have been at least a hundred and ten. There she was, trying her hardest to lift boxes. It was the most pathetic thing I think I've ever seen. But all day it got me to thinking."

"Thinking about what?"

"About our lives," Stacia said under her breath. "I hate to put it like this, but that attack made me wake up, as hateful as it was. Things need to start changing. This hotel room is nicer than our house. I still live in the damn ghetto after all these years." Stacia clenched her teeth before coming to a deep pause in her tirade. "I'm still not married after all these years."

If there was one point in her conversation that seemed to make Dixon perk up, it was the beleaguered "M" word. The man began to step forward until he was within arm's reach of Stacia.

"It almost all ended that night." Stacia began to whimper. "I got my babies staying inside a hotel room because some sorry bastards are too lazy to go out and get a job; meanwhile, my black ass is working at a warehouse, lifting boxes all day long like I'm some machine. I had plans for my life?"

Stacia stared straight into Dixon's face. She could spot what resembled a blemish of compassion begin to seep its way from out of the man's granite interior. She wasn't exactly trying to gain his sympathy, but it helped her all the same to know that at least he understood where she was coming from, above all else.

Pointing to the hotel room door, Stacia continued, "Those babies in there are the only things that matter to me. Things have got to change. I'm not gonna end up like that old woman, crippled and broken down. I'm tired of thugs and the way things used to be. It's time to move forward."

The moment she was done talking, Stacia put out her right hand. Dixon took it into his own mammoth paw and held it tight.

The breeze that passed by was cool and unsettling, but Stacia could hardly even feel it, she was still coming down from her zealous rant. But it was then that she realized that the fury she thought she had expunged the day before hadn't been exhaled to its fullest extent.

With his head to the ground, Dixon mumbled, "Do you think we could get away for at least twenty minutes somewhere?"

Stacia only twisted her lips and giggled before saying, "Leave it to a man to have one thing on his mind."

CHAPTER 6

Lunchtime was always a cultural event at the warehouse. No matter who was on the work floor during the day, inside the lunchroom, every individual of just about every ethnicity, tribe, sex, origin and social status all gathered at once for thirty minutes to take part in the human event referred to as eating.

For a half an hour people stood in line to wait to use the several microwaves or the vending machines that rarely ever worked, no matter how much money a person would insert inside the contraptions.

Tables, both round and rectangular, were lined with people all trying their hardest to eat in time before having to head back on the floor again. Then again, just finding a table in such a crowded room seemed always to be a task reserved for the most fearless spirits. That is if patience was on a person's side.

Stacia, however, being a second tier supervisor, always seemed to carve out for herself a nice little space in a room behind the cafeteria that she shared with Max and a couple of the other female workers. It wasn't that the tiny pack was too good to eat with the others, but after so many years of hard labor at the same job, a person tended to take advantage of the perks of their longevity; one of the perks being that "if I don't want to eat with you, then deal with it."

Lunch for Stacia took only fifteen minutes. Once done, she and two other of her female friends took off outside to a designated corner to smoke it out for the other fifteen.

"So when was the last time you two fucked?" Stacia asked Veena, a large, black woman who was blowing out a large plume of cigarette smoke from her mouth.

The woman stared back at Stacia with an almost shameful expression before dashing her cigarette and replying, "Last night."

"Last night?" Both Stacia and Lucinda, a white woman beside her, said out loud in unison.

"Wait a second, didn't you say that you and Paul were just friends?" Lucinda asked.

Blushing like a teenager, Veena remarked, "Yes, I know, but I just couldn't help myself, girl. He just came in and started lookin' at me with those peek-a-boo eyes. Next thing I knew, I wake up butt ass naked in the bed next to him."

Stacia and the Lucinda glanced at each other before busting out in laughter. Stacia then blew out another smoke bomb and said, "Shoot, I don't blame you, girl, I had to get mine the other day."

"What, did Dixon come and lay you out?" Lucinda asked.

Smirking, Stacia answered, "He sure did, and damn good, too. I needed it though, after what I went through."

"How is the house hunting coming along?" Veena inquired while chewing away on a Snickers bar.

"I must've been on that computer of mine for hours each night this week looking." Stacia bemoaned. "And it's not like I don't have the money, it's just that some of the places in this city are either too far from the kids' school, or too far from work. Searching for the right place is like walking through a maze in the dark."

"You better hurry and find something soon," Lucinda said, "before you end up running out of money paying for that hotel."

"She's right, girl, you'll end up burning your money on a hotel room before you can even get a house."

Stacia stood against the stiff wind that was blowing while listening intently to her friends rattle on about her situation. Everything they were saying was filtering through, but with the excuses that she was handing out, not only to her friends but also herself, Stacia still had an apprehensive nerve nagging at her like a busy bee. She couldn't explain to herself why that nerve was still there, or why it tortured her so vehemently, but it was strong enough to cause her to come up with one more daily justification, just one more day to perhaps procrastinate.

Veena giggled before saying, "I just don't understand why you and the kids don't go and stay with Dixon. Hell, you all are practically family now as it is."

Stacia dashed out the remains of her stubby cigarette into an ashtray beside her before sighing and saying, "With me and Dixon…we just have to iron out some details before we can—

"Maybe you've been looking too hard." A feeble voice from around the corner all of the sudden spoke out.

Stacia and her cohorts all jumped before standing at attention and gawking all around to see just who was speaking.

Lucinda took a few steps forward and rounded a corner. Stacia stepped up behind her to see none other than Judy sitting on a bench all by herself. The woman was wrapped in a heavy, grey winter coat and matching knit hat. She was holding her little self like she was freezing half to death, even though the temperature outside was at least in the mid-fifties.

"Oh, we were wondering who said that." Lucinda looked in a strange fashion.

Judy continued to sit, huddled up inside of herself. She had her face pointed to the ground as though she was studying the cracked pavement.

"Judy, honey, do you need to go back inside?" Stacia steadily and carefully stepped to the woman. "You look cold." Then, as if a spark had been lit, the old woman looked up at all three before her and methodically scanned each individual before eventually directing her attention solely on Stacia.

Stacia could feel the coldness not only on Judy's face, but also in her grey eyes. It wasn't a hateful stare, but rather a more startled manifestation, like the old lady hadn't laid eyes on her ever.

"I couldn't help but to overhear your dilemma." Judy's scratchy voice struggled to say out loud. "I don't mean to pry, but I just happen to know of a house."

Stacia was inexplicably stuck in place. Just Judy's voice seemed to send a sliver of electricity down into her wobbly belly.

"Oh really," Veena grinned. "What place do you have, Judy?"

Without taking her eyes off of Stacia, Judy replied, "833 Husk Drive. It's a lonely house. It's been lonely for years now."

Just to amuse the woman, Stacia asked, "Okay, where is this place?"

"It's over near the old quarry."

"Down on the East side?" Lucinda turned up her face with a gasp. "That's in the bottoms!"

Still, Judy kept her eyes focused on her intended target. "It's a lonely, old house, but it'll take care of you."

Stacia watched as Judy got up from off the bench and began for the backdoor. Stacia then walked up to the woman and extended her hand for a shake.

"Well, I uh…I thank you for the information." She uttered with a kind smile.

Judy stood perfectly still before Stacia. The old woman stared down at the gracious hand before her and glared at it as though it were a weapon before she stated, "My brother wouldn't like it if I did that."

At that, Judy resumed her stride back into the building, leaving Stacia and her right hand hanging oddly in the air.

Slowly turning around to her friends, Stacia, with her smile still attached to her face, said, "What the fuck was that?"

Laughing out loud, the others ladies stood by with confused, yet fun loving expressions on their faces, as to say that they, along with Stacia, were seemingly amused by the peculiar woman.

"How long has she been here?" Stacia pointed behind her.

"She actually started back on Monday, but you were in that meeting all day." Lucinda explained. "Then of course you missed her on Tuesday."

Stacia pulled out her cell phone from her hip pocket and looked down at the time. "Oh well," she sighed, "back to hell again."

Like three battle weary combatants, the ladies all carried on back inside the building. There was something heavy hovering over Stacia however. It caused her feet to drag a little more than they usually did upon going back inside from a break.

The woman actually strolled in behind her two friends like she were dreading something or someone around each and every corner.

It was the street name that just would not let her go. As hard as Stacia tried to shove it out of her head, or at least to the back of her mind, no matter what, 833 Husk Drive stayed with her like an incurable rash.

CHAPTER 7

I'm dreaming; I know I am because my feet are floating across the ground. I'm dressed in that white nightgown that I saw at Macy's, the one that I wanted so badly.

I can hear that weird music, it sounds like something or someone whining. It gets on my damn nerves every time.

As I'm floating, I see nothing but fog all around me. I can hardly see anything else. That is until something appears in front of me. It's big alright, big enough to almost be a skyscraper. Okay, maybe not a skyscraper, but it's a huge son of a gun all the same.

The closer I float to the house, the more I can see people; they're all standing to the side clapping for me. Some of them I know, like grandma, Deontae and even my own mother, she's actually clapping for me. I can't imagine what I could have done to warrant such an accolade, but I'll take all the same.

As I reach the porch, I can see the house number, good old 833. Here we go again.

Before I can even reach for the front door, it opens all by itself. The second I float inside, the living room is all lit up with such beautiful lights. All this gorgeous furniture, the kind I see on The Real Housewives of Atlanta. It all must have cost thousands of dollars, more than I can ever afford.

I'm still floating. The house is so elegant; now, if I could only get rid of the damn whining noise then it would be perfect.

Then I reach the dining room. There's this long table, the kind you see in these movies where all the rich folks sit and eat every meal.

Behind each chair there are black butlers, each of them smiling from cheek to cheek, like their duty was a heavenly calling. The black maids all stand around the table waiting to serve the meal that was prepared.

I float my happy ass over to a chair and sit down before one of the butlers gently pushes my seat up to the table. Clear down at the other end of the table sits Judy. Her hair is actually combed for a change. She's wearing this pretty black dress that has sequins all over.

She's smiling for once. That depressed look she wears everyday is gone. The woman actually looks halfway descent. But there's something different about her. Something that I can't quite put my finger on.

Oh yeah, it's her eyes. She has those same beady, white eyes that they used in the old Incredible Hulk TV show, just as the guy was about to turn green.

As disturbing as they look, it's Judy's gracious smile that keeps me calm. It's like she's saying to me that everything is going to be ok. It's like she's telling me that you've finally made it, Stacia Taylor. All the years you've worked so hard, the blood, sweat and tears are finally paying off.

Then the butlers present the meal. They place down in front of me and Judy these silver platters that are covered with silver tops. I can't wait to eat.

They then lift the tops off of the platters, and lying on the platters are these pictures of me and the kids. I pick up the pictures, there must be at least twenty of them in all, and in each one is just us three.

Judy then opens her mouth. "You all have earned it, Sweet Sapphire. Just don't tell my brother."

Ever so abruptly, Stacia's eyes popped wide open. She immediately glanced over to see the kids fast asleep together in the bed right next to hers.

The room's heater was set on low; just to give everyone a more comfortable night's sleep just in case the temperature outside happened to dip past thirty degrees that evening.

Stacia wasn't terrified of the dream, just more or less perplexed. To her, it was as realistic and vivid as if she were wide awake viewing it all.

She turned her head to the left to see the digital clock read 2:38 a.m. Coughing a bit, Stacia carefully climbed out of the bed before sneaking over to her pants that were lying on the floor and reaching in for her pack of cigarettes and lighter.

From there, she gently opened the door and stepped out onto the balcony. It was a cold night, not bitterly cold, but rather just brisk and windy. Her undershirt and sleeping pants would suffice for at least the few minutes she needed to hurry up and smoke.

The breeze made it difficult for her to light the tip of her cigarette, but after several attempts the feat was accomplished.

Stacia leaned up against the balcony's railing and smoked away while looking down at the parking lot below at a white man and woman unloading luggage from their van and carrying it inside the building.

The dream she awoke from hadn't evaporated from her memory, it was still sitting there waiting to be pondered on some more. No, it wasn't a bad dream, just mysterious, and after so many years of cryptic dreams, Stacia became quite adapt to the ones she should let go, and the ones that should be heeded with caution. Ninety-seven percent of the time her night visions had a hidden message buried deep within, but for some reason, she couldn't quite unearth the meaning behind 833.

She was wise enough to realize that in time the meaning would reveal itself as the days dragged along. Until then, she wanted to hang on to the part where everyone was wishing her glad blessings and comfort for finally moving forward, without any more excuses.

Before Stacia could take another puff, her ears caught the buzzing of what sounded like whimpering coming from inside the room.

Stacia wasn't all too alarmed, but her stride was hasty all the same. She dashed her cigarette out on the ground before stepping back inside to find Devon hanging precariously off the bed.

Before the child's descent to the floor could be completed, Stacia rushed right over and scooped the boy up into her arms before rocking him back and forth like he were a newborn.

"Don't shoot me." Devon whined in his sleep.

Stacia looked over at Sidney who was still sleeping before staring back down at Devon and whispering soft words of comfort in his ears.

At last, her contempt was complete.

CHAPTER 8

～

Saturday lugged on like cold sludge. From morning till the late afternoon, Stacia, the kids and Dixon tooled around the city of Lane in search of suitable accommodations.

For Stacia, it was exactly what she envisioned; some houses were too far from work, the kids' school, too expensive or too much like what they were trying to escape from in the first place.

It was aggravating, depressing and downright miserable. The children were hungry and fidgety, Dixon's cursing was increasing by the hour and much to her dismay, Stacia had to crack open her third box of cigarettes for the day or else she would have crashed her car in the river out of sheer rage.

The second they pulled onto a street where the sidewalks were lined with nothing but mini pine trees, Stacia's stomach immediately dropped. The houses in the neighborhood were nice looking, but not so much to where she thought she would go completely broke paying the mortgage.

They were modest looking homes. Fairly lower middle class. It gave Stacia a spark of hope that perhaps the day wasn't a total loss after all.

"Look there," Stacia pointed, "I see a 'For Sale' sign."

Stacia pulled her car in front of brown, ranch style house and parked. All four persons inside the vehicle sat for a while and gawked at the home. Across the street were three, little black children who were playing on the sidewalk.

"Someone already lives here, grandma." Sidney said.

Stacia looked over to see a young, white man and a white couple walk around from the backyard into the front.

"They don't live there, baby girl." Dixon corrected. "They're here to see the house."

"Hold on for a sec." Stacia held her breath while waiting for the three to complete their business on the front lawn.

It seemed to take forever, but after a full half an hour the young couple eventually went on their way. Stacia wasted no time in jumping out of her car and running towards the man like a madwoman.

Out of breath, Stacia said, "Excuse me, I don't mean to bother you, but is this house still for sale?"

Appearing a bit confused, the man stood back and said, "Uh…yes it is."

Realizing that she both appeared and smelled like a rancid mess, Stacia extended her hand for a shake and continued, "I uh, I was just in the neighborhood and wondering."

"Yeah, we saw you speaking with those other folks and wanted to know if we had a shot." Dixon announced as he suddenly appeared behind Stacia.

"Well, as a matter of fact, the people I just got done showing this property to decided that it wasn't what they were looking for. But, if you'd like to take a tour I'd be more than happy to show you both." The young realtor gladly remarked.

With a mountain of hope building up inside, Stacia motioned for the children to come along before following Dixon and the realtor inside the home.

The house had a scent of fresh linen that seared Stacia's nose. It was a pleasant aroma, one that made the house feel even more welcoming.

The white carpet felt soft and spongy beneath her rubber soles. She almost felt ashamed to tread upon it. The white walls looked brand new, even though the house itself appeared to be at least three decades old.

There was a downstairs family room, as well as an adjacent laundry room. The three bedrooms upstairs were roomy enough to where a person could relax in each one without having to retreat to the living room.

There was a two car garage, along with a kitchen with an island. The second all five individuals stepped out onto the back patio that overlooked a sprawling backyard, Stacia looked over at Dixon who was wearing a subtle, satisfied appearance on his face and said to the realtor, "I like it a lot." She sighed pleasantly. "It's a little far from my grandkids school, but, at least the house itself is nice."

"Yeah, now, how much," Dixon asked the man with an intimidating frown.

Snickering like he was buying himself time, the young man replied, "Well, we're talking $280,000.00.

Right then and there Stacia could have a melted into mush. Her eyes snapped wide open before her knees buckled. She was completely speechless.

Looking down at Stacia, Dixon said, "Damn, you got that covered, babe."

Stacia couldn't even look back at the man; she kept her frazzled eyes locked on the brown grass ahead of her like she was entranced.

Like an excited little boy, the realtor reached into his brown suitcase and said, "We can get started on the paperwork right away and—

But before he could even finish what he was saying, Stacia grabbed a hold of Sidney and Devon and ventured around to the front yard and back to the car.

The instant all three got in, Dixon came racing around the house with a puzzled stare on his face. "What's the matter?" He tossed up his arms. "You can buy this place outright!"

"Get in the car, Dix." Stacia steadily said as she started the vehicle.

"But you got the loot for this place!"

Too embarrassed to look anywhere but at the road ahead of her, Stacia calmly, yet sternly said to the man, "Get in the damn car, now."

Without wasting another second, the man stormed over to his side of the vehicle before Stacia took off down the road, leaving the realtor standing dumbfounded on the front lawn behind.

"What the hell was that about?" Dixon griped.

Coming back down, Stacia replied, "The place was two hundred and eighty-thousand dollars."

"So," Dixon shrugged. "You got half a mill."

"And that house takes almost the half."

Shaking his head in bewilderment, Dixon asked, "So what are you gonna do now? That place back there was a steal."

"That place looked like it was built back in the sixties or seventies. And they want two hundred grand for it?"

"It costs that much because of all the amenities, Stacia."

"I'm not out to spend that much money on a house."

"So what, are you gonna spend it all on an apartment again? Or are you gonna stay cooped up that damn hotel for the rest of your lives?"

Stacia remained quiet while Dixon continued to rant on and on about how foolish she was for running away from such a supposed good deal. She wanted the house more than anything; everything but the price was right.

The more she listened to the man rage on, the guiltier she began to feel, like she had let everyone down. But every time that shameful emotion came around, all she had to do was remind herself that she had a plan, and whether the love of her life could see it or not didn't seem to matter much anymore.

Stacia glanced back at the children in the backseat. They looked more afraid of Dixon than disappointed at their grandmother. That was exactly when Stacia decided to pull the car to the side of the road and get out, away from Dixon's bluster.

She got out and walked over to a nearby bench. Stacia wanted a cigarette more than anything, but rather than reach in and whip one out, she instead went for her phone and began to punch numbers and words at a rapid pace. She knew where she was and what she was doing, but she was surprised at how quickly she was doing everything all at once; it was like she wanted to hurry before Dixon got out of the car and came at her with even more fury.

Over the past few days Stacia had typed in and looked for a lot of houses on her phone, but for the life of her she couldn't once recall punching in 833 Husk Drive. It was dead last on the list.

Ironically, all that day, the four had visited every address but Husk. Stacia glanced at the waiting car before turning her head to see other vehicles fly by her like they were on a racetrack.

Stacia hung her head low and listened as busy cars and trucks carried on past her like she wasn't even there.

CHAPTER 9

The dull, bitter hangover from the day before was still looming over everyone's heads that Sunday morning. Much like the day before, Stacia wanted to get out and about early. She really didn't want Dixon to join along after his tirade, but the man insisted nonetheless. She understood his protective actions, but Stacia would have rather gone it alone, even the kids would have seemed like a detriment in her pursuit.

For at least an hour, the Saturn was completely quiet. It was as if everyone inside felt like speaking would cause yet another eruption. The children in the backseat, who upon any other event, would be chatterboxes a' plenty, kept their lips sealed to the point where one would believe they were born mute.

Both Stacia and Dixon kept their faces directed towards the road ahead. She couldn't speak for her man, but Stacia had not one word to speak to anyone that morning. She wasn't mad, just focused on her task at hand. She wanted the whole house hunting ordeal to be over sooner than later. And as much as she tried not to deliberate over it, Stacia realized that it should have been dealt with years earlier. Coping with such a fact caused her eyes to sting.

Stirring alive from his half-awake stupor, Dixon opened his mouth and asked, "So, where are we supposed to be going to now? You've been driving around in circles for over an hour."

At first, Stacia didn't want to respond, she kept her mouth shut long enough to come up with the nerve to blurt out what she had to say to everyone all at once.

With her face still pointed at the road, she explained, "The other day, this old lady at work gave me the address of this place down near the quarry."

"The quarry," Dixon questioned with a sour grunt. "That's down in the bottoms."

"I'm aware of that. But I think it's worth a look."

"And just who is this old lady you've been talking to?"

"She's just some woman that works down at the warehouse."

For at least ten seconds there sat a tense quiet inside the car before Dixon eventually said, "You know there ain't nothing but white folks that live down there."

Sighing and rolling her eyes, Stacia remarked, "Who cares? All I want is a damn house."

Glancing down at her GPS, Stacia realized that her destination was approaching a lot faster than she expected. She turned down one street and across an alley before eventually pulling onto Husk Drive.

Much like the rest of the bottoms, Husk Drive was an unimpressive, small strip of a neighborhood. Just two rows of outdated houses that the city left behind or forgot all about.

All of the houses looked like they had been built around the turn of the twentieth century. Every person inside the Saturn looked on in silent repulsion. Stacia held her breath up until she reached 833.

The very moment she stopped the car in front of the house, she exhaled, the house didn't appear anything like it did back in her dream, she didn't expect it to.

It was a white, two story house. The porch was big. There were two large windows on opposite sides of the second floor, as well as a window directly in the middle of those. It appeared to also have an attic. No, it looked nothing like her dream house, and that alone set Stacia at ease. She had no reservations or bad omens whatsoever about the place. Even the crippled old trees that surrounded the house seemed settling to her. She knew that come spring they would flourish and provide shade.

Stacia cut off the ignition before climbing out of the car and opening the door to let the children out.

"You're going in there?" Dixon turned up his nose.

"Yep, you can stay in here if you like." Stacia boldly replied before taking off with the kids towards the home.

"It's a big house, Grandma!" Devon said out loud.

"It sure is, baby." Stacia responded while ogling over the chipped siding.

The second the three stepped up onto the first porch step, the flooring acted as if it wanted to collapse. Stacia yanked Devon out of the way before carrying on towards the front door.

Coming up right behind everyone was Dixon. With a salty frown on his face and rolling eyes the man commented, "Damn place is probably filled with rats."

Without even looking in his direction, Stacia said, "Better rats than gunshots."

The four carried on around to the backyard where a small toolshed sat directly in the middle of the large lawn. An old, blade lawnmower sat by the porch steps, as rusted and crippled as a fossil.

The back porch itself was leaning to the side. Lawn chairs and a small table were strewn all over its floor. A birdhouse was lanced to the backdoor, as well as broken flower pots that were hanging overhead.

To Stacia's naked eye, the house's exterior was something that could be overlooked for the time being, it was the inside that she desired to inspect. Once more, she had no misgivings about the house, to her it was just another broken down, old piece of property.

"Excuse me, can I help you folks?" A portly, middle-aged white man called out as he came racing into the backyard to meet up with the group of four.

As if they were caught in the act of doing wrong, all four individuals spun around and froze in place.

Out of breath, the man, behind his thick, grey mustache, inquired, "Are you folks lost or something?"

Before Stacia could even open her mouth, Dixon stepped forward and snidely remarked, "If we are, what's it to you?"

Appearing stunned at first, the man took a pace backwards before saying, "This is private property."

"We, uh, we just wanted to take a look around. I'm looking for a house for me and my grandkids."

The man stood at full attention at that second, seemingly even more stunned than before at what he had just heard.

"Man, c'mon, this cat's probably just some nosey ass neighbor!" Dixon griped as he began for the front yard.

"No, no," the man implored, "I've just never seen you people around here before."

"You people?" Dixon scowled as he advanced towards the skittish man.

With his hands outstretched in a defensive fashion, the man beseeched, "Hold on, hold on, I didn't mean it that way. I was just saying that—

"My name is Stacia Taylor, and I would really like to have some information about this place." She impatiently marched past Dixon. "You see, me and my kids really need to find a place. We're not here to cause any trouble; we just want to take a look at the place."

"No we don't!" Dixon blasted back.

"Yes we do!" Stacia stood defiantly.

Everyone gathered stood and stared at each other like they were locked in the midst of a duel. No one at that point didn't seem to have anything to say.

"My name is Stanley Ewing." He announced with his hand out for a shake.

Stacia shook the man's hard hand before looking back at the decrepit home and asking, "Do you know if the place is even for sale?"

With a nervous laugh, Stanley replied, "Well…to be honest with you, I've never known anyone who wanted to even live here. Not that I'm trying to scare you away or anything, but… someone did die here a long time ago."

"That's okay, I don't believe in ghosts." Stacia nonchalantly waved off. "Is it possible for us to take a look inside?"

"Well, uh…if you'd like to, I guess." Stanley stuttered before stepping up onto the back porch steps and prying open the door. "You may wanna hold your noses; it's been a while since someone's been in here."

Stacia, with the children attached to her, ventured into the dingy house, with Dixon reluctantly behind them. The kitchen's walls and floors were stained from top to bottom with grime and filth. A dead rat lay next to where the stove once sat.

From the kitchen to the dining room is where the group meandered next. Once more, Stacia was set at ease knowing that the dining room she encountered in her dream wasn't anything like what she was experiencing there inside 833. It was dark, smelly and downright miserable, as was the living room.

Stopping short of the stairs that led to the second floor, Stacia asked Stanley, "Are you the realtor or something?"

"Oh no," Stanley chuckled.

"Then how the hell do you know so much about this place?" Dixon brazenly chimed in.

Glancing daggers back at Dixon, Stacia turned to Stanley and blushed, "The reason I asked was because I needed a price quote."

"No, I'm not the realtor. I actually live across the street there at 877 with my mother." He pointed backwards. "You see, this is deemed a historic community. This house here was built way back in 1921. There's not much here on Husk Drive anymore. And with most of this area, the city has pretty much forgotten all about us down here. So those of us that are still here try and keep up with what's left while we're still able to."

Stacia stood and pondered hard before heading up the stairs. The hallway was long and slim and lined with brown hardwood flooring. There were three large bedrooms, the master being the biggest. Stacia marveled at the fact that the master bedroom had its own fireplace, as well as two closets.

"Hey, grandma, can I have my own room and put up my wrestling posters, too?" Devon's eyes lit up.

"The little guy likes wrestling?" Stanley smiled.

"Yeah, he likes wrestling." Dixon grimaced hard at Stanley.

"We'll see, baby." Stacia replied with a terse grin. "We'll see."

"Yeah, they sure don't make houses like this anymore." Stanley said. "This flooring is darn near impossible to find in any of these new houses today. I'm 62 years old, and I still love it here on Husk."

Pointing at one of the other bedrooms, Stacia said to Sidney, "Look, honey, you can finally get that bookshelf you always wanted. Now that your bedroom is big enough."

Sidney looked up at her grandmother with a wide-eyed astonishment and asked, "Are we really getting this house?"

Stacia had to actually remind herself that she was still in search mode. She had become caught up in her own hype to the point where she believed the place was hers.

"Can we see the attic?" Stacia asked.

At once, Stanley pulled down a rope that was dangling from the ceiling above to release a series of steps. Stacia ordered the children to stay put while the adults went up.

The attic space was completely empty, which set Stacia at comfort for the time being. The last thing she wanted was to have any long hidden surprises leap out at her.

Coming back down the steps, Stanley said, "Well, there's still the basement, if you're up to it."

Stacia shook her head yes before taking the children and heading back downstairs, through the living and dining rooms and into the kitchen to find a door next to where a refrigerator once stood.

The second Stanley opened the door, the pungent stench of must escaped the blackness of the basement, causing everyone to stand back and cough.

"This whole place is probably filled with asbestos!" Dixon covered his mouth.

"What's asbestos?" Sidney questioned while pinching her nose.

"It's something that can kill us all if we're not careful." Stacia replied before following Stanley downstairs.

The sun outside shined bright enough to where a person could see clearly inside the dank and gloomy basement. It wasn't a big space, but it was large enough to where ample storage could be permitted. On a wall was nailed an enormous, tattered and worn Confederate flag. Right away, Stacia wanted to shield the children's eyes from such an image.

Grunting as if he were in the know on things, Dixon spoke up, "I should've figured, the fools that once lived here were probably part of the Klan or something."

Promptly taking down the flag, Stanley blushed, "Sorry about that. My mom never really talked too much about the last occupants."

Stacia continued to gawk all around until her eyes caught sight of a piece of paper that was lying on the floor near where a chest sat. She walked over, picked up the frayed sheet and began reading. Dixon stepped up behind her and read alongside.

"My Sweet Sapphire," he huffed. "Another racist thing about this place; but then again, that's the bottoms for you."

"Look, we're nothing like that here." Stanley insisted. "That old crowd left this world a long time ago. Now, all we have around here are a few of old folks, several young people down the way and a few gays that live further down."

Stacia dropped the letter back down to the floor before aimlessly strolling about the basement. She was once more secured in her thought mode. Dixon was getting on her nerves, but she understood his hesitation and cautions nature. Yes, the Rebel flag was unsettling, but it was a relic that was left behind.

She wanted to hate the house, but she had no reason whatsoever to do so. Out of all the places that she searched online and driving by, 833 seemed to fit like a glove. No, she wasn't going to thank God for Judy's intervention, but Stacia was thankful all the same.

"I'm curious, how did you folks come across this house?" Stanley scratched his head. "I've never known anyone who even bothers to take a second glance at this old place."

"A lady I work with told me about it. She said that it was a lonely house, bless her heart." Stacia giggled.

Stanley laughed back before saying, "I guess so. Well, are you actually interested in buying this place?"

As though time stopped all of the sudden, Stacia stood in place and allowed her brain to blunder back and forth before she stopped spinning and blurted out the very first thing that appeared in her head. "Yeah, I want this place."

"You what," Dixon shouted out in amazement.

Looking at the man strangely, Stacia said, "What's the matter with it, dammit?"

"It's a piece of shit!"

"But I can apply for the first time home owners' credit and get most of this place fixed up, Dix."

"The last time I checked about a couple of months ago, the asking price was around $10,000.00." Stanley stated.

Stacia glared deep at Stanley, looking as if the man had just tossed gold coins at her. "Ten grand," she asked with a gasp in her throat.

"Like I said, that was a couple of months ago; it could be lower now for all we know."

"And that means the mortgage could possibly be around say, four to five hundred a month?"

Shrugging his shoulders, Stanley replied, "Give or take a few, sure."

Stacia's stomach flipped with delight, even the miserable looking basement began to appear in a more joyous light right then. She wasn't overwhelmed to where her better judgment was clouded, but for that one moment in time, she was content.

Stacia took one more glance around before she looked down at the kids who were completely silent in their awaiting an outcome.

Like a giddy girl, Stacia shrugged her shoulders and simply said, "I like it. I think we'll take it."

"You can't be fuckin' serious!" Dixon angrily yelled before storming back up the stairs.

Stacia waited and listened as the backdoor slammed shut before she meekly glanced at Stanley and said, "You'll have to forgive Dixon, he gets a little emotional sometimes."

Laughing off his embarrassment, Stanley replied, "I guess I understand. Home buying can bring that out of a person sometimes."

Blushing, Stacia remarked, "He's an ex-marine. He's a great guy, mind you; he just gets a little wound up sometimes."

"Yes, well." Stanley exhaled. "I can get in touch with the realtors that lease the property and you guys can take it from there."

With a subtle grin written all over her face, Stacia calmly said, "Okay, Stanley, the sooner the better."

"I didn't mean to come across like I didn't want you guys to move in here earlier, it's just that we get some kids running around, trying to creep in here and do God knows what."

"Don't worry about it, I understand."

"It'll be nice to see the old place up and running again. And don't worry about this thing," Stanley pointed to the flag he was holding, "it'll see a trash can before you know it."

"Good, I'm glad!" Stacia chuckled.

For the next hour or so, both Stacia and Stanley worked out the particulars of the house before exchanging phone numbers and going their separate ways.

By the time Stacia and the children made their way back out to the car, Dixon was already seated inside. Stacia knew from the jump that she was in for a storm, the likes she didn't want either of the kids to be a party to. From just a few yards back she could see the man's evil pout from within the car.

Stacia and the children all climbed inside. Before Stacia could even open her mouth to speak, Devon right away began chirping in. "We got us a house, Dixon! And now I have a room of my own so I don't have to sleep with Sid anymore!"

"We don't sleep together, Devon!" Sidney quickly corrected the boy.

Ignoring the children's outbursts, Stacia took her phone and pointed it at Dixon explaining, "Stanley gave me the number of the realtor agency that owns the property. He's said that they've wanted to get that house sold for years."

Dixon, with his head turned to the road in front of him, said not one word. Stacia could feel the heat of his fury emanate off of him.

Giving a sort of light-hearted chuckle, Stacia continued, "Stanley said that his mother would try and stop people from buying the house because she didn't want to see the place sold. But apparently she suffered a stroke two weeks ago and is laid up, so we don't have to worry about her."

Still, Dixon said nothing. The man was a picture of absolute solitude, which in turn only made Stacia all the more tense and upset.

Exhaling, Stacia asked, "Okay, what's the matter? Why aren't you speaking? What's got you so mad?"

Slowly turning his head, Dixon answered, "You don't know anything about that house, this neighborhood or the folks that live around here. And there you go, just buying a place just like that. You had a perfectly good place yesterday, and yet, here we are, at this shithole."

"What's the matter with it?" Stacia shrugged. "Okay, it's needs fixing up, I'll admit that, but like I said, the tax credit—

"Fuck the tax credit!" Dixon bellowed. "You could've had a perfectly good looking place yesterday!"

Stacia sat and stared at the man with poison in her eyes before she steadily placed her phone down on the dashboard. "First of all, I told you about cursing or even yelling in front of these kids. You did it yesterday, and it's enough. Second… listen to that."

Dixon turned up his face at that instant before gawking all around and saying, "Listen to what? I don't hear anything."

"That's just it, you don't hear a thing. When was the last time you were in a neighborhood that didn't have any cars blasting by, or people yelling and screaming at each other? Is that place a dump? Yes. But it's a dump that can be fixed up. Was that house we saw yesterday nicer? Yes. But it was too expensive, and it was too far from the kids' school. Not only can I manage the mortgage on this place, not only will it not eat up at the money I have, and not only is it near the kids' school, but it's not ghetto! It's right here in the center of the city!"

Dixon just sat and twisted his lips while Stacia went on and on. "You were the one that made this big speech the other day about what I should do with my money! I'm 43 years old, I should be able to do with my money as I choose! And I choose to spend it right here! How long are we supposed to stay cooped up in that damn hotel anyways? Another month?"

"I bet this woman who told you about this place is related to that fuckin' Max at work, isn't she?" Dixon sneered.

Stacia sighed and said, "That woman has only been working there for the past week! And please don't start that Max bullshit again!"

"I don't see why I shouldn't, you used to fuck 'em years ago!" Dixon screamed into Stacia's face before getting out of the car and walking away down the street.

Stacia sat and listened as birds chirped and a dog barked nearby. She wanted to look back at the kids, but their hushed silence amidst the mayhem caused her to sit still while focusing on the Saturn logo that was printed in the middle of the steering wheel in front of her.

"Is he coming back, grandma?" Devon meekly asked.

Pressing her lips together as tight as she could, Stacia said, "Maybe, honey… we'll see." Stacia then gathered the courage to turn back and look at the children with a smile that she had to fake. "In the meantime, you both have your own rooms, and you have a backyard to play in."

"Can we get bikes, too?" Devon blushed.

"I don't see why not, love."

"Does this neighborhood have people that shoot at everyone?" Sidney spoke.

Stacia sat and stared hard at the girl. "I don't think so, baby." She tenderly uttered. "I don't think we'll have to worry about that anymore."

CHAPTER 10

"He said that the house was built around nineteen-twenty or something. So yeah, it's pretty old." Stacia explained to Max who was standing next to a file cabinet inside his office with an offhanded grin on his bearded face.

"Did Dixon like it?" He asked with a sly smirk.

Stacia rolled her eyes before replying, "No. He wanted me to get a house that would have bankrupted me. We had it out, but he'll be back around before you know it."

"So, all in all, are you happy with your decision?"

Shaking her head confidently, Stacia said, "Yeah...yeah, I am. I truly do feel like this one could be it."

Max laughed, "Let's just hope you don't find anymore Jim Crow-type memorabilia left in there."

Laughing back, Stacia said, "I know, I about had a heart attack when I saw that thing yesterday. That's all I need, the kids going back to school saying they live in a house with a Rebel flag down in the basement."

"Well, I'm happy for you," Max humbly imparted. "Hopefully now you three can get your lives back in order and away from that nightmare once and for all."

"Tell me about it. I got nervous thinking I wouldn't be able to find anything that was just right. Yeah, the house needs a lot of work, but for the first time, we'll actually have a place to call our own. No more renting."

"I hear you, girl. Well, we'd better get down to it before the ten-thirty rush comes in." Max exhaled as he began for the door. "Oh, by the way, we got another new one in today."

"Another one," Stacia moaned. "How many more temps are they gonna send us?"

"I don't know, but I do know I'm getting real sick and tired of training new people every week."

Stacia and Max both carried on out of the office and into the work area where the usual crowd was busy bustling about. Max gave the work detail for the day before everyone took off for their assigned quarters. Stacia, however, still riding her wave of refined euphoria, chose to seek out the one person that pointed her in the direction she had been waiting for.

Stacia went up and down one row after another in search of Judy, but after so much fervent skulking, the woman was seemingly nowhere to be found. Stacia looked up at the clock that was perched on the wall; it was well past nine that morning, which meant that either the woman was late or had called off.

"Hi, can I have a pair of gloves, please?" a small voice asked from out of nowhere."

Stacia spun around to see a young, skinny black girl standing there in front of her. "Oh, what's your name?" she asked with a subtle surprise.

"My name is Charmaine; this is my first day here."

Stacia shook the young lady's hand before going over and retrieving a pair of gloves for her to use. She then explained the work detail to Charmaine before seeing Veena walking by.

"Veena," Stacia called out, "have you seen Judy anywhere?"

Walking towards Stacia, Veena answered, "Nope, I ain't seen her anywhere. She probably finally went on to a nursing home, with her old self."

"Old Lady Judy?" Charmaine inquired all of the sudden.

Both Stacia and Veena turned around at that instant. "Yeah," Stacia glared strangely at the woman. "Do you know her?"

"If we're talking about the same old woman, she used to work at this other warehouse where I was just last month. She was real strange. Always sat by herself; never really talked to anyone."

"Always muttering?" Veena smirked.

"Yep, that's Old Lady Judy," Charmaine laughed out loud.

"So she's been making the rounds at other warehouses, huh?" Stacia asked.

"Judy's all over the city. I heard she even worked at this one warehouse down near the bottoms. That one that shut down after all those people were burned to death."

Stacia stood and stared for a moment at Charmaine before wandering away. "Hey, girl, did you find yourself a house?" Veena excitedly asked as she followed Stacia.

Shaking herself awake, Stacia said, "Uh...yeah. Believe it or not, I ended up going to the same place Judy referred me to."

"For real," Veena marveled. "What did the place look like?" "Like a dump, but that can be fixed," Stacia commented. "We're gonna take it."

Veena hugged Stacia before congratulating her. Stacia went along in explaining all that went down over the weekend while keeping Old Lady Judy fresh in her head.

It upset her to no end that she couldn't thank the woman face to face.

CHAPTER 11

S tacia, Sidney and Devon all stood at the front door of their former hovel in a stunned, restrained and dismayed triad of emotional tribulation. Stunned to see that since their departure a week earlier, someone had entered the home and destroyed it even more than before. Restrained for the simple fact that it was common; everyone in the neighborhood knew the Taylors were gone, it was bound to happen. The dismay, however, came from Stacia, she had lost all hope for the people she was forced to live amongst for the past two years; at that juncture she honestly wanted nothing more to do with black people altogether. If their new neighborhood was full of nosey neighbors and rebel flags, then all Stacia had to do was embrace the new living and never look back again.

With her 38. locked tight in her sweaty, right hand, Stacia turned to the kids and sighed, "Okay, gang, gather up the rest of your clothes, toys and whatever else, and bring it out to the car. We're never coming back here again."

Without saying a word, both Sidney and Devon carried on inside the house and towards their bedroom. Stacia followed in behind them, making sure that they and they alone were the only persons still left inside the house.

Like diligent ants, the children gathered what remained inside their ram shackled bedroom. Stacia could tell that whoever had entered the house while they were away possibly had kids of their own, judging by the fact that they managed to get away with most of Devon's wrestling action figures and Sidney's Easter dresses.

Devon looked back at his grandmother with a befuddled muse on his face. Before the boy could even open his mouth to protest, Stacia stepped forward.

"It's okay, baby, we'll get some more once we move."

"What about my clothes, grandma?" Sidney sniveled.

Wanting to scream, Stacia rubbed the girl's back. "Easter is right around the corner, sweetie, we'll see what we can do."

"Can I get another wrestling ring, too?"

Not wanting the children to see the rage on her blushing face, Stacia turned and began for her own bedroom before exhaling in a faraway tone, "Yeah, baby, we'll get it all back."

As it was before she left the house days earlier, her bedroom floor was still littered with clothing and shoes, expect the nice clothes that she had bought for herself were all seemingly gone. Stacia didn't even have to root through the piles to notice, she could tell simply by seeing more sweatpants, t-shirts and tennis shoes than anything else.

But rather than allow another outburst to take form, she placed her gun down onto the dresser and gingerly began picking up the remainder of clothing, pictures and whatever else was left on the floor. Stacia wanted to just leave everything behind, but taking what she still could gave her the sense that she got back a bit of revenge upon the community that had terrorized her and her family so viciously.

Before Stacia could gather another pile of clothing into her already packed arms, out of the corner of her eye appeared a large, dark shadow. She dropped the clothes to the floor and darted for her gun only to notice that it was Dixon standing near the doorway.

Catching her breath, Stacia slipped the weapon into her pants pocket and turned away from the man as though he were not even there at all.

"So you gonna treat me like that?" Dixon tossed up his hands.

Stacia only rolled her eyes before resuming her packing duty. The very last thing she wanted that day was another fight; she didn't even want to look at another human being for that matter.

Approaching Stacia from behind, Dixon softly uttered, "Look, I think I know who it was that robbed ya'll, but I—

Before the man could speak another word, Stacia grabbed Dixon by the arm, led him out of the bedroom and past the children who were cowering in a corner in their own room like two scared kittens.

The second they reached the front door, Stacia looked Dixon dead in the eye and growled in a whisper, "First off, don't you ever scream in front of my children again. We talked about that shit before. Second, I don't want you talking about killing anyone in front of them ever again."

Holding up his hands, Dixon relented, "Okay, okay, I'm cool with that."

"Those kids are scared to death enough as it is. And who the fuck cares who did it? We're leaving this place anyways."

Dixon heaved a heavy sigh before stuffing his hands into his pockets and looking bashfully at Stacia. "Why do you have your gun on you?"

Stacia glanced around before saying, "Someone was up in here while we were gone."

Dixon's face took on a reddish hue as the man balled up his fists. "What the fuck?" He barked.

"Keep your damn voice down."

"Keep my voice down for what?"

"Stoppit," Stacia clapped her hands as hard as she could in the man's face.

Dixon stood at full point attention at that instant. For a moment or two Stacia felt a surge or energy breeze upon her body.

"This shit ends now." She pointed. "We're out of here. And what happened the other day won't ever happen again."

"That's what I came over to talk about. I'm…sorry." He stuttered as though saying such a thing hurt beyond belief.

Shaking her head in disbelief, Stacia said, "I've heard this before, Dix. It's old. And you know what else is old? The whole Max thing. That happened years before you and I met, and you said yourself that it wasn't a big deal. Why do you always bring that up whenever you get mad?"

Dixon turned his head away before looking down at the floor and saying, "Look…I just worry about this whole house thing."

Shrugging, Stacia asked, "What's there to worry about? You know good and well why I didn't want to buy that other house. This place is perfect for us."

"It just seems like a waste of money."

"Believe me, that money is being put to good use. It doesn't make any sense to spend the majority of that money on a house that's too far from everything. Me and the kids wouldn't be left with anything once I was done just laying out the down payment for that place. But we've been over this before, Dix."

For a few moments a bitter quake of quiet hovered over the two. Dixon appeared as if he wanted to say something, but the man seemed too compliant to even open his mouth.

With her hands shaking, Stacia muttered, "I need some kind of assurance from you. I'm not saying that I want you to marry me tomorrow, or even next month for that matter, but… you and I can't keep going on like this. Either you're gonna be there for us…or you need to move on."

Dixon and Stacia stood and stared at each other for at least an entire minute before Dixon took her hands into his and said, "I've been there since the beginning. You're all I got in this world."

Stacia glared into the man's partially wrinkled face as hard as she could. She wanted to believe that out of all the disagreements that they had in the past that their current dilemma would put a sense of closure to their fragmented bonds. Stacia wanted to throw away the broken record that she had been listening to for far too long.

"Did they take the kids' toys and stuff?" Dixon whispered.

Stacia stood and studied the man before replying, "They need more than just toys…grandpa."

Dixon pulled Stacia into his heaving bosom and rubbed the back of her head before kissing her on the forehead.

From there, they went back through the living room and into the kids' bedroom to find them both still rummaging through what was left of their possessions. Dixon stepped into the room and gathered Sidney and Devon into his arms.

The children looked uneasy around Dixon, like it was the very first time they had ever seen the man. It unsettled Stacia, but after so many blowups between them, she became aware of something very stark, the man had a magic about himself. It worked on her, and the children were almost elementary. Stacia knew that all she had to do was stand back and observe.

Looking at both children, Dixon said, "So, I hear you guys are gonna move into another house."

Sidney and Devon just shook their heads yes before glancing up at their grandmother who remained still by the doorway.

"Here's how it's gonna go, my nephews are gonna come over and help pack up the rest of this stuff, and then we're all gonna go out and eat."

"Can I get some new wrestling men again?" Devon sheepishly asked.

Dixon gave Stacia a brief glimpse before looking down again at the boy and saying, "I'll tell you what, when I see another A on that report card of yours, then we'll talk about wrestling men, 'cause that D in math just isn't gonna do. Alright?"

Devon shook his head yes. "If I get an A, then can I have another Kofi Kingston poster, too?"

"Devon, no one cares about your stupid wrestling." Sidney moaned.

"And you, young lady," Dixon said, "it's almost Easter, that means you need some new dresses. But then again, I've been hearing that you got detention because you took your cell phone to class. So, from here on out, until that mess stops, you can forget about a new dress."

Sidney gazed up at her grandmother in astonishment, looking as if her whole world had just been flushed down the toilet. Stacia simply smirked before turning and walking back out to the living room.

Before she could even reach the kitchen, a knock at the front door interrupted her stride. With her hand clutching the butt of her gun, Stacia carried on over to the door to find the young woman from across the street standing on the other end with one of her little boys.

"Hey, girl, where ya'll been all this time?" The woman asked while wrangling with the boy that seemed to have a difficult time standing on his own two feet for some reason.

Stacia just stood there at the door and stared at the individual like she were the most disgusting thing she had laid eyes on. Her hair was wrapped in an African scarf while her filthy tank top shirt hung off her chest.

Nonchalantly lighting a cigarette right there in front of the woman, Stacia took a couple of puffs before saying, "We had a few things to do, Jamarcia."

"Stand up, motherfucker!" Jamarcia screamed at her little boy. "Damn, one of my baby's daddy's said he saw the dudes that ran into your house last night."

"Someone was here last night?"

"Yep, he said that they ran out the backdoor."

Stacia continued to casually smoke away. Behind her in the background were the sounds of Dixon and kids moving things around and about.

"Is ya'll movin' away?" Jamarcia asked with a surprised angst.

Arrogantly blowing smoke in the opposite direction, Stacia commented, "Yeah, we're getting out of here."

"For real," Jamarcia's eyes exploded. "Where is ya'll movin' to? Do they take Section 8?"

Stacia stood and gazed on at the thing before her for a few seconds longer before stepping back and slamming the door right in her face.

CHAPTER 12

March 7th, Day 1

A light layer of March snow covered the ground as the finishing touches on 833 were being laid down. The furniture was all set inside. All three bedrooms were perfectly positioned the way each member wanted them.

For Devon, his remaining wrestling posters were nailed to the walls to where whenever he walked into the room John Cena would be very first one he would see. Upon a two shelf bookcase sat not only numerous math instruction textbooks and WWE magazines, but also his famed wrestling action figures, all set out like collectible mainstays, only to be touched and admired by him and him alone.

Within Sidney's room was a seamlessly made bed complete with pink and blue sheets and a blanket. Along the four walls were plastered posters of Kanye West and Beyoncé. On the pink nightstand that sat next to her bed was not only her beloved cell phone, but also a collection of necklaces.

Stacia's bedroom, despite being the biggest of the three, remained fairly simple, a closet full of clothes, a bed and two nightstands on opposite ends of the bed. Sitting on the nightstand to her right were framed pictures of Sidney and

Devon, Dixon and her son. All four persons would be the first thing she laid eyes upon awakening in the morning.

The age old stench that once overwhelmed the house was gradually sifting away to a scant aroma that could be ignored with the passing of time. Stacia had already called in repairmen to fix up the leaning back porch, as well as the busted pipes down in the basement.

All in all, after several weeks or planning, calling and cleaning, the house was slowly but surely coming together a lot quicker than anyone had expected. Obviously there were still major improvements to be cared for, mainly new carpeting throughout and a set of new basement stairs, but nothing that couldn't be worked around for the time being.

Trying her best not to slip and fall in the snow, Stacia, with her brand new plasma TV in her arms, carried on out of the U-Haul truck and into the house.

"You two stop that running around here before someone falls on their asses!" She hollered at the rampaging children that were ripping through the living room like feral cats.

As soon as Stacia was done placing the television down onto its stand, she managed to catch Devon who was being chased down by his sister.

"Listen here," she yelled into the boy's face, "instead of acting like fools, you both go out to that truck and get those end two tables! You can help each other bring them in!"

"Yes, ma'am," the children both exclaimed as they raced out the front door.

Stacia wiped the sweat from off her forehead before plopping herself down on the loveseat and breathing in the house she purchased. The smell was still rampant, the walls needed cleaning and she needed a new refrigerator, but there was that small wisp of fire inside her belly that wanted to burst into flames, not flames of fury, but of completion.

Even though the work wasn't done, Stacia Taylor exhaled. She wanted to say it out loud, "It's all mine." Just thinking those three words felt nearly orgasmic. The home invasion was still lingering in her head, and it would for a long time to come, but she knew that there would be an eventual finality down the road.

Within the dank walls of the house was her absolution. Stacia didn't except perfection, no matter how long she resided at 833, but she demanded at least one positive result from all the hard work she had laid down over the years, even if it meant living down in the bottoms.

She wanted to shut her eyes and fall right asleep, but before her eyelids could drop, in came two of Dixon's nephews with the couch.

"Where you want this, Stacia?" One of them asked.

Immediately, Stacia got up and pointed, "Right over there, Trey."

Both of the young men carried the heavy sofa across from where Stacia was once sitting. Just as soon as they were done putting down the couch, Dixon came inside, as did another young man who was carrying a washing machine upon his back.

"Tavon, be careful taking that thing downstairs, those basement steps aren't all too stable." Stacia said. "Where are those two at?" She griped while looking outside the window. "I told them to bring in those end tables."

"They're out there playing in the snow." Dixon said.

"What?" Stacia growled as she started for the front door. "I'm gonna tear them apart!"

But before she could take one more step, Stacia was yanked back by Dixon who then pulled her into his arms and kissed her on the lips. "That furniture ain't going anywhere." He uttered. "Let 'em play for a while."

Stacia awkwardly gazed around at the remaining nephews who saw fit to promptly excuse themselves. Once they were out the front door Stacia saw fit to wrap her arms around her man's waist.

"I'm surprised you were able to get your nephews out of bed today, being that's it a Saturday and all." Stacia smirked up at Dixon.

"Shit," Dixon sucked his teeth, "those niggas do nothing but sit around, get high and watch TV. This is the most work they've done in a long time."

Stacia giggled at the man's comment before taking a long gander around the living room and sighing, "I'm sure glad we were able to get the electric turned on."

"That reminds me, we still got that mini freezer out there, too. I'll have them bring that in so you guys can get your food in there for now."

Stacia unhooked herself from Dixon and placed her hands on her hips while wandering around the living room in a meditative fashion.

"Whatcha thinking about, baby girl," Dixon observed.

Stacia waited for a few moments before turning back to the man and replying, "You want the truth?"

"Heck yeah," he smirked.

"I was sitting here just a while ago thinking to myself, just how this all feels. This is what I've always wanted to give to… Deontae." She sniffed.

"Yeah, but you got it now." Dixon said as he came up behind Stacia and began rubbing her shoulders. "Wherever he is out there, he's gotta understand that his momma is doin' just fine."

"I think you got a big ass rat down there in your basement." Tavon announced as he came in from out of the dining room from the kitchen. "I heard it messin' around down there while I was trying to put the washing machine in."

"Whereabouts did you hear it?" Dixon asked.

"Down by the water heater."

"I'll go and buy some traps tomorrow." Dixon said as he took off for the kitchen.

"Knock, knock!" Stanley chimed in from the front door.

"Oh, come on in." Stacia said in a surprised tone. "I wasn't expecting company so soon." She smiled.

"I didn't want to intrude, just thought I'd stop by to see how things were coming along."

Spreading her arms, Stacia answered, "Well, as you can see all we're still moving stuff in."

"Wow, the place looks and smells a lot better than it did before." Stanley marveled before taking a long look at one of the rough looking young man before him.

"Oh, this is Tavon, one of Dixon's nephews."

"How do you do," Stanley warmly greeted the men.

"Wassup," Tavon lazily replied.

"Oh, Mr. Dixon is here, as well?" Stanley timidly asked.

"Grandma, Sid threw snow at my glasses!" Devon came in the house crying.

"He threw snow at me first!" Sidney came bawling right up behind her brother.

"I hear the damn thing down there, too. It sounds pretty big." Dixon said as he all of the sudden came back into the living room.

There stood a six person showdown right in the middle of the floor. All Stacia could do between unruly children and a jealous boyfriend was crack a shy grimace and insert herself in the center of it all.

"Honey, Stanley stopped by to see how we were doing."

"Oh yeah," Dixon raised his nose in the air. "Tell me something, how big are your rats down here in the bottoms? Because it sounds like you got a monster down there."

"Well, uh...I've seen some pretty nasty ones over the years." Stanley stammered. "Do you have any poison? Because if not I've got some over at my—

"That's alright, man, I'll get some traps myself." Dixon hastily interrupted.

"Well, alright then." Stanley chuckled his embarrassment off while slowly backtracking to the door. "Like I said, I just stopped by to see how you folks were holding up."

"We certainly appreciate you stopping by, Stan." Stacia kindly said.

At that, Stanley let himself out the same door he entered. Stacia then turned to Dixon with a somewhat perturbed frown on her face. "Why do you have to be such a negro?"

Grinning from ear to ear, the man responded, "Just havin' a little fun with the man, no harm in that."

"Uh, huh," Stacia shook her head. "Well, we still have more furniture out there, 'Mr. Fun.' Being that these two knuckleheads would rather play in the snow than do what I told them to do in the first place."

Dixon and Tavon carried on outside, but not before Dixon popped Stacia on her behind in a playful fashion.

Stacia swatted away at the man before looking down at Devon and Sidney. She wanted to tear into them for disobeying her earlier, but she was still riding her euphoric high of home ownership. Instead, the woman brusquely wiped snow from out of Devon's hair before pulling them both close.

"You two see this?" She looked all around. "I want you both to remember this moment for the rest of your lives, because this is what it's all about. It may not look like much, but it's far away from whatever madness we were once around. And this is only the beginning, too. You both are going places in this world. It all starts coming together now."

"Can we go to WrestleMania, too, grandma?" Devon looked up with stars in his eyes.

Stacia rolled her eyes and snickered while rubbing the boy's head. "You and that ridiculous wrestling are drive me and your sister crazy."

"Grandma, Tracy at school said that what if our house is haunted?" Sidney commented.

Stacia twisted her lips before saying, "Tracy is a fool, darling. There is nothing wrong with this house."

"What's haunted mean?" Devon squinted.

"It's nothing, little man." Stacia patted him on the back. "Now, you both get upstairs and out of those wet clothes before you catch colds."

Stacia watched as the children rampaged up the stairs and to their individual bedrooms. That image alone nearly caused Stacia to faint from bliss.

***

10:38 p.m.

"Grandma, now that I have my own room, can I flash my Kane light in the dark?" Devon asked while pulling out his little plastic flashlight from underneath his pillow.

Setting out the boy's Sunday best clothes, Stacia said, "I don't see why not, honey. You won't be bothering your sister with it anymore."

Piece by piece she placed one article of clothing after another onto a chair that sat near the child's bed before walking over and kissing Devon on the forehead.

"And I don't want you to be up all night playing with that flashlight, young man. Your sister is fast asleep, and that's how I want you, too."

"Yes, ma'am," Devon replied while shining his light all over the walls.

"I love you, baby."

"I love you, too."

Stacia shut the door and cut off the hallway light that was located just across from Devon's room. Like a creeping cat, she ventured to Sidney's room to find her knocked completely out. The girl could sleep through a tornado if it were to strike, a habit that always bothered Stacia to no end.

Once she was done observing the child, Stacia ever so carefully shut her door and took herself across the hall to her own bedroom. Her entire body was as sore as though she had ran a marathon, but it was all worth it; the pain was momentary, being away from her previous surroundings was permanent.

Stacia shut her bedroom door and dropped her weary body down onto her bed where she proceeded to take off all her clothes. From there, she reached up under her bed and pulled out a nine inch dildo. Usually, she would have some kind of soft R&B music playing while taking care of herself, but that evening she chose to go it alone.

Ever so gently, she slid the toy inside her vagina and began to pump it in and out while imaging Dixon's hulking body bouncing up and down upon hers.

As the minutes went by, so did the thrusting action. What started off as soft insertion eventually turned into vigorous motion. With every stroke Stacia wanted to moan, but she realized that even behind the doors of her bedroom her most modest groan would possibly be heard by the young ones. Stacia instead pressed her lips together as hard as she could while nearing the emotion that she had waited for nearly a week. She wanted it all out.

11:33 p.m.

From out of the belly of the basement it crept. It was well aware of its new tenants, ever since they first arrived weeks earlier.

The basement door creaked wide open. It looked all around at the kitchen that appeared brand new to it all of the sudden.

From the kitchen to the new dining room and living room where it saw the plasma TV sitting next to the fireplace. It stepped in front of the television, its reflection never once appearing in the glass.

Sounding like it was wearing a pair of heavy workman boots, it went about upstairs, clopping around. It crept along the hallway, one room at a time. From Stacia's room where it heard her whining in ecstasy behind the door. From her room it ventured down to Devon's where the boy was still shining his light wildly.

After Devon's room it carried on down the way to Sidney's. Ever so brazenly it opened the door and stepped on in. It stood above the girl watching her sleep while it breathed in and out. It remained there next to her for at least five whole minutes before scooping the comatose child up into its arms and walking away with her into the blackness of the quiet house.

CHAPTER 13

Day 2
8:17 a.m.

Stacia, clothed in a pair of loose pajama pants and a sweat shirt came yawning out of the bathroom and into the hallway. To be truthful, she hated waking up early Sunday mornings; the weekends were to be hers. But she wanted the children to be in church, another blessing that she wished she could have imparted to her son.

Her body, the day after so much moving, still felt worse than it did the day before. Her legs were sore and her arms felt as if they were on fire, and yet she felt it her duty to get her grandchildren off to Sunday school more than anything.

As for herself, going to church and praising God was something she wanted to do, but never had the will to undertake. Stacia still repressed a lot of hardness towards God. She had come a long way, but the resentment was still present. Nonetheless, she sang along, she prayed the prayers and she shouted "Amen" whenever someone next to her shouted it first. It was show, a "put on", and that's the way she wanted it for her present life.

Stumbling down the hallway, Stacia knocked on Devon's bedroom door and sluggishly said out loud, "Get up, boy! It's Sunday morning!"

From there, she strolled on down to Sidney's door and suddenly realized that not only was it wide open, but that the girl was not in her bed. Stacia was too sleepy to take notice when she first got up to go use the bathroom. As much of a heavy sleeper as Sidney was, it subtly surprised Stacia to see the girl at least up and at it.

Stacia carted her two ton body down the cold steps and cut on the television. The very first thing that was showing was none other than *SpongeBob Squarepants*. Neither of the children cared all too much for the cartoon, but she realized that the louder she turned up the volume, the more it would motivate the kids to move along.

To the kitchen Stacia went next. Sunday morning breakfast wasn't all too different from Monday thru Saturday. Perhaps some eggs, maybe toast and or bacon, and if everyone was lucky, a bowl of cereal. Not all too much thought was put into the ordeal, being that after church service all three would come back home and go right back to sleep for a few hours.

Stacia opened the cabinet to find a full box of *Frosted Flakes*. She then opened another cabinet and took out three bowls before placing them down onto the table that sat in the middle of the floor.

Time had passed, the TV was at full blast inside the living room and Stacia still could not hear Devon scatter about upstairs. She wasn't angry, just impatient. With bleary-eyed energy, Stacia sashayed back into the living room and yelled upstairs, "Devon, get up and get down here, now! Your sister is already up!"

Once she was done hollering, Stacia went back for the kitchen, but something was out of order, and it really didn't hit the woman until she crossed the kitchen's threshold. Stacia stood for a moment or two and looked from her left to her right. After a few more seconds, it finally donned on her.

Stacia speed walked back through the dining room, living room and eventually upstairs back to Sidney's bedroom. The bed was unmade, which wasn't unusual. Stacia stepped inside the room and looked from top to bottom. She opened the closet and searched inside there.

Stacia wasn't all too nervous, just concerned, she knew that Sidney wasn't one for uncharacteristic behavior, so there was still a rational explanation to unlock.

From Sidney's bedroom she ventured into Devon's to find the boy dragging himself out of his bed like a drunkard after a hard night.

Stacia stood at the threshold and gawked all around before asking, "Where's your sister at?"

Devon just shrugged his shoulders and yawned, "I dunno."

Stacia turned and went for her own bedroom to search, but when that turned up no result she raced back down the stairs and hollered out, "Sid, where are you?"

From the living room and its closet, to the dining room and back to the kitchen Stacia investigated. By then, her search, which began at concern, had turned into a frantic tear.

With only her socks on her feet, Stacia stepped out onto the back porch and screamed the girl's name at the top of her lungs. She raced around to the front yard only to find nothing but snow and an alley cat strolling by.

Stacia ran back around to the backyard and into the house to see Devon standing by the table in his pajamas with a bewildered look on his face.

"Where the fuck is Sid at?" Stacia frantically yelled.

Devon only stood in place, seemingly too afraid to even speak. Stacia stared the boy up and down before realizing that she hadn't checked the basement yet. Without wasting another second, she flung open the basement door and hurried herself down the rickety steps as fast as she could.

"Sid, where are you?"

Stacia skulked about the dark and cold basement, hoping that something or someone would jump out at her.

The more she walked about, Stacia's feet suddenly connected with something on the ground. Nearly falling, Stacia caught herself and looked down to see none other than Sidney lying on the freezing floor of the basement, curled up in a ball.

As cold as it was in the basement, Stacia couldn't stop sweating. A breath of relief gripped her entire body at that instant as she stooped down and breathlessly began to shake the girl awake.

"Sidney! Sidney, wake up!" She shouted into the girl's face.

Steadily, the child awoke before gawking all around at her dark surroundings. Stacia continually tried to awaken the girl to full attention.

"I'm up, grandma." Sidney slurred.

"What are you doing down here?"

Sidney once more looked all around before staring hard at her grandmother and saying, "I dunno. I went to bed last night."

Stacia held Sidney in her arms and glared around at the quiet basement before gazing up the stairs at Devon, who looked more petrified than anything.

"C'mon, let's go up." Stacia said as she led a shivering Sidney back up the stairs. Shaking herself, Stacia then said, "Go on up to your room and get warm, baby."

Stacia stood by and watched as Devon helped his flummoxed big sister along the way. Stacia, however, was still shaking in her wet socks. She glanced back down at the black basement with a claustrophobic anxiety. She honestly didn't want to entertain the musings of just how or why the girl was down there, she was found, and that was more than enough relief for the present day.

Taking her eyes away from the basement, Stacia closed the door as gently as she could.

CHAPTER 14

Day 3

Stacia pulled her car in front of her house and got out. As the case with any other day, work had worn her out completely. She didn't have to pick up the kids for another ninety minutes. All day long the only thing that hung on Stacia's mind was going inside and pleasuring herself. She and Dixon worked opposite shifts, so getting together was a challenge that they both loathed but understood.

Before she could even find her house key, right across the street was Stanley who was flagging down Stacia like he was directing an airplane.

"Hi there, neighbor!" He shouted.

Not wanting to appear a mirror image of her boyfriend, Stacia waved back, but as soon as she saw the man start towards the curb, she realized that a conversation was brewing. Talking to anyone at that time of the day was nowhere on her agenda, but she pasted on her best fake smile while making her way over to the other side of the street to meet the man.

"How are you?" Stanley smiled while holding his metal lunchbox in his hand.

"I'm doing okay. How are you today?"

"Well, you know you're getting too old to work when the days get shorter and shorter." He sighed while still smiling.

Chuckling, Stacia replied, "I feel you. I feel like I've been working for a hundred years at my age."

Stanley squared his eyes at Stacia before saying, "C'mon, you've only just begun to work. I'm the old fart here."

Stacia blushed and then asked, "How old do you think I am? Or better yet, how old do I look?"

Stanley himself blushed and blew off her question like he was too embarrassed to answer. Stacia was accustomed to it.

"So, how do you folks like your new home?"

Stacia glanced back at the house with a humble grin and replied, "It's okay so far. A bit drafty in some spots, but all in all, not bad. It's a whole lot better than where we came from."

"Well, these old houses were built to last a long time. Nowadays, they build homes the way they build cars, strictly for show and tell. These houses today are no sturdier than if they were made out of straw it seems." Stanley griped. "I've been trying to tell the contractors I work with the same thing for years, but of course, they just look at me like I've lost my marbles."

"You build houses?"

"I'm the foreman down at Raiden Construction. We're the ones that are putting up that new tower downtown."

"Oh, I see." Stacia commented, sounding slightly surprised.

"Yeah, I used to work over at the old rendering plant across the way before they shut it down back in the eighties. My dad worked there, too."

Stacia happened to glance over Stanley's shoulder at the mammoth building that could be seen for a least a mile away. The bottoms got a bird's eye view of the place every day.

"Stanley, did you bring that medicine?" A white woman called out from the front door of Stanley's house.

"Got it right here, Ashley," Stanley shouted back. "Hey, you wanna come in and meet Ashley and my mother? If you have the time that is."

Stacia stood and pondered for a few moments. Dildo, or play nice? "Sure, I can stop by for a second." She kept her smile up.

Ever so reluctantly Stacia followed Stanley inside his home. The instant she stepped in, Stacia was bombarded by a menagerie of nothing but pictures upon pictures of white people all over the walls, old and young persons in both color and black and white photos. It was all too much for the woman to take in with one or even ten glances.

Stacia Taylor, this is Ashley Forrest. Ashley, this is Stacia. Stacia lives in the house across the street."

Ashley was a young lady with short, blonde spiked hair. Stacia could right away sense that she was one half of the gay couple that Stanley mentioned when she first arrived weeks earlier. She could tell right off the bat that she was the dominant one.

"Nice to meet you," Stacia smiled at the woman.

"Good to meet you, too." Ashley smiled back.

"Ashley here watches over mom while I'm away at work." Stanley explained while taking a bottle of medicine from out of his coat pocket and handing it to Ashley.

"Great, your mother has been going nuts for this stuff."

"Is she awake?"

"Yeah, and as ornery as ever," Ashley sighed.

"Believe me, Stacia, ornery is actually well-tempered for my mom." Stanley expounded as he began for the second floor.

Stacia and Ashley followed in behind the man. Much like the downstairs, the upstairs walls were littered with pictures. To Stacia, it was like visiting a museum.

"A lot of pictures, huh?" Ashley smirked at Stacia.

Catching herself off guard, Stacia looked over at the woman and said, "Uh…yeah. They must have a lot of family."

"Not really, mom just can't stand to have the damn walls bare," Stanley sneered.

"I see." Stacia giggled.

"So, how do you like here in the neighborhood so far?" Ashley asked.

"It's nice." Stacia modestly remarked. "Like I told Stanley, it's a lot better than what me and my grandkids are used to."

"You have grandkids?" Ashley gasped. "Tammy and I thought those were your kids."

"I get that all the time, girl. No, they're my grandbabies," Stacia carried on.

"Wow, it must be hard caring for grandkids and working. You must be tired of taking care of children after so long."

Before Stacia could reply, just around the corner was a bedroom. Inside the bedroom was a television that was playing *Adam-12*, along with a bed that had an old, white lady lying on her side. The second Stacia stepped inside the room she could have passed out from sheer heat exhaustion. It was almost too stifling for her to even breathe.

Stacia waved her hand across her face to fan off from the overbearing temperatures that prevailed inside the room.

"Sorry it's so warm in here," Stanley turned around and whispered, "mom thinks it's 30 degrees everywhere in this house."

Stacia turned to face Ashley who herself was wearing a perturbed expression. Stacia began to realize that her luck would have her stay in the house longer than just a mere spell.

"Mom, mom, are you awake?" Stanley yelled into his mother's face.

The woman's eyes were wide open, but they were locked solely on the television in front of her. Every so often she would stir about in her bed like the thing was made of nails.

"Mom, this is Ms. Stacia Taylor!" Stanley pointed.

The woman, with her pointy eyeglasses, looked up and all around before focusing her blue eyes on everything but Stacia.

"I know who she is!" "Mother grumbled." "She's been here all day!"

Laughing and shaking his head, Stanley reiterated, "No, mom, not Ashley, this is Stacia!"

Stacia warmly waved her hand for the woman to see her, but the very second she pointed her face directly at Stacia, the woman's facial appearance went from disgruntled to downright puzzled.

"Who are you?" She coughed uncontrollably.

Stepping forward, Stacia, with her hand extended and her smile still caressing her face, loudly proclaimed, "Hello, I'm Stacia! I live across the street! Good to meet you!"

The old lady looked on and on at Stacia until her eyes began to water. She then turned back over in her bed and whispered something to Stanley.

Scratching his head, Stanley asked, "What did you say, mom."

"I said get her out of here, and don't let her back in this house again!"

At that, Stacia turned up her nose before spinning around and heading for the stairs, with both Ashley and Stanley right behind her.

"Agnes, that wasn't nice!" Ashley scolded the old woman.

"Stacia, I'm so sorry about that." Stanley constantly repeated over and over. "Sometimes mom comes and goes."

Stacia was in a hurry to get out of the house, not so much for the Agnes' sake, but for the simple matter that she was tired, too tired to put up with crotchety elderly folks for the day.

By the time Stacia hit the bottom floor she could hear Agnes up above crying like a baby. Stacia looked up in a mystified manner.

"What is wrong with her?" Ashley, too, looked on amazed. "She was fine all day."

Sighing, Stanley replied, "I don't know, like I said, she comes and she goes. I just want you to know, Stacia, that I'm sorry for that. Mom is cantankerous, but not like that."

Not wanting to take the subject any further, Stacia waved her hand in the air and said, "Don't worry about it, I work with cantankerous people all day long. But I do have to get home."

"I understand," Stanley said, "have a good night."

Ashley followed Stacia out the door. The two women carried on until they reached the sidewalk. Before anything else, Stacia immediately saw Dixon's white Denali parked across the street in front of her house. Right then, a tidal wave of refined elation whipped her body.

"I think that old bat is on her last leg if you ask me." Ashley grimaced while glancing back at the house behind her.

Stacia, too, took a quick glimpse behind her before spinning her head back to the Denali where she could see Dixon seated inside. Stacia could hear Ashley, but the woman might as well have been a world away; both her mind and hormones were elsewhere.

"Did you hear me?" Ashley poked at Stacia.

Stacia all of the sudden snapped to before looking back at Ashley and squinting, "Huh…I didn't understand you?"

"I said, how do you and your grandkids like the house so far?"

Modestly giggling, Stacia responded, "Oh, I mean…it's okay. Still a bit drafty, but at least it's a roof over our heads."

"Agnes can't stand the place. Did you notice that she had the blinds in her room facing your house shut?"

"No, I wasn't paying much attention." Stacia tried keeping up with Ashley's inquiries.

"Don't ask me why only those blinds. Tammy, my roommate, said that she and the woman who used to live there years ago used to have a thing for each other, if you know what I mean."

Stacia squared her eyes strangely at Ashley before saying, "Um…I don't mean to be rude, but, the man who's supposed to be fixing our basement stairs is waiting for me there."

Appearing surprised, Ashley jumped back and said, "Oh, I'm sorry. Here I am, babbling like a dork. Have a good evening, Stacia. And don't hesitate to stop by anytime. We live down there at 823."

With a hasty smile, Stacia waved at Ashley before speed walking across the street to Dixon's truck. The second the man climbed out Stacia noticed his eyes fixated upon Ashley who was carrying herself down the sidewalk.

Twisting her lips, Stacia said to the man, "Forget about it, that girl is straight up gay, and she lives with her partner."

Smirking, Dixon commented, "Oh yeah, your boy did mention that there was some of them living on this block."

Taking the man by the arm and leading him towards her house, Stacia said, "So, why are you off from work so early?"

"I had to run a few errands here and there."

The closer Stacia's nose came in contact with Dixon's jacket, the more she could smell the aroma of weed smoke emanate off of him. The woman just frowned at the man before turning her face away and taking her keys out.

"What's the matter?"

Stacia didn't say anything; she just silently unlocked the front door and slammed her purse down onto the couch before walking over to the stairs. But before she could even get one foot on the first step, Dixon caught her by the arm and asked with a tender tone, "What's goin' on, girl? I came by to see you before the kids got out."

Without turning her head to face him, Stacia said, "We've talked about this."

"About what," Dixon sulked.

Stacia turned to the man with a face that suggested he knew exactly what she was talking about. Dixon turned around in a shameful fashion; his eyes couldn't even connect with hers.

"I just smoked one with my nephews." Dixon pleaded. "You know all the pressure I've been going through down at the plant. Now they're threatening to lay about half of us off before the end of the month. You know I can't retire yet."

"I've been under pressure, too." Stacia retaliated. "But I haven't smoked that shit in years. And you know I don't want the kids smelling that stuff."

Glaring into her eyes, Dixon scaled his hands up Stacia's right arm. It was a sensual gesture that at any other time would have Stacia drooling all over herself, but at that moment, just the sheer scent of weed felt burned sulfur in her nostrils. She despised it, and she hated it even more knowing that Dixon was still indulging.

But as angry as she was at that juncture, not once did her hormones cease to settle down. She was a cauldron of fire ever since lunchtime, and just knowing that her man had made an untimely trip to her home before the kids got out of school made her even more horny.

She allowed the man to keep on rubbing her arms before he took off her blue thermal hat and tossed it behind him. From there he kissed Stacia on the lips before scooping her up into his arms and running up the stairs directly into her bedroom.

Without even closing the door behind him, Dixon dropped Stacia's body onto the bed before he hovered over her and began kissing and sucking all over her neck. Stacia held onto the man's head before she eventually went down and unzipped her pants. All Stacia hoped at that instant was for no interruptions, even the children would be a nuisance at that point.

Dixon then rose back up and pulled off his jacket and t-shirt. Stacia rubbed all over the man's rippled, tight stomach before she unzipped his pants and yanked out his dick. Dixon drew closer as so to give Stacia a mouthful of all eight inches. Stacia sucked and licked all over the thing while listening to Dixon grunt and groan in rapture. Just hearing the man enjoy her work actually made Stacia all the more excited, so much so that she stuffed the entire rod into her mouth, causing her to gag and nearly vomit all over the bed, but before that could even happen, Dixon pulled it out of her mouth and pulled his own pants off. He then spread open Stacia's legs as wide as he could and slid his member inside her slippery snatch.

Stacia wanted to get off so bad, but she held it in a while longer while feeling his rock hard rod slide in and out of her with such great ease that even she couldn't believe how wet she was.

Stacia held Dixon's back as he rocked back and forth on top of her. She wrapped her legs around the man's waist as tight as she could while gritting her teeth and holding on to the orgasm that wanted ever so much to be released.

At least five times she screamed out "Oh God!", and that was all the harder Dixon pumped in and out. He would speak nasty words in her ear, asking her if she liked it, and if she wanted to be fucked any harder. Stacia would always reply in a grunting whisper, "Yes.", as if the man had to ask to begin with.

It was approaching, the moment that Stacia was trying her almighty best to keep at bay. The orgasm was right there, waiting to be let loose, all it would take was two more pumps.

"What the fuck?" Dixon suddenly screamed as he jumped up off of Stacia and gawked all around the bedroom.

Stacia sat up in the bed and gazed around with him before asking in a startled voice, "What is it?"

At first, Dixon said not one word, he stood there in the middle of the floor butt naked to the world and still staring around as though he were searching for either something or someone.

"What's the matter?" Stacia's jaw trembled. "What are you looking for?"

Without looking at her, Dixon replied, "I felt something hit me on the back."

Stacia stared out into the hallway, but of course could see nothing. She then re-directed her attention back to Dixon who looked as though he was lost in space. Never before had she seen the man so stunned and frightened. For a moment or two it actually scared her.

"Maybe you're still feeling the effects of your high." Stacia rolled her eyes.

"No, no, that ain't it." Dixon breathed in and out. "Something slapped me on the back. It was cold."

"Oh, Dixon, please," Stacia griped as she got off the bed. She wasn't going to make it known to him, but she was more upset at not getting off than she was at what he thought he was experiencing at that second.

"You think I'm playing, but I know I felt something touch me." Dixon continued to fervently rant.

"You felt me." Stacia tossed up her hands.

"No, it wasn't you. Like I said, it felt cold and it smacked me. You don't smack."

Still raving naked, Dixon ventured out into the hallway. In all her nakedness, Stacia followed until they both were standing right underneath the attic door. No matter what, the man would not be settled. He prowled about like a paranoid cat, keeping his eyes wide open for anything that would possibly pounce at a moment's notice.

Not wanting to get caught up in his obsessed enthusiasm, Stacia irritably began for her bedroom, but not before the attic door that Dixon just happened to still be standing under fell open and onto the man's head, sending Dixon to the floor.

Stacia screamed out loud before racing over and moving Dixon away from the door that was dangling down along with the steps that were attached to it.

"Are you okay?" She hysterically begged.

Holding the back of his bleeding head, Dixon slurred, "Yeah…what happened?"

Looking up at that open attic, Stacia said, "I don't know, baby. The thing just came down."

Dixon looked up as well before rubbing his head back and forth. "This shit would happen when my ass is gettin' some." He grinned.

Stacia, too, cracked a subtle grin before getting to her feet and heading for the bathroom. "Stay right there, I'll get some Band-Aids and alcohol."

Just as soon as Stacia was about to open the medicine cabinet, five knocks at the front door shook her every movement. She quickly looked down at her watch just to make sure she didn't forget the kids. When the time checked out, she immediately ran to the bedroom to retrieve her robe. From there she went downstairs and opened the door to see Detective Paulson standing on the other end with a heavy winter coat covering her body.

Stacia was already a ball of unwrapped nerves; just seeing the detective there at her new house only caused the woman to break out into a brand new violent sweat.

"Glad to see your home, Ms. Taylor. You're a hard lady to find." Paulson beamed.

Stacia, with her robe wrapped tightly around her naked body, peeked out the door before turning to Paulson and frowning, "What…what do you want? How did you find me?"

Appearing surprised, Paulson said, "With all due respect, Ms. Taylor, we're the police, we can find almost anyone. I'm actually here to discuss your case a bit further."

Dropping her shoulders in anguish, Stacia said, "Look, I've moved on. I don't want anything more to do with that."

"I understand, Ms. Taylor, but we believe we may have a lead on the culprits, but we still need some more questions answered."

Stacia rolled her eyes before glancing behind her to see Dixon standing clear up on the very top of the stairs, looking as if he were too afraid to come down.

"Ms. Taylor, we recently discovered that your home was broken into again. Can you tell me why you never reported it?"

"What for," Stacia shrugged. "Me and my grandkids were already moving out. Whatever was left there was worthless to us."

"One of your former neighbors there said they saw four men break into the house and take more property. Don't you think it's odd, Ms. Taylor, that four more men would assault the same house?"

Stacia plunged her head. She wanted to scream at Paulson more than anything; she was already leaning on the edge with what just took place with Dixon back upstairs, and now the most harrowing event of her life was being thrown back in her face all over again, from out of nowhere, no less.

Sounding exasperated, Stacia stepped forward and adamantly proclaimed, "Look, I don't want anything more to do with that house or the people who broke into it. Me and my grandkids have moved on. Do you understand me, Detective? We've moved on!"

Detective Paulson stood in the brisk wind that passed by on the porch as a dejected frown came upon her chubby face. She straightened her coat and quietly uttered, "Ms. Taylor, I fully understand what you and your grandchildren went through was traumatic. Believe me, I understand it more than you think. But if these guys are the same ones that attacked you three, then we may be onto something. They just broke in and assaulted an elderly couple last week. They broke an eighty-five year old man's collar bone, Ms. Taylor."

Stacia stood as straight as she could while listening to Paulson go on in her desperate plea. It touched her bitterly inside to know that there was someone out there in the world that could be so cruel, but all that mattered to her was that she and her litter were as far away from it as possible.

"Now, you mentioned that you were able to recognize at least one of the voices that night. It would help us out a lot if you could come down to the station and—

"No!" Stacia fired back, holding in tears. "I'm done, and that's that."

Detective Paulson dropped her head before looking back up at Stacia with sympathetic eyes and saying, "Okay, I understand. You have my number. Please contact me if anything comes up."

Stacia stood and watched as Paulson walked herself back to her brown sedan and pulled away. She then shut the door and turned to see Dixon trotting down the stairs fully clothed and in a rush.

"Where are you going?" She asked in a confused stutter.

Putting on his jacket, the man huffed, "I gotta get outta here."

"Why were you hiding up there?"

"Are you crazy?" He crunched up his face. "I still got the skunk on me. That cop would've smelled that a mile away."

Stacia stood and watched Dixon stare out the peephole in the front door before the man swung open the door and began out.

"Aren't you gonna at least stay for dinner?" Stacia exhaled.

"Tell the kids I'll see them later." Dixon quickly replied as he kissed Stacia on the cheek and bolted out the door and to his truck.

Stacia looked on as the man cold-started his vehicle and tore away. She then shut the door and looked all around her in the lonely and quiet living room.

From Stanley's mother, to Dixon's paranoia spell and Paulson's unexpected visit; everything happened so quickly and in such a short amount of time that Stacia was still chasing after her own breath.

Dropping her shoulders in a defeated fashion, Stacia dragged her limp carcass back up the stairs and away from the day.

CHAPTER 15

8:43 p.m.

"It's going on nine 'o clock, you two!" Stacia announced from outside the front door. "Start getting ready for bed!"

"Yes, ma'am," both Sidney and Devon said in unison while keeping their faces tuned to the television in the living room.

Once she was done speaking with the children, Stacia closed the door and went back outside on the porch where she was both smoking a cigarette and texting Dixon all at the same time.

The twenty degree breeze that stalked the neighborhood that evening didn't seem to bear all that much difference upon Stacia, as a matter of fact, it never really did. She had her smokes and a soothing conversation to keep her warm on such nights.

Stacia: So get this, the very second I get home today, Stanley asks me to come and meet his mom. She stays up in her bedroom all day long. That house is hotter than hell.

Dixon: Oh yeah? What was she like?

Stacia: She's a mean old bag. The second she looked at me she told me to get out and to never come back again.

Dixon: I tried to tell you about those bottoms motherfuckers, but you wouldn't listen to me.

Stacia: Whatever. Stanley and Ashley are nice.

Dixon: Who's Ashley?

Stacia: She's the girl you saw walking down the street.

Dixon: Oh, the lesbo?

Stacia giggled while taking another drag of her cigarette before she attempted to type again on her cellphone.

Stacia: Yes fool, the lesbo.

Dixon: What's her girlfriend's name?"

Stacia: I think her name was Tammy or something. I was in such a rush to get out of that old bat's house that I wasn't paying much attention.

Dixon: You should get to know them better.

Stacia: Why?

Dixon: You never know, we could make it a foursome, if they're up to swinging that way at least for one night. Lol

Stacia only twisted her lips and rolled her eyes before dashing her cigarette out on the porch floor.

Dixon: You're still up for that aren't you? A threesome?

Stacia raised herself up from the porch banister where she was leaning and roamed about the rickety floor in deep thought. Just the mention of a three-way sent a sharp pain down her back, as it did every time it was brought up by Dixon, and only Dixon.

Dixon: Hello?

Stacia: I'm here.

Dixon: So, what's up with that girl?

Stacia: Need more time to think.

A long pause on Dixon's end caused Stacia to freeze right where she stood at that moment. She knew that her hesitation aggravated him.

Dixon: Cool.

Just seeing that one word gave Stacia the motivation she needed to resume her march around the porch once again.

Stacia: I was talking to this one lady at work, and she said that all it took for her to start her online business was about $1300.00. That got me to thinking, if I could just get my website on track, then by the start of the summer I could have the money to open up my catering service.

Dixon: I can give you $1300.00.

Stacia: No, you do more than enough for us as it is. This is something that I have to do.

Dixon: There you go again, trying to prove something to someone. If we're gonna be married one day then you have to let me help you along the way.

Stacia stood and pondered for a few seconds. She could spend the whole night trying to explain to the man her reasons as to why it was hers and only hers and he still would have never grasped it. Instead, she chose to switch gears as fast as she could.

Stacia: So, why did you bail out like you did earlier today when that bitch showed up?

Dixon: What bitch?

Stacia: The detective.

Dixon: I told you, I was still smelling like skunk. Those cops can smell that stuff a mile away. I don't want nothing I do to come down on you three.

Stacia: Then why do you still do it after all these years?

Much like moments earlier, a long pause carried on over the phone. Stacia expected it, deep down she wanted it. It only meant that Dixon was thinking hard on the matter.

Dixon: I'm trying baby girl. You and those kids are the only reason I've even bothered to change my ways after all these years. To be honest, before today, the last time I smoked was back in January. You know how I get when I'm around my nephews.

Stacia: Then perhaps you need to find new hangout partners. Both of the kids asked if I had an animal in the house when they came home from school today.

Dixon: I'm sorry, it won't happen again.

Stacia had heard it before. She wanted to light another cigarette, but she realized that she had chain smoked at least five in the past twenty minutes.

Dixon: What did you guys have for supper?

Stacia: Just some leftover spaghetti.

Dixon: Lol. And you wanted me to stay and have leftovers?

Stacia: Whatever, nigga. Lmfao.

Dixon: Has anymore crazy shit happened there since I left?

Stacia: I don't know what you felt today, but it all had to be in your mind.

Dixon: I told you, I felt a hand slap me on the back.

Stacia: It was me.

Dixon: Your hands ain't never been that hard. This was a hard slap across the back. It felt like a dude hit me.

Stacia: If you think that's strange, I found Sidney sleeping down in the basement yesterday morning.

Dixon: WTF?

Stacia: Yep, I looked all over this place for her. Then I went downstairs and there she was, sleeping away on the freezing basement floor.

Dixon: What the hell was she doing down there?

Stacia: She can't remember. I'm afraid she may be sleep walking now. With her being such a hard sleeper as it is.

Dixon: Next thing you know she'll be sleepwalking out of the house.

Stacia: Don't say that, that's all I need, another—

Stacia caught herself in mid-sentence right then. Her fingers didn't have the ability to type any further. Without allowing another sour thought to enter her head, Stacia right away began to type speedy words.

Stacia: Listen, let me get these kids off to bed. I'll talk to you tomorrow. Love you, baby.

Dixon: You okay?

Without replying to his text, Stacia stuffed her phone back into her pocket and carried herself back inside to surprisingly find the kids still seated and watching television.

"I thought I told you both to head off to bed!" She shouted.

Stunned, Sidney and Devon jumped to attention. Devon spun around and desperately pleaded with his grandmother, "Please let me stay up till ten. Daniel Bryan is gonna fight."

"Boy, I don't care who's fighting! Cut off that TV and get to bed!"

Stacia watched as Devon dragged his little body off the couch and over to the coffee table to retrieve the remote.

Right before the television could be cut off, a large, black shadow all of the sudden crossed directly in front of the set and in front of everyone watching in the living room.

"What was that?" Sidney ran away from the TV in shock.

Stacia stood behind the couch, too astonished to even speak at that moment. She wanted to believe that what she saw was just a flicker of sleepiness, or perhaps she blinked for longer than a half a second.

"What was that, grandma?" Devon stammered as he came running to his grandmother's side.

Stacia gathered both kids to her and stood back. All three individuals remained absolutely still there on the floor and watched as a commercial came upon the screen.

Stacia didn't want to shake, but she couldn't help it. It was the fact that all three of them saw the same thing that made her hands sweat all the more profusely. It wasn't a "brain fart."

"Grandma, did you see that?" Sidney looked up in fright.

Stacia couldn't speak, all she could do was continue to stand idly by and wait for another possible occurrence to strike.

Then, with as much courage as she could assemble, Stacia pulled herself away from the children's strong grips and carefully ventured over to where the remote was still seated on the table in front of the television.

As if the contraption were electrified, Stacia quickly pushed the "off" button before tossing the thing onto the couch and rushing both of the kids up the stairs and to their individual rooms.

Clearing her dry throat, Stacia said, "You two go on and get ready for bed. And lock your doors, too."

Without muttering a single word, Devon and Sidney ran off. Stacia, however, only stayed behind to do something that she would have rather not done, make sure all was well downstairs.

The lights needed to go out. There were two that sat on both ends of the sofa. Shaking violently in her sneakers, Stacia ever so vigilantly went over and clicked off both lamps before racing back for the stairs and gawking around in the hushed darkness.

The living room was completely black and quiet. Stacia herself was sweating from head to toe. She didn't want to see anything else. All she wanted to do for the rest of the night was lock herself in her bedroom and come up with rational solutions as to what her and her grandchildren could have possibly all seen with their very own eyes.

"Grandma, are you still downstairs?" Sidney screamed from upstairs.

Scaring Stacia half to death, she screamed back, "Yes, dammit! Go to bed!"

Leaving the darkness of the living room behind her, Stacia carted her own self up the steps, all the while yelling, "And don't forget to lock your doors!"

CHAPTER 16

Day 5
2:51 a.m.

I'm dreaming. I can tell because I can hear myself talking. I'm in that old shithole house we used to live in. The big guy has his shotgun pointed at my fucking head. I can feel it pressing against my skull. It hurts me so much because he's using such force to press it.

I can hear his hateful voice, it sounds so evil. I've never heard anything so ungodly in my life. He sounds like he wants so bad to kill me, and I don't know why. I can't remember ever causing anyone else so much harm to make them want to do me and my babies like this.

I can see Devon and Sidney crying their little eyes out. I wish to God they never had to be a part of such an evil thing. They'll never be able to live it down for as long as they live.

I've tried so hard to keep them both away from the ugliness of the streets, but no matter what, the streets keep finding their way back into our lives once more as usual.

There he goes, yelling and screaming at me. No matter what, I can't give in. I can't give him what he wants, even though my life is on the line.

I just pray to God that no matter what happens to me, they won't harm the kids, if they do, then they're no better than the Devil himself.

Here it comes, I can feel it, it's like a train about to hit me square in the head. The shell from the gun goes straight into my skull and cracks my head wide open. The noise from the blast is loud enough to wake me up.

Stacia awoke from her slumber in a sweaty heap. The second she caught her breath she rolled over and gulped down the water that was in the glass next to her bed, she then fanned herself with her hands before sitting up in the bed and staring off at the window straight ahead.

Stacia knew that ever since her return meeting with Detective Paulson that the nightmares would resurface, all she was doing was waiting for them.

She wanted to be mad at Paulson for finding her, but Stacia realized that the woman was only doing her job, which was why she didn't lay into her as much as she may have desired. What took place back at the old house was something that Stacia wanted erased permanently. She was sorry for the others that felt the sting that she and the children endured, but as far as she was concerned, that wasn't her problem.

Stacia tried to calm herself by counting from twenty. The gunman's voice roaring in her head felt like grinding iron, and counting as slowly as she could didn't seem to silence him at all.

Stacia then laid back down. There was the overbearing pressure to please herself back to sleep, but that would have only kept her awake longer than she would have wanted. Instead, she closed her eyes as tight as she could and began thinking of work, the only thing in the world that bored her silly.

After ten whole minutes of pondering on tally sheets for the next station delivery, Stacia's attention began to fade, so much so that she was beginning to lose conciseness.

Right before she slipped away, something from within the house hollered. Stacia struck back awake. She immediately sat up in her bed and listened as the sound echoed all over the house. For a while, the noise sounded like it was in the hallway. Thinking of the children, Stacia jumped up and flung open her bedroom door. The noise no longer sounded close, but rather far away.

Devon and Sidney both came out of their separate rooms and stood next to their grandmother. The hollering sounded painful, almost like a large animal screaming out in terror while being tortured.

"Grandma...what is that?" Devon shivered while holding on to Stacia's leg.

"You both go on in my room." Stacia whispered before running back to her bedroom and reaching up under her mattress for her gun and her cellphone that was placed on the nightstand. "Stay in here, and don't move."

Stacia closed the door behind her and dialed 911 on her phone before slowly going downstairs where the noise only grew louder.

The second she heard a voice on the other end, Stacia immediately interrupted the operator. "I need someone here now. I think I have an intruder in my home."

"Okay, ma'am, where are you in the house right now?"

"I'm going downstairs with my gun." Stacia stammered.

"Ma'am, do not engage the intruder! I repeat, do not engage the intruder! Stay away until help arrives! Give me your address!"

Stacia recited her address to the operator before sliding her phone into her pajama pants pocket. But instead of listening to the operator's urgent command, she persisted downstairs.

To say that Stacia was scared was hardly the appropriate word; she was nearly having a stroke at that point. The hollering only intensified the closer she seemed to draw to the kitchen.

She couldn't for the life of her explain why she was being so hardheaded, it wasn't her nature to be so nosey, but it was her house, her last stand against the world, and perhaps that alone gave her the blind courage to proceed.

The hollering was vicious. Stacia honestly couldn't tell if it were human or not, it just sounded ugly and awkward.

As she rounded the corner that led to the kitchen, the noise was all but apparent. It sounded as if it were right behind the basement door. No matter what, Stacia wasn't going down there, she was adamant about that. But who or whatever happened to be down there would surely meet a deadly demise if they came upstairs, because her gun was locked and loaded. Her hands were shaking incessantly, but that surely wouldn't stop her from doing what she had to do in order to save her babies and herself.

Stacia stood there in the middle of the kitchen floor waiting and listening to the noise carry on while wondering if anyone else in the neighborhood could hear it as well.

She began to cry, so much that she was losing her grip on the gun. Stacia wanted ever so badly to cut and run out the backdoor; she actually had to remember that her children were still upstairs in her bedroom.

Soon, the sounds of sirens in the distance caused Stacia to bolt from the kitchen and to the front door like a hungry cheetah. She swung open the door to see one cruiser pull up behind her car. Two, male, white police officers came rushing towards the front door with their own weapons drawn.

"Ma'am, are you okay?" One of the officers asked.

"Yes," she stuttered. "They're inside. I think down in the basement."

"Stay here, ma'am." The other ordered before he and his partner went inside.

Stacia stepped back inside the house. She wanted to see how the children were doing upstairs, but before she could even set one foot on the first step, the television suddenly came on all by itself.

Stacia was stuck solid in place. She could still hear the hollering. She wondered if the policemen had encountered whatever it was. But the TV came on all by itself. Some many distractions all at once only sent the woman into a free-fall. All Stacia could do was stand still and wait for something else to happen. It's not that she wanted something to take place, but by then, she realized that it was beyond her control, whatever "it" was to begin with.

After nearly ten minutes, the hollering ended, that was when the officers came back up and into the living room along with Stacia. Stacia unhinged herself from the bannister and cut on one of the lamps before shutting off the television.

With staggered expressions on their suddenly pale faces, both of the officers glanced at each other before turning to Stacia. Then, placing his piece back into its holster, one of the policemen uttered, "Okay, ma'am, whatever was down there is gone."

Shaking her head in disbelief, Stacia breathlessly asked, "How so? Did you see who it was?"

"We saw nothing down there, ma'am."

"Didn't you hear that, too?" She urged.

They both gave a brief pause before the other replied, "We heard it, ma'am, but like he said, we saw nothing. The second we got downstairs it stopped. We searched all over, but we found nothing."

"Not unless there's a hidden room down there." The other man speculated.

Stacia shook her head no before dropping herself down onto the couch and exhaling as hard as she could. The officers stood there above her just waiting.

Stacia then spun around and said, "Wait a minute, if you two and my grandbabies all heard the same thing, then that means we're not crazy, right?"

"You have grandchildren in here, ma'am?"

"They're upstairs," Stacia pointed to the steps. "But you did hear it?"

"Yes, ma'am, we heard it as well. We can't explain what it was, but we did hear it."

Stacia breathed a sigh of relief, for a second she thought she may have still been asleep and dreaming. Knowing that she wasn't the only one slipping caused her shaking to cease.

"Well, ma'am, if there is anything else we can do, don't hesitate to call us."

Stacia got up from off the couch and escorted both officers out the door. Without a moment's hesitation she then turned off the lamp and bolted right back upstairs to her bedroom to find Sidney and Devon hiding underneath the covers.

Stacia shut the door behind her and locked it. From there, she went over and pushed a chair up against the door's knob.

"Grandma, what was that down there?" Devon wept.

Stacia placed both her gun and cellphone down onto the nightstand before climbing in the bed with the children and wrapping them both up in the covers like they were infants.

"Listen to me, both of you." She whispered. "It was nothing. The police were just here and they didn't find a thing. Okay?"

"Is it gonna happen again?" Sidney wept also.

"No, baby, it's all over. Just go back to sleep."

"Can we leave the light on?" Sidney asked.

Stacia reached over and turned on the lamp to her nightstand before cuddling up with the kids as tight as possible.

For the remainder of the night, all three Taylors laid in bed and held on.

CHAPTER 17

Day 7

The rain steadily pelted the plastic hood under which both Stacia and Max were standing and smoking. Stacia made extra sure that no one else was around.

"Have you told Dixon yet?"

"Yeah right," Stacia twisted her lips, "he still thinks I'm crazy for buying that place. I wouldn't have told you, but I need to tell someone so people won't think I'm losing my fucking mind."

Max took a long drag of his cigarette before asking, "How are the kids taking it? I mean, I could excuse the TV coming on by itself, but the screaming is something that would have scared me shitless."

"They're scared to death, Max." Stacia desperately replied. "They sleep with me now. I don't mind that, but I'm sure they're going to school and telling everyone there about what happened. That's all I need is some teacher calling me or coming over to my house asking me a whole bunch of questions about my parenting skills. I went through that shit with Deontae."

"Okay, okay." Max insisted. "Now listen, I'm not saying that I believe in that kind of stuff, but I've known you for far too long, Stacia, if there's something going on in that house then I believe you. I'm not saying I believe in spirits, but I believe in you."

Stacia put out her cigarette and stared long at Max. He was exactly what she needed, common sense without the lecture.

"I don't believe in that shit either, but if me, the kids and two cops experience the same thing, then something stinks."

Max shook his head up and down before dashing his cigarette on the wet ground. "Okay, now that we got that out of the way, let me ask you a question. What do you know about the previous owner of the house?"

"Not much," Stacia shrugged her shoulders. "Judy was the one that refereed me to the place."

"That nut." Max snorted. "She was a hundred years old and half crazy. Who knows what kind of haunts she left there."

"I don't care anything about her; I just want whatever is going on to end. I don't want any crazy shit up in there. You know what I've been through all these years. I can't take anymore surprises."

"I think you'd better care about Judy, Stacia, because if she was the last owner, then perhaps she can give you some clues as to what's happening."

Stacia only sighed before turning away and saying, "Who knows where in the world she's at anyways? She just came and went like the wind."

"I can get in touch with the temp agency that sent her ass here. They'll find her. In the meantime, I've got several suggestions."

Stacia turned back around and waited with bated breath for the man to say what he had to, and without pause.

"You can call a medium, and they can—"

"No," Stacia stubbornly fussed, "I don't want some voodoo woman, or someone chanting spells and throwing up that ectoplasm shit all over the place. I've seen these movies."

"But a medium may be able to tell you if you have a spirit up in there." Max urged.

"No, Max! I don't want the kids to see that. Knowing my luck, they'll end up conjuring something even worse."

"Okay, okay, how about a minister?"

Stacia stopped and looked on at Max. "You mean a pastor to do an exorcism?"

Fidgeting from side to side like he was too shy to reply to her question, Max said, "Not that, but perhaps you could have him come in and pray over the house. He doesn't have to know your business. All you want is to have your house blessed."

"Do you think that'll work?"

"Stacia, at this point, anything is possible. But, if that doesn't do the trick, then I have one more solution. Do you remember my half-wit nephew Scotty? The one that's spent seven years at OSU, still trying to figure out what he wants to do with his life?" Stacia quaintly smiled before saying, "Yeah."

"Well, for a while now, he's been doing research with this little team of paranormal investigators. Now, before you go off on me again, these guys aren't mediums or voodoo priests, they just investigate. Apparently, they've been all over Ohio examining ghost sightings and whatnot. Now, once more, I'm not saying that I believe in such things, but it's what they do for a living."

"Are they Ghostbusters or something?" Stacia broadened her eyes.

"I wouldn't go that far, but they do have experience in these sorts of matters. Scotty seems to enjoy it. For the first time in his life, he's actually sticking to an occupation. Hell, whatever keeps him out of trouble is okay with the family."

Stacia thought long and hard, weighing her options while trying not to appear too desperate to the one person in the world that still had faith in her.

"Okay…I'll try the minister first." Stacia cracked a timid smile.

"Good, it can't hurt."

"There's a church about two blocks away from the house, I'll see who's there. And if that doesn't do the trick, then we'll try dear old Scotty."

Right then, Max's phone began to ring. The man answered the call and snapped back at the person on the other end before hanging up and saying, "Its dock nine, they got another spill over there."

"Get to it, bossman." Stacia grinned.

Just as Max was about to turn and storm away, he stopped right in the middle of the rain and said, "I don't think for one moment you're crazy, Stacia. As a matter of fact, I'd do the same thing myself if it were me."

Stacia stood and watched as the heavy man ran back into the building. Her lunchtime was nearly over, which only meant that it was close to quitting time for the day. That was the last thing she wanted to know was that it was almost time to go home.

CHAPTER 18

"Freddy, you need to come out here and see this!" Margaret loudly proclaimed.

Zipping up his pants while grinning at his wife's constant urgings, Frederick made sure to remember to wash his hands before exiting the tiny bathroom that he had been stuck in for so long.

From the hallway, Frederick could hear the bluster outside the church. It was so loud that for a moment he believed he should have contacted the police.

Straitening his glasses, Frederick stepped up behind his inquisitive wife and viewed the carnage outside the window where she was perched. In the parking lot was a group of young, white boys, all who were hurling curse words at each other while using their overactive bodies to threaten physical violence.

"Oh my," Frederick moaned in a slight German accent, "those boys will never learn."

"It's a shame they have absolutely nothing to do after school lets out." Margaret complained while stepping away from the window and carrying herself back to her desk.

Frederick examined the melee further before turning and heading for the backdoor which was only a few feet away from the church's office.

"Where are you going to?" Margaret all of the sudden looked up startled.

Frederick stopped for a second before turning around and saying, "I'm going out to see what all the hullabaloo is about before someone gets hurt again."

Getting up from out of her seat, the elderly Margaret raced around her desk and said straight into Frederick's face, "What if they have weapons? You're not exactly fifty years younger, Freddy."

Frederick took his wife's delicate face into his hands and said, "My dear, you give me far too much credit."

With that, Frederick went about his business, and as he was about to exit the door, he went out saying with a charming tone, "I'll be back before sundown!"

Before Frederick could even round the corner that led to the parking lot, the uproar of the young men could be heard clear across the neighborhood. Frederick buttoned up his heavy sweater and picked up his slow pace.

In all, there were exactly eight boys, four on opposite sides of each other, yelling and screaming into the others faces. Frederick recognized several of the youths, but the remainder was brand new to him, which in turn caused the man to perhaps second guess his decision on whether or not he should interject himself.

"Okay now, boys, what is this about?" Frederick screamed at the top of his lungs.

The boys fussed for a few seconds longer before eventually halting their feud and looking at Frederick. One of the young men stepped forward with a disgusted frown and bawled, "Get the fuck outta here, old man! Ain't nobody call you!"

"Don't talk to the reverend like that, motherfucker!" Another one of the boys screamed.

"Alright now, boys, let's calm this down!" Frederick stepped in between the eight. "Now, let's start from the beginning, what's going on here?"

"Reverend Fred," another one of the familiars spoke up, "these faggots came down here lyin' and sayin' that my brother got his hoe ass sister pregnant!"

"Bitch, my sister ain't no hoe!"

"Alright now, let's leave all of the colorful language out!" Frederick protested.

"Who the fuck is this anyways?" one of the boys grimaced.

"The man said to stop cursin'!"

"I'll fuckin' curse if I want to!"

Just like that, the fight erupted all over again. At that point in the day, Frederick was far too weary to put with any kind of out of control confusion, especially when it came to a group of foul-mouthed youths. The old man used his arms to separate the two factions before screaming them all to a standstill.

"Now, we all need to just stop this loudness and settle down!"

"Fuck settling down, I'm gonna shoot his fuckin' ass!" One of the boys hollered before pulling out a revolver and pointing it at the other faction.

Frederick saw only the gun. Without even thinking twice, the man jabbed the youth straight in the mouth before snatching the weapon from his hand. All eight young men stood back and stared on at the Reverend as though they were in the midst of a giant among men.

Frederick himself, still standing in between the two factions, looked back at the injured individual and his group and sternly ordered, "Now, I suggest you boys head on home, before I contact the authorities. Whatever quarrel you have with these young men can be worked out rationally at another date."

Grumbling amongst themselves about their enemies and the old man's surprise takedown, the four stumbled away into the nearby alley. Frederick, with gun still in hand, turned back to face the group he was familiar with. He had a stinging expression on his face, like he was thoroughly disappointed in them all.

"Man, I ain't never seen anything like that before, dog!" One of the boys exclaimed.

At once, all four boys began to clamor around the Reverend. Frederick only stood by and allowed the young men to fawn over him, all the while keeping his scowl attached to his face.

"Okay, boys, that'll do." Frederick calmed them all down. "Now, why don't you all head on home and be good?"

Frederick watched as the youths carried on down the other end of the alley. Forgetting he still had a revolver in his hand, the man took himself over to a nearby trash can and pitched the weapon inside before heading back into the church.

Even before he could reach the door, Margaret met him with a worried frown and a towel. "Look at you, you old fool!" She frantically sobbed while wiping his sweaty face and hands.

"I'm fine, Margaret, I'm fine." Frederick tried to console the woman. "Just a bunch of hotheaded boys with nothing to do, that's all."

"And that's the problem with the world today."

Frederick happened to glance down at his right hand to notice that it was bleeding. Gradually, he was coming back to life once again. The punch and the gun were becoming more and more recognizable with the passing seconds.

"What on earth possessed you to do that?" Margaret griped.

"I honestly don't know, my dear. One moment I was trying to keep the boys apart, the next thing I know, I have a gun in my hand." Frederick sighed.

"Well, while you were out there playing Superman, you had a call."

"Really," Frederick lit up. "From who, The Reverend Moore?"

"No, it was a woman by the name of…Stacey, or Stasha. I can't quite remember how she pronounced her name. Her number and address is there by the phone."

"Did she say what she wanted?"

"She needed to know if you would stop by her place and bless her house."

Frederick stood straight up at that instant, seemingly amazed and perplexed all at once. "I didn't think people did that sort of thing anymore." He chuckled.

"Well, she sounded quite the desperate one." Margaret said as she wrapped gauze around Frederick's right hand.

The moment she was done, Frederick stepped over to the desk where the phone sat and picked up the piece of paper underneath. The man studied the address closely before grunting far off, "Husk Drive. Where have I heard that name before I wonder?"

"It certainly doesn't sound familiar to me."

Clearing the cobwebs, Frederick stuffed the letter into his pocket before looking back at Margaret and saying, "Oh, and please remind me to write a letter to The Reverend Moore. I've been saying that I'm gonna do it, and I never get to it."

"He'll be back in America again before you end up writing to him." Margaret laughed before exiting the room.

Frederick, too, laughed before gawking down at his bandaged right hand. He was still upset at the boys, but for a brief moment in time, the old man felt like one the youths he had to put in place. He was still stunned to know that he had the reflexes he needed to move into action.

A slight, proud grin found its way onto his face before he playfully shadowboxed his way out of the church's office.

CHAPTER 19

Day 9
4:33 p.m.

S tacia, along with both Ashley and Tammy, all sat at the
dining room table staring at the images on the laptop
that sat in front of them.

The ladies she was surrounded by went on and on about
the various websites that they were showing Stacia, but all Stacia
could seem to do was keep her eyes and attention tuned to the
children in the kitchen who were milling about looking for
something to eat while carrying on in their usual sibling enmity.

Every so often Stacia could hear Tammy ask her questions,
and all Stacia would do was hand off a simple grunt or an "uh
huh", whenever the inquiry sounded like something important.

Stacia was waiting, waiting for something to happen inside
the kitchen, or anywhere else in the house. Ever since the noisy
incident from four nights earlier she didn't want either Sidney
or Devon out of her sight. If they weren't inside the house
with her then they were at school, and that was the way she
expected it.

"Wix is probably your best bet when it comes to making
your own website." Ashley explained. "It's easy because all you
have to do is—

For the past ten minutes or so, Stacia heard sounds in her head, but to her it was all gibberish. She just couldn't seem to focus on one thing at a time. The very moment the sounds ceased, she suddenly snapped to and looked up to see both Ashley and Tammy staring at her with simple grins on their faces.

Waving her hand in front of Stacia's face, Tammy said, "Earth to Stacia, are you in there?"

Shaking her head from side to side in an embarrassing fashion, Staica looked up and blushed, "I'm sorry, you two, my mind is elsewhere."

Tammy, a chunky, middle-aged white woman who wore eyeglasses, sat back in her chair and placed her hand on Stacia's arm saying, "It's okay, the sex convention isn't until later tonight, we've got all day."

All three women laughed out loud before Stacia reached over and picked up her writing tablet and pen. "Believe me, I am glad you guys stopped by, it may be a couple of months still before I can get Wi-Fi again."

"Don't mention it," Ashley replied in a careful whisper, "the only time we use ours is for porn."

"I used to do the same thing, until I got grandkids." Stacia whispered right back in a witty fashion.

The ladies carried on and on about websites, porn and children. For Stacia, it was a delightful little respite from the uncanny happenings that had been taking place as of late. Catching brief breaths in between life's occurrences was something that Stacia reached for like water in a desert. No matter what situation she happened to be caught in.

Still talking low enough so that the kids couldn't hear, Stacia locked her eyes on Ashley and asked, "So, when was the last time you sucked Stanley's dick?"

Shrugging her shoulders as to say it was just a thing, Ashley answered, "About five months ago."

Glaring oddly at the young woman, Stacia glanced back at the children before looking at Ashley. "Are you bi?"

Shrinking into her seat, Ashley said, "Not really, I guess I kind of felt sorry for the guy."

"Stanley has been through a lot in his life," Tammy explained, "losing his wife, son, and his dad. All that he has left is his mom, and you met her already."

"Don't remind me." Stacia rolled her eyes.

"Yeah, she's a real trip alright." Ashley added. "She's getting more anal as she gets older. Poor Stan just puts up with it. I'm afraid one day he'll end up having enough of her and next thing you know, here comes the paramedics."

"Speaking of paramedics," Tammy stared over at Stacia, "was that the meds or the police the other night racing down this street? I thought I dreamt that."

Stacia's stomach caved in at that moment. But rather than allow the question to bog her down, she instead fixated her attention upon the computer in front of her.

Stacia then looked up at the front door that sounded as if it were about to crash right in from the loud knocking that was being laid upon it.

"Wait here, I'll be right back." Stacia said as she got up and went to the door.

Without giving a thought to who was on the other end, Stacia flung open the door to find Agnes, dressed only in a white girdle and slippers. It was around forty degrees that afternoon, and there stood the old woman with two gaping eyes that stared at Stacia like they were ready to fall right out of their sockets.

Completely staggered by not only the woman's unruly appearance, but also by her very presence at her front door, Stacia caught her breath and stammered, "Uh…can I help you?"

At first, Agnes seemed to be at a loss for words. Her eyes were still bugging out while her jaw trembled. Stacia was in no ill mood for the insufferable old thing, but just then she realized that she had arrived for a reason, what that reason could have been only made Stacia all the more uneasy.

"You heard him, didn't you?" Agnes anxiously muttered.

"What?" Stacia twisted her face, trying to figure out what the woman said.

"Did you hear him in there?" Agnes spoke a bit louder.

Stacia began to shake at that point, not only from the fact that there was someone else who heard the voice, but from Agnes' sheer fright.

"What…what are you talking about?" Stacia shuddered in her shoes.

Stepping in closer, Agnes said, "I've heard him before. He's spoke to me before."

"Who, dammit," Stacia began to get agitated. "Who's he?"

"Stand up to him. Do you hear me? Stand up to him, and don't back down."

Stacia broke out into a soaking sweat right there at her own front door. Beyond Agnes, a maroon Chevette pulled behind Stacia's car. From out of the Chevette appeared Frederick.

Stacia only wanted the moment with Agnes to end. She kept on looking past the old lady and to the old man that was slowly, but anxiously making his way towards the house.

"You need to go, Agnes, right now." Stacia adamantly pointed.

"Good afternoon, there!" Frederick called out as she stepped up onto the porch. "The name is—

But before the man could finish what he was about to say, he was inexplicably caught off guard by the sight of a scantly clothed Agnes.

"Agnes, please go home, now." Stacia continued to implore.

"Agnes?" Frederick questioned. "Agnes Ewing? My stars, it has been ages since I last laid eyes on you!" Frederick exclaimed to the world.

Everyone, all at once, seemed to be at a loss for words, Stacia especially. The entire event was taking place so fast and sudden that she felt like she was spinning around.

"Don't you remember me?" Frederick pressed. "Reverend Freehoff. I gave the eulogy at your husband's funeral fifteen years ago."

Agnes didn't reply. She simply turned and shuffled her way back across the street to her house. That left only Stacia and Frederick at the front door.

"I'm sorry about that; she's a little batty in the head." Stacia blushed.

"Don't apologize, my dear. We all get that way sometimes. My name is Frederick Freehoff. You left a message with my wife."

"Oh yes." Stacia caught herself. "Come right in." She gladly invited.

Stepping inside and taking off his winter hat, Frederick looked all around at the spacious living room before saying, "I knew Husk Drive sounded familiar when my wife took the message. I haven't been down to these parts in years. I wonder how Stanley is doing these days."

"He's doing okay."

From out of the dining room came both Ashley and Tammy, packing up their laptop along the way.

"You two don't have to go." Stacia halted their progression.

With dual, cordial smiles on their faces, Tammy pulled Stacia to the front door and whispered into her ear, "There's a saying amongst our ilk. A preacher a day keeps the homo away."

Stacia stood back, and with an amused face she said, "You're bad, girl."

Stacia let both ladies out of the house before turning back to a waiting Frederick. "I'm so sorry, here I am letting you into my house and I haven't even introduced myself. My name is Stacia Taylor."

"Glad to meet you, Stacia." Frederick kindly shook her hand.

From out of the dining room came both Devon and Sidney. Devon had in his hand a wrestling action figure, while Sidney carried in with her a bowl of cereal.

"Well, what do we have here?" Frederick knelt down.

"These are my grandkids, Sidney and Devon."

"Good to meet you both." Frederick smiled from cheek to cheek. "So, you're a big wrestling fan, are you?"

Devon glanced back at his grandmother before turning to Freehoff and shaking his head yes, as if he was too shy to open his mouth.

"That boy loves him some wrestling." Stacia said.

"Tell me, my lad, have you ever heard of Gorgeous George, or Nature Boy Buddy Rogers?"

Devon squinted and said, "No, but I know John Cena and Triple H."

"Those names sound familiar, but then again, my wife rarely allows me to watch TV anymore." Frederick patted the boy on his head. "What a pretty young lady we have here." He said to Sidney. "How old are you, darling?"

"I'm nine." She bashfully responded.

"Ahh, I remember nine, a long, long, long time ago." Frederick laughed.

Taken aback by the man's accent, Stacia said, "Not that it matters, but are you foreign?"

Struggling to stand back up, Frederick replied, "I was born and raised in Bavaria. I came here to America when I was twenty. Oh, I didn't see you, sir. How are you?" Frederick waved towards the dining room.

In unison, Stacia, Sidney and Devon all spun around to see nothing but the dining table behind them.

"Who were you talking to?" Stacia shook all over again."

"The gentleman in the other room there," Frederick innocently answered. "Where did he go that quickly?"

"There's no gentleman in this house." Stacia's tongue fumbled about inside her mouth.

Snatching Frederick by the hand, Stacia pulled the man towards the front of the living room. "Um, did your wife tell you why I wanted you to stop by?"

"Well, she mentioned that you desired to have your home blessed. I'll admit, I haven't done such a thing since the nineteen eighties." Frederick grinned.

The man's charismatic and genial manner was a settling tone for Stacia, but the pleasantries could be flushed as far as she was concerned. "You see, we believe that God's blessings will watch over this house all night and day." Stacia explained from out of the side of her mouth. "We don't need anything elaborate or fancy, just a simple blessing."

"I wholeheartedly understand." Frederick beamed at Stacia. "Would it be okay if I started upstairs?"

"That would be fine."

All four ventured up the stairs. The children couldn't help but stay attached to their grandmother like they were conjoined. Stacia made sure to remain close to Frederick as the man started at her bedroom, then to Sidney's, praying a prayer for peace to come upon the house and those who resided therein.

From Sidney's room, the four went down a few steps to Devon's. Out of nowhere, Frederick stopped on a dime right before entering the child's bedroom.

"What's the matter?" Stacia eyeballed the still man.

Frederick glared strangely all around the hallway before turning to Stacia and asking, "Where…where is that music coming from?"

Stacia and the children all began gawking around their area and back to each other, appearing as if the old man had lost his mind.

"What music are you hearing?" Stacia nervously questioned.

"You don't hear that? It sounds like…like Hank Williams."

"I don't hear anything." Devon looked up at Frederick.

"It sounds like its coming from inside this room here. Do you have a CD player running in here, son?"

"Look, I don't mean to be rude, but can you please just finish the blessing?" Stacia pleaded.

Frederick stared awkwardly at all three Taylors for a moment or two before turning back to Devon's room. "Dear

Lord, Heavenly Father, please send down your blessings upon this room and all its inhabitants. Send your Holy Spirit to comfort and protect—

Right in the middle of Freehoff's prayer, the man stopped to sneeze. One sneeze was followed by another and another after that.

"Please forgive me," Frederick pulled out a handkerchief and wiped his nose, "my allergies tend to get the best of—

Once more, Frederick was halted in his speech, but rather than repetitive sneezing seizing him, hard, mucus filled coughing took control. The man coughed so viscously that blood actually came out of his mouth.

"Eww, grandma," Sidney shrieked while backing away.

"Oh my God," Stacia gasped before going to the bathroom to retrieve some paper towels to hand to the man.

Frederick continued to cough before he leaned up against the wall. "I can't imagine what has come over me!" He gagged, "I…I've never had such an attack in my life."

"Are you gonna be okay?" Stacia attended to the man.

Coughing into the paper towels, Frederick replied, "I believe so. I just have to…catch my breath."

"Sid, go in the bathroom and get a cup of water." Stacia said.

"Please, don't make a fuss over me." Frederick insisted. "I'm an old man who's seen better days."

Stacia stood next to the Reverend with a concerned frown on her face. She looked all around the hallway and into Devon's bedroom in frightened dismay. She wanted to break down and cry right there, but not in front of the children. She gritted her teeth while not allowing the fretful appearance on her face to be noticed by Sidney and Devon, who themselves looked as scared as two kittens up against mad dog.

"Here, let's go downstairs so you can catch your breath." Stacia urgently coaxed the man down the hallway towards the steps.

"Oh my Lord God in heaven," Frederick bawled with his hands covering his ears.

"What's the matter?" Stacia screamed back.

With his hands still shielding his ears, Frederick groaned, "Who turned up the music? It's so loud!"

Stacia at that point didn't have a clue as to what to do. All she could think of was helping the man down the stairs. She was more concerned with aiding him than what insanity was taking shape inside the house.

The second they all reached the living room, Frederick uncovered his ears. Stacia saw that both of them were bleeding profusely.

"Shit!" She hollered before racing to the kitchen to retrieve a towel.

The second she came back into the living room, she found Frederick falling to his knees in agony. "Please, just give me a few moments to…to collect myself." The man beseeched in pain.

"But your ears are bleeding!" Stacia handed Frederick the towel. "Do you want me to call 911?"

Frederick took the towel and wiped his ears with it before crawling his way to the couch. "I…I cannot believe for one moment that none of you heard that music." He struggled to speak. "I haven't anything like that in my life."

"I don't hear anything, sir." Devon said next to the man.

Frederick compassionately patted the boy on the head and smiled before looking up at a worried Stacia and saying, "My dear…please do not take this the wrong way. I'm seventy-three years old. I've never had this happen to me before."

Stacia sat down next to Freehoff and held the man's clammy hands in hers. She peered deeply into his startled eyes as though it was desperation propelling her to do so.

"Please tell us, do you feel something in this house? Something out of the ordinary," she asked with a tone of panic in her cracking voice.

Frederick sat and stared broodingly at the Taylors while breathing in and out deeply. To Stacia, he looked as though he wanted to throw up all over the floor.

"Stacia, I am not a man who believes in superstition. I am a—"

"No, no," Stacia adamantly stopped Frederick, "I need to know what you felt back upstairs, as one human being to another."

Frederick seemed to be at a loss for words. The startled look on the old man's face told Stacia that he was just about done, which in turn didn't give her one moment's harmony.

Frederick fought his way up off the couch. The man then grabbed his coat and hat and headed for the door.

"Is he leaving, grandma?" Devon looked at Stacia.

Stacia didn't respond to the boy, she just stood and watched as Frederick turned around. She wasn't mad at the man, in fact, she understood his actions all too well.

With the front door wide open, Frederick stood by and gave the Taylors what seemed to be a final look. He then focused his eyes solely upon Stacia. For Stacia, he didn't have to say a mumbling word; his disheveled appearance told the bitter story of a man that had just fought an unexpected battle the likes he wished he never had.

"Stacia…what can I say?" Frederick gasped. "Lean on God. All three of you. Lean on God."

The Taylors watched as Reverend Freehoff walked out the door and to his car. "Is he coming back, Grandma?" Sidney held Stacia's moist hand.

Stacia had nothing to say to the girl. Once Rinsinky's car was out of sight, she gazed hard across the street at the Ewing's house. Stacia hadn't forgotten about Agnes or her ramblings from earlier. No, she wasn't mad at the Reverend, but someone had to give up something.

Taking both Sidney and Devon by the hand, Stacia charged directly across the street and banged as loud and hard as she could on the front door. After about two whole minutes, Stanley came running to the door.

"Stacia," the man looked bleary-eyed, as if he had just awoken from a nap, "what can I do for you?"

"I need to speak with you mother?" She desperately replied. "Mom's asleep now."

"Stanley, she was just over at our place a while ago."

Opening his eyes wide, Stanley said, "What? What was she doing over there? She can hardly even walk, for God's sake." "She kept going on and on about—

"Stanley, Stanley, get up here, now!" Agnes shouted from upstairs.

"Mom, just hold on!" Stanley yelled back. "Stacia, look, I'm sorry if mom bothered you guys, it won't happen again."

"No, Stanley, you don't understand, she came over talking about someone else living in our house."

Waving off the complaint like it was frivolous, Stanley said, "Mom has been doing that for years. For some reason or another she can't stand anyone living in that house. Like I said, I'll keep her out of sight the best I can."

"Stanley, get your fat ass up here right now, boy!"

"I'm coming, ma!" Stanley rolled his eyes. "I'll talk to you guys later."

Stacia and the kids all stood and watched as the man shut the door in their faces. Speechless, and downright infuriated, Stacia dragged both herself and the children back across the street to their house. The second they got inside, Stacia slammed the door as hard as she could behind her before looking down at the kids and screaming, "You both go into the kitchen and stay there until I call for you!"

Sidney held Devon's hand as they both walked side by side into the kitchen. The sound of Devon's crying only broke Stacia down to her knees. Without making a whimpering sound, she herself began to weep into her hands, all alone there on the living room.

For once, Stacia wished she, too, could hear the overbearing music that Frederick was hearing, anything to drown out her grandson.

CHAPTER 20

At his dining table, where the light shined down a soft, dim hue, Frederick sat with a piece of notebook paper in front of him and a ballpoint pen fumbling about in his right hand.

It was so quiet inside the home that the man for a moment actually believed that he was all by himself in the world. It was only hours removed from his visit at the Taylors, and yet, it was those thirty some odd minutes inside their house that caused the man to reconsider much.

He wanted to write something down on the paper, but his thoughts caused his hand to feel like led. He just couldn't seem to focus upon writing.

Frederick wanted more than anything in the world to help the Taylors, but he couldn't explain or admit to himself just what he could have been possibly helping them against.

Their pitiable faces caused his knees to knock together. He was a man that always prided himself on being able to aid those in need. Being there for those who required his help was not only his job, but also his life's passion. But on that day, he felt like a lowlife.

"You've been sitting here now since dinner, and that was two hours ago, Freddy." Margaret came into the dining room. "Don't tell me you haven't written anything down yet."

Frederick awoke from his stupor and looked up at his wife with hazy eyes. "I've written a bit, my dear."

Margaret peered down at the paper in front of Frederick and said, "So far all you have written is", 'A letter to my dear friend.'

Frederick glanced at his writing before grinning. He then sat up his seat and took Margaret by the hand before looking up at the woman and smirking. "Humor an old man, will you?" He humbly requested.

Margaret's face took a grimmer glare; it was the emotion that Frederick desired. "What's on your mind, Freddy? You've been awfully quiet since you got home this evening."

"I know," he softly stated. "Tell me something, Peggy, in all the years you've known me, have you ever known me to be an irrational man?"

"Besides taking on a group of well-armed young hoodlums, no," Margaret sarcastically replied.

"No, I don't mean that. I mean…when it comes to my beliefs."

Squaring her eyes, Margaret said, "I don't know what you mean."

Sighing, Frederick said, "You see, I believe in everything the good book has to say, but…it never occurs to someone who preaches it that perhaps one day…you may be forced to believe a little bit more."

Appearing confused, Margaret said, "Freddy, what's going on? What happened to you today?"

"I don't know for sure. But I feel as though I may have left a family in certain peril today. Stacia Taylor asked me if I felt something inside her house, and for the life of me, Peggy, I could not answer the woman."

"What went on there?"

"I won't go into the graphic display that I put on today, but I know for a fact that something very ugly lives there with those people. That woman called me there for a reason. She needed me for more than just a blessing. Those people are in danger."

"Freddy, you're scaring me now." Margaret began to fidget about.

"I don't mean to frighten you, my dear, I only need to say this because I need to get it out. I believe the good Lord sent me there to help those people, and I failed them today. I failed to inform them of a presence that resides there with them."

"Are you saying...a ghost?"

"I'm not so much saying that, but...if that it may be, then so be it. I saw someone inside that house today that had no business being there. And I seemed to be the only person that could see that individual."

"Oh, Freddy," Margaret lamented, "you must do what you think is right. Do you think these people should leave this house?"

Frederick tightened his lips. "God help them...yes."

"Then you need to call them and let them know. If you, of all people, have a bad feeling, then you need to follow it."

Fredrick leaned over and kissed Margaret's hands before getting up and carrying himself in the other direction.

"Are you going to call them now, Freddy?"

"Right after I answer nature's call, my dear." He grunted.

Frederick trotted himself into the bathroom of his one floor house and locked the door behind him. As he stood over the toilet, he couldn't help but to reflect on the Taylors faces that by then had become a permanent fixture inside his brain. He wanted to reach out to them in the worst way imaginable. By that point, even if he had to move them in along with him and his wife then it would be worth it.

Frederick zipped up his pants and reached into his pocket to pull out the Taylors phone number. Before anything, the man washed his hands in the sink. From there he wiped himself dry.

Before the man could even pull himself away from the mirror in front of him, a force from behind grabbed Frederick by the neck and rammed him face first into the glass.

Frederick, along with shards of glass, went crashing down to the floor. Shaking profusely, the man gawked all around the tiny bathroom before feeling streams of blood cradle down his face.

"Freddy, what on earth is happening in there?"

Frederick couldn't even speak; he was too enthralled in both pain and shock to believe what was happening to him. Shaking from head to toe, the man attempted to get to his feet, but not before a punch to the face caused him to hit the floor again. That punch was soon followed by another strike which ended up knocking out two of Frederick's teeth.

The old, bleeding man was too afraid to even lift his head. He laid there on the floor shaking and crying in his own pool of blood.

"Freddy, open the door, I can't get in!" Margaret hysterically screamed while twisting the door's knob left to right.

Frederick, unable to talk, tried to lift himself at least to the knob, but before the man could even propel himself up to the sink, he felt his entire body slowly ascend off the floor. Just two feet above the tile Frederick Freehoff serenely levitated.

"Our Father who art in heaven, hallowed be thy name." He whispered in a stammer, and with his eyes closed.

The man desperately repeated the first stanza of the *Lord's Prayer* at least ten more times before what felt like a breeze in his right ear slowly groaned, *"Leave… them… alone."*

It was that same eerie, threatening groan that caused the Reverend to pray even harder than before. But after so long in mid-air, ever so gradually, Frederick's body came back down to the floor and remained there.

"Freddy!" Margaret screamed at the top of her lungs as she rammed her way into the bathroom. "Oh my God, my Freddy," she wept as she went down to her beloved.

Frederick held on so tight to Margaret to where her arms began to turn blue from the strain. The Freehoff's laid there together on the bathroom floor, cradling each other while sobbing.

CHAPTER 21

L aw & Order: Special Victims Unit ran on the television in front of Agnes that evening, as it did every night, just as she expected it to.

She kept the lights on in her bedroom all night long, a habit that enraged Stanley to no end. Agnes was well aware of the fact that Stanley struggled to pay the electric bill, but her cares never seemed to touch on her son.

Agnes laid there in her bed, holding the covers on her frail body as though the room was freezing cold. From her bedroom she got a bird's eye view of 833 straight across the street from her. Rather than watch the television, she chose instead to keep her attention locked on those she had scared half to death earlier in the day.

From her bed she could see Stacia's bedroom light turn on. It stayed on for about five minutes before it went out. From there, Sidney's bedroom light came to life. Agnes had no clue as to where in the house the Taylors were, but something deep inside told her that it wasn't them going from room to room like a crazed rat.

After about six or seven minutes, Sidney's light went out. Agnes waited for Devon's light to come on. She waited and waited until an entire half hour went by. When the light never came on, she rested her body in her bed and resumed watching TV.

Agnes' eyes were watching the television, but her mind was far away. She had a hungering inside her body that would not budge. She wanted to get up and go back over to the Taylors house again, but she realized that she had used up all of her reserve energy just going over there earlier in the day. By that time in the evening, she was as feeble as an invalid.

Before her eyes could even blink, the hallway light in the Taylors house came on. Agnes looked up to see a masculine figure stand in the window, staring right back at her.

Agnes immediately turned her head away and ducked underneath the covers. The woman's body almost immediately broke out into an intense sweat. Both the blanket and the bed's sheet underneath her stuck to her skin like flypaper.

Agnes closed her eyes as tight as she could. Before long, the sound of the television could no longer be heard. Agnes peeked out from under the covers to find her room completely black; the lights had gone out as did the television.

Her frightened eyes gawked all around the room before they finally connected with a lone, hulking figure standing in front of her bed.

"I…I tried to tell them." Agnes salivated. "You know I…I went to the hospital. I couldn't warn them."

The old woman pleaded her case over and over again, but the dark figure before her would neither speak nor move. It stood there staring her down. Even though she couldn't see its face, Agnes knew that the individual was angry with her; the weight of its stare caused her breathing to become stifled.

"Go away from here!" She forcefully screamed. "Get away, and stay away!"

But the figure stood, it stood as though the woman hadn't said a single word. Agnes then began to cry as she held tighter than before to her covers.

"Stanley, come in here!"

As soon as she was done shouting for her son, the same covers that Agnes was clinching were suddenly ripped right out of her hands and off the bed. Agnes laid there shivering from head to toe. "I'm so sorry! I tried so hard!" She screamed ever so dreadfully.

"Mom, what's going on in there?" Stanley struggled to open the door.

Agnes laid in her bed and helplessly watched as the windows that were beside her and in front began to vibrate. They shook and bended so much that they began to crack. Before long, all four windows broke into pieces, pieces that went flying towards Agnes.

Agnes watched in horror as the glass came right for her face. The old lady couldn't even lift her hands to shield herself from the onslaught.

Stanley burst open his mother's bedroom door to find the room dark. The man reached over and cut on the lamp light to see his mother lying in her bed with shards of glass stuck to just about every portion of her body. From her face and neck, all the way down to her stomach and feet.

CHAPTER 22

Day 10
7:05 a.m.

Stacia remained perched at the front window downstairs studying Stanley's house across the street with cagey eyes, waiting for the man to come out.

She had heard the sirens from the night before. She saw the paramedics carry the blanketed body out of the house and into the ambulance. Stacia wanted to go over and hand Stanley words of comfort, but she realized that approaching the man so soon could have been a bit hazardous. Instead, she chose to lay back and bide her time. He would make an appearance sooner or later.

Suddenly, the children's usual Sunday morning chaotic routine interrupted Stacia's peeping session. The woman rolled her eyes before dragging her stiff body up the stairs and to Devon's bedroom to find both the boy and girl arguing in the middle of the floor.

"What are you two doing now?" Stacia sighed with her arms folded.

"Devon has one of my socks!" Sidney fussed with a finger pointed at her brother.

Stacia turned and looked down at Devon with a confused frown before asking, "What on earth would your brother be doing with your socks?"

"He stole them because I wouldn't let him use my magic markers!"

"But they're my markers, grandma," Devon urgently insisted.

Too wound up and spent to even care, Stacia snatched the sock out of Devon's hand before tossing it at Sidney and yelling, "You go in your room and get ready for church, and you, young man, go in that bathroom, get your face washed and quit taking things that aren't yours!"

Sidney took her lone sock and went about her business before Stacia whipped her body out of the bedroom and back downstairs. Before she could even reach the door, she could see both Tammy and Ashley walking across the street to Stanley's house from her window.

Stacia wasted no time putting on her jacket and carrying herself outside to join in the fray. As soon as she reached the three, Stacia stepped up to Stanley and immediately said with a sympathetic frown, "I'm so sorry for what happened, Stan."

Appearing subtly distraught, Stanley turned his head back to his house before looking at the women and saying, "Thank you. Thank you, all."

"What happened?" Stacia asked.

Stanley right then dropped his head before looking back up. "I, uh…I honestly don't know. Last night, mom was in her room watching TV. Next thing I know, she was screaming. I tried to open the door, but she had somehow managed to lock it."

"I don't know how that's possible," Ashley said, "Agnes could hardly even move."

"I know, but I sure as heck couldn't get myself in there. When I was able to get inside…she was dead." Stanley shamefully muttered.

Stacia, Ashley and Tammy all gave each other quick glances before Stacia looked at Stanley and carefully asked, "How did she go?"

Stanley hesitated at first, appearing as though Stacia's question had cut right through his soul. The man kept gawking around the neighborhood like he was looking for something.

"It…it wasn't a pretty death, I can assure you of that. But…I have one question, Stacia. Why did my mom come over your place yesterday?"

Ashley and Tammy stared at Stacia like she was the accused. Stacia only stared back at the three before saying, "Well, I was trying to tell you yesterday that she came over talking about some man that was supposedly up in my house."

"Some man," Tammy questioned with a gasp.

"Yes. She kept going on about how I should stand up to him, and asked if I had heard him."

"I still can't believe Agnes was even walking." Ashley's jaw dropped.

"Mom was full of character, but I honestly can't imagine what go into her yesterday, Stacia." Stanley explained.

"Didn't you say that she was always trying to keep people from buying that house?" Stacia asked.

"Yeah, but I never really took it to heart. Mom was hard. If she had her way, she would have lived to be two hundred, just so she could torment me even longer. When she was bedridden last month, she kinda settled down."

"That is until Stacia and her grandchildren moved into the house." Ashley stated. "Ever since that happened, Agnes went nuts."

"Wait a minute," Stacia held her breath, "I need to know something. Do any of you know of anything that could be wrong inside that house? Because ever since we moved in, a lot of strange things have been happening. All three of us have been hearing some pretty weird noises coming from the basement."

"What kind of noises?" Stanley squinted.

"Like something was screaming in pain. That's why I called the police the other night; I thought there was something in there with us."

"I dunno, maybe Agnes was trying to keep folks out of there for a reason." Tammy said.

"Mom never talked about the house, at least not to me."

"What about the people who lived here before us?" Stacia remarked. "The woman that referred me to this house was named Judy."

Stanley stood and thought long and hard before saying, "Judy McFord?"

"She used to work down at the warehouse where I do." Stacia anxiously replied.

Scratching his head, Stanley said, "Wow, I haven't heard that name in years. Judy was the person that owned the house, but that was way back in the seventies, for crying out loud. I remember her and mom were inseparable."

At that moment, the light at the end of the tunnel that Stacia had been searching for was becoming brighter by the second. "I need to know everything you know about Judy." She eagerly implored. "She may be the only person that can explain that house to me."

"Well, way back in the sixties—

But before Stanley could even blurt out another word, the thumping and bumping of a white Denali came into earshot. Every person standing outside turned to see what the commotion was. But it was Stacia that felt the sting more than anyone else. It was Dixon, and the man was driving with a purpose, which in turn only gave her all the more reason to become scared; she never once called the man to begin with.

The very instant the Denali parked up on the curb in front of Stacia's house, Stacia immediately took off back across the street. Before she could even reach the vehicle's driver's side door, Dixon, along with his three nephews, hopped right out and angrily began across the street.

Standing in front of the rampaging man and his crew, Stacia tried to halt Dixon's infuriated progression. "What are you all doing here?" She yelled.

Dixon only shoved Stacia aside before racing towards Stanley and grabbing a hold of the man's neck where he proceeded to choke the life out of him.

"What are you doing?" Stacia screamed, trying to pull the huge man off of Stanley.

Stanley tried to fight back, but he was overpowered and outnumbered. All three of Dixon's nephews had the beleaguered man pinned down from behind.

"Get off of him, dammit!" Stacia pounded on Dixon's back.

Dixon released the man before turning to Stacia and yelling, "I fuckin' told you that this motherfucker was up to no good, but your ass wouldn't believe me!"

"What the fuck are you talking about?" She hollered back.

"You know exactly what I'm talking about!"

"No I don't! What are you doing here to begin with?"

"Devon called me!"

Stacia spun around to see the little boy peeking out the front window like a frightened cat. "Why did he call you?"

"You tell me! That fat motherfucker put something up in that house!"

"Put what in the house," Stanley stood to his feet with the aid of Ashley and Tammy as he coughed and gagged.

"Devon said that someone painted something in his room!" Dixon screamed into Stanley's face.

Shaking her head in bewilderment, Stacia ran back to her house. Once she got inside, she saw both Devon and Sidney cowering in a corner. "What did you call Dixon over here for, Devon?" Stacia shouted.

Devon appeared to be too frightened to even answer his grandmother. The boy held on to his big sister for dear life.

"I asked you a question, Devon! What is in your room?"

"It's…it's a painting, grandma." Sidney stammered.

Stacia, along with Dixon and his nephews, all raced upstairs and into Devon's bedroom to find one of the four walls painted all red with a giant swastika planted directly in the middle.

Stacia wanted to fall over and faint at that second; the woman could hardly even stand, let alone see straight. The bright red shocked her eyes and mind so vividly.

"I…I was just in here a moment ago!" Stacia reached for air.

"I tried to tell you, but you wouldn't listen!" Dixon ranted on. "These bottoms motherfuckers are all racist!"

Stacia turned to the man and screamed, "This wasn't in here when I was up here a moment ago!"

"Well, someone sure as hell painted it! Fuck this place!" Dixon roared before storming out of the room along with his nephews.

Stacia stood and stared at the stunning wall in all its ugly glory. The words that she wanted to say were locked away inside. Her body at that point couldn't even shake or tremble. The woman just stood and gawked on and on.

"We some ridas up in here," the rowdy four hollered from outside the house.

Still, Stacia just would not be torn away from the wall that shined its deep, red shade down upon her. Even the swastika had her jaw hanging down to the floor.

CHAPTER 23

10:52 p.m.

Stacia took one final, embittered look at Devon's wall before retiring for the evening. For hours, ever since first seeing the image, she didn't have all too much to say. Even explaining it to the children was all the more painstakingly difficult. She couldn't imagine what was racing through their minds when they first laid eyes on the symbol. Just the very thought caused her to shudder.

Like she was dragging a bag full of bricks behind her, Stacia pulled herself away from the wall, shut off the light and closed the bedroom door before going for her own bedroom to find both Sidney and Devon lying in bed watching television.

Stacia didn't want to look them in the eye, she could feel the desperation and confusion emanate off of them like heat. She picked up the remote control that was lying on the table beside the bed and hit the "off" switch before climbing in the bed and laying her tired body down.

For at least five whole minutes not a single sound was uttered between the three, not even so much as a cough or grunt was let out. Just hard silence like someone had done something terribly wrong and was ashamed to bring it up.

"Grandma," Sidney all of the sudden spoke up, "are you gonna paint Devon's room all over again?"

Stacia sighed heavily while staring up at the ceiling. "I reckon I will, baby." She softly verbalized. "It'll take some days, but I'll eventually get to it."

"I'm sorry I called Dixon, grandma." Devon whimpered.

Stacia exhaled before reaching over and caressing the little boy's head. "Don't be sorry, honey, you know how Dixon can get sometimes."

"I got really scared when I washed my face and came back and saw my room."

Holding back emotion, Stacia gritted her teeth and said, "I'm sorry you had to see that, baby."

"I saw it once in a book at school." Sidney said. "Mrs. Belini said that racist people use it."

"What's racist people," Devon asked.

Stacia didn't want to respond to any statement that the children were making for fear that their juvenile minds were already cluttered with more than enough happenings already inside the house. But she bore down as hard as she could and swallowed.

"It's a symbol. A symbol of hatred for people who don't look like you do," Stacia prudently explained. "People who are simple, and are bored with their lives do stupid things sometimes."

"But who put it up there?" Sidney questioned. "We didn't see anyone in here when it happened."

Stacia shut her eyes for a second or two before opening them and turning to the children. "Listen, we just have to be strong for each other right now. I don't know how that happened, but I promise it won't happen again."

"Is this place haunted like Tracy said?" Sidney sniveled.

"Don't say that." Stacia adamantly stated. "Tracy doesn't know what she's talking about. She's a silly little girl who watches too much TV."

"But she said that she watched this one movie where these ghosts took this little girl into a closet, and the house disappeared into thin air."

"Sidney, stoppit," Stacia grabbed the girl's hand. "That stuff isn't real. It's all fake."

"I wanna leave this house and go find another house to live in, grandma." Devon began to sob.

Right then, Stacia gathered both of the children into her arms and held them tight. "Listen to me, the both of you. I don't know what's happening here, but this is our house, and no one is gonna make us leave. Remember what I told you when we first moved in? It's far from where we once were. All the gunshots, people chasing you down, no one breaking into the house. I know it all seems scary now, but after a while, it'll all go away."

"Why can't we go over to Dixon's house, grandma?" Devon asked.

Instead of answering the boy's ardent plea, Stacia held her breath for as long as she could while looking on into her grandchildren's worried eyes and wondering just how much more they could possibly endure.

She herself wanted to believe every word that had come out of her own mouth, but Stacia's resiliency was beginning to melt away, much like the snow outside.

"Can we keep the light on, please?" Devon shuddered underneath the covers.

Stacia held her kids in her arms and closed her eyes. She kept reciting her speech over and over in her head, hoping that everything she said to her babies would come true.

The longer it remained quiet, the more Stacia could hear what in her ears sounded much like thousands of roaches scraping across the floor in rampant succession.

The woman kept her eyes shut and tried in earnest to keep the racket out of her head.

CHAPTER 24

Day 13
4:17 p.m.

A knock at the front door.

Stacia opened the door to find a young, fat black man, a young Asian woman who wore a blue thermal hat, and a young, skinny, bearded white man.

The entire crew was carrying what appeared to be heavy, black duffle bags, along with metal rods and two television monitors.

"Good afternoon!" The black man announced with his arms loaded with the TV's.

"Hi there," Stacia smiled awkwardly while standing aside to allow the three inside her home.

"Hi, my name is Dee, and this is my fiancé Patrick, and our friend Scott." The perky Asian woman shook Stacia's hand.

"Good afternoon, my name is Stacia Taylor, and these are my grandkids, Sidney and Devon." She pointed to her right.

"Hi, guys." Dee waved at the children.

Both Sidney and Devon sat on the couch and waved back at the young lady before resuming their staring detail at all the equipment that was being hauled into their house.

Stacia as well looked on in awe at the hardware that was being heaved inside. Briefly she turned back to the kids and handed them both a confused, grinning shrug before walking over to the crew.

"Uh, what is all of this?" She pointed at the bags.

Placing one of the monitors down onto the floor, Patrick turned around and smiled, "I guess you could call it our own little cache of ghost detecting equipment."

"Oh, I see." Stacia stood back and grunted as if she had no idea what he was talking about.

"He means it's the stuff we use to do our job." Dee whimsically explained. "You have to forgive Patrick; he likes to exaggerate his profession."

Right off the bat, Stacia got a comfortable vibe from the group. She could sense that they actually took her plight seriously even before anything was ever explained.

After about ten minutes of settling in, Stacia and the group of the three all sat down on the couches in the living room, with Stacia seated right next to her grandchildren.

"So, you two are getting married?" Stacia grinned at Patrick and Dee.

"Yep, we hope by the summer." Dee said.

"Why do you hope?"

"Because when you're a college student living off of Ramen Noodles and paying for a one bedroom apartment, summer gives us enough time to get everything worked out." Patrick lightheartedly explained.

"Believe me, I remember those noodle days." Stacia giggled.

"Yeah, our grant money is nearly running out." Scott said. "We take these jobs around the state in the hopes that we come up with something viable enough to bring back to our sponsors."

"Yeah, your uncle Max tells me that you've been struggling to fit in here and there."

Scott blushed at that moment before both Dee and Patrick laughed out loud at their comrade. "Uh oh, sounds like news travels fast, bud." Dee poked at the man.

Sighing, Scott asked, "What all did Max tell you about me?"

Grinning from ear to ear, Stacia replied, "Just that you're having a hard time figuring out what you want to do with your life, that's all."

Smiling back, Scott said, "Hey, in my defense, I'm still young. At least I'm not out there doing what my other cousins are doing."

"Yeah, he told me about them, too." Stacia sniggered.

Once all the laughter died down amongst the group of adults, Stacia pointed her attention to Patrick who in her eyes seemed more like a curiosity.

"You have to forgive me, but…I didn't think black folks were into this sorta thing." Stacia squirmed.

The room suddenly grew quite before Patrick smiled, "I'm a nerd and I'm not ashamed to admit it."

"Believe me, he's telling the truth." Dee added.

Once more, the collective carried on laughing for a few moments before Patrick sat up in his seat and took out a mini tape recorder. "Okay, let's get down to business. I know you guys are looking at all this equipment and asking yourselves what the heck is going on here. We travel across the state searching for paranormal incidents and activity."

"You mean like the movie?" Sidney spoke up in an excited manner.

Stacia looked over at the girl in wonder and asked, "How do you know about those movies?"

"They talk about them in school." The child blushed.

"Something like that, Sidney." Dee said. "What we do is come in and try to find the source, if any, of any hauntings. We take a look at the history of a place and go from there."

"All this equipment is sorta like our mobile ghost detecting laboratory." Scott stated. "It aids us in our search for whatever supernatural experience someone is encountering."

"To be clear, we are not mediums or spiritualists. We only investigate and try to discover why the haunting is taking place at all." Patrick clarified. "So, in your own words, Staica, what makes you believe your home is haunted?"

Stacia steadied herself before glancing down at the children. "Well, to be honest, I can't even believe I'm actually talking about this. I didn't think black folks went through this sort of thing." She exhaled.

"As a matter of fact, you'd be very surprised." Dee said. "There was an incident in Baltimore where a black family was haunted. But with the kids here, I won't go into detail."

"Well, to be exact, ever since we first moved in here, we've been experiencing some pretty strange stuff. One incident happened a few days back when we heard this screaming noise down in the basement. It sounded like something or someone was down there yelling for their lives. I called the police. They went downstairs to check it out, and when they came back up, they looked more terrified than me."

"What did they discover?" Patrick inquired.

"Nothing at all," Stacia shrugged. "The noise stopped the moment they got down there."

"What else have you guys experienced?" Dee asked.

"At night I can hear something crawling across the floor. It sounds like its coming from down here in the living room. My fiancée swore that he felt something touch him one of the last times he was here."

"And my room," Devon blurted out.

"Oh, yes, and his bedroom," Stacia sighed. "If you want we can go up there and check it out."

At once, everyone got up. Both Patrick and Scott began rooting around in various bags. Patrick gathered his camcorder while Scott got himself what appeared in Stacia's eyes to be a black cellphone like contraption that had a red screen lens directly in the middle of its core.

She led the group upstairs and straight to Devon's bedroom. At once, Patrick, Dee and Scott's mouths all hung down to the floor at the sight of the painted wall.

"Back on Sunday, I was getting the kids ready for church. Mind you, this was not painted here when I went outside for a few moments. When I got back inside, here it was."

"You gotta be kidding me." Patrick gasped while pushing against the wall. "I'm just checking to make sure we're not dealing with an interchangeable wall here."

"You mean to tell us that this was painted here within a matter of minutes?" Dee's eyes bugged out.

"That's right, out of thin air. The kids never saw anything. They were too busy getting ready for church."

Using his contraption to scale the wall up and down, Scott commented, "I'm getting some pretty heavy readings here, guys."

"What is that thing?" Sidney pointed.

"It's an EVP reader. It detects temperature changes." Scott elaborated. "It can tell if there is a presence located within a structure. And it looks like we may have a nudge on the line."

Everyone followed Scott out of Devon's bedroom and into the hallway. The young man followed his trusty device from room to room before stopping at Stacia's room and looking around.

"I'm getting some real strong readings in here." Scott stretched out his words.

Stacia stood back with the children huddled behind her. She wanted to know what he was finding, but not that badly.

"What are you getting, Scott?" Dee asked.

Scott hesitated at first before saying, "Something very heavy, but it's not exactly confined to just this room. It's all over the house."

"Stacia, can you tell us who owned this house before you?" Patrick inquired while scanning his camera around the room.

"There was this woman that used to work down at the warehouse I work at. Her name was Judy. She was the one that referred me to this place. We're still trying to figure out where she went to though."

"What do you mean?" Patrick asked.

"Soon after she told me about this house, she up and quit. No one can seem to locate her. She looked crazier than a loon."

"Did the realtors ever give you an exact name?" Dee probed.

"Not really. The house was condemned for so long that the city took it over."

Everyone took off back downstairs. From the living and dining rooms, to the kitchen and eventually down into the basement the investigation carried on. All in all, the entire event took well over an hour. Once the tour ended, the gathering took up at the dining room table where both Patrick and Scott began to rummage through their duffle bags for more equipment.

"Well, Stacia, what the guys are gonna do is set up cameras around various points throughout the house. The cameras are going to record any kind of activity, from sights to sounds and everything in between."

Stacia sat and watched as the men went about their duty of placing their camcorders in numerous points within the home. From the basement, kitchen and living room, all the way upstairs; wherever they saw the need.

Once the detail was completed, Scott called for Stacia to come into the kitchen, along with Patrick and Dee who were standing by the backdoor.

With the four huddled together, Scott whispered to Stacia, "I didn't want to say this in front of the kids, but I was just telling these two that the readings I got from the EVP were some of the strongest I've ever received."

"What does that mean?" Stacia held on.

"It means that there's possibly something very wrong in this house." Patrick seriously stated. "We've been doing this now for six years, and the readings Scott got are off the charts. Much like any state, Ohio, too, is haunted, but this house has a history."

"Stacia, the last thing we want to do is scare you. And believe me, we don't say this to everyone we meet." Dee compassionately explained.

"Yeah, no disrespect, but we don't get paid to do this." Patrick offhandedly snickered.

Inching in closer to the three, Stacia commented, "I didn't wanna bring this up in front of the kids, but a few days ago, I brought in this preacher. He was blessing the bedrooms, and then out of nowhere, the man just starts coughing and throwing up blood all over the place. He couldn't finish the blessing. We haven't heard from him since. But that man swore he saw another person in this house."

Patrick, Dee and Scott all stared at each other with apprehensive glares on their individual faces before turning back to Stacia who appeared even more shell-shocked than they were.

"We want you to know that we believe you." Patrick reassured. "We're gonna delve deeper into this house's history and see what we can find."

"Yeah, we've met some pretty outlandish people in our travels." Scott said. "People who only want to be famous; or those who wish their houses were haunted. But we think this place takes the cake."

"Stacia, try not worry, we'll let you know if there is a danger here or not. We promise, we won't abandon you guys."

Dee wrapped her arms around Stacia's neck and squeezed, Stacia returned the gesture, only her embrace was more desperate and forceful.

"We'll be back in three days." Patrick said as he handed Stacia a card with his name and number printed on it.

Stacia took the card and watched as the gang walked out of the house. The very second she closed the door, Stacia apprehensively turned around to see the children seated on the floor getting ready to play video games on the PlayStation 3 that Dixon bought them.

Seating herself down onto the couch, Stacia said, "You two come here." Sidney and Devon did as ordered and stood before their distraught grandmother. Once more, Stacia wanted to utter bold words of both encouragement and strength, but the words were as transparent as the air she breathed. She just wasn't feeling it.

"Listen to me, I don't want you two to be going to school telling everyone about the people that came here today, or about all the cameras that they put up. Okay?"

"Yes, ma'am," the children said in unison.

"It's no one's business what goes on inside this house. Dee and the others are here to help us."

"Are they gonna beat up the ghosts, grandma?" Devon anxiously asked.

Stacia shook her head and snickered, "We'll see, sweetheart. You just remember what I said, don't tell anyone else about this, not even Dixon. We don't another call from the school."

"Are they gonna make a movie about us?" Sidney's face blossomed.

Astonished, Stacia laughed at the girl before saying, "A movie? Child, we could only wish this was just a movie."

CHAPTER 25

Day 14
12:37 p.m.

Dixon: I just wanted to say that I'm sorry.

Stacia: How many times are you going to be sorry? You always bolt out whenever something doesn't go your way. That's something the kids do whenever I tell them no.

Dixon: I know, and like I said, I'm sorry. You know how I get whenever you three are in danger. I go crazy.

Stacia: And that's the problem, you always fly off the fucking handle. This temper of yours has to be curbed. You know I don't want the kids around that. They're going through enough now as it is.

Dixon: I just wish you had listened to me on the house situation.

Stacia: Did you have another place for us to live? Because if so, then you should have come clean.

Dixon: Anywhere but there. Now you got someone painting racist shit on the walls.

Stacia: Dixon, I really don't have the time or patience to go over this right now.

Dixon: Can I come over and see you guys tonight?

Stacia: Now you want to drop by? Any other time whenever I invite you, you make up an excuse. Like I said, I'm really busy right now. I'll talk to you later.

Stacia slipped her cellphone back into her pocket before leaning up against the wall that was located right around the corner from the bustling lunchroom.

She stood and listened to the everyday commotion of workers eating and talking. No more did she revel in partaking in the rabblerousing, Stacia desired only solitude. There was far too much consuming her; just being around people at that point was becoming an aggravating ordeal.

Stacia lifted her body from off the wall and began down the hallway that led outside. Before she could even reach the upcoming door, Max came running around the corner.

"Hey there," he huffed, "glad I caught you."

With lazy eyes, Stacia asked, "What's up"

"Two things, first, when you get back from break, Kohler wants you to make sure you secure docks two and three."

Stacia dropped her shoulders and rolled her eyes. "I just did that yesterday." She griped. What are the people down there doing, picking their noses?"

Shrugging his broad shoulders, Max replied, "Who knows? If you ask me the whole crew should be fired."

Relenting, Stacia sighed "Alright, I'll see what I can do when I get back. "What else you got?"

"I also got a number for you. The temp agency finally got back to me this morning about Judy."

All of the sudden, Stacia's drowsy attention perked up the very instant Judy's name was dropped.

"What did they tell you?" She panted.

"Not much, if anything at all." Max said as he handed Stacia a piece of paper. "They said to call that number."

Stacia took the paper and studied the number before looking back at Max. "Thank you." She mumbled.

"No problem. So, Scott and his gang stopped by, huh?"

"Yeah, and they said that there's something definitely there in the house. But then again, I don't know what to think anymore, Max."

Max's face took on a more disheartened appearance the longer he stared at Stacia. "Do they have a clue as to—

"No." Stacia hastily cut in. "And honestly, I don't think I wanna know when or if they do find out something. I feel like I'm locked inside of a bad dream." She began to chuckle. "I still can't believe this is all happening."

"What did Dixon do about the wall?"

Twisting her lips, Stacia said, "Please, all he can do is get mad at the world and run away. Don't get me wrong, Scott and his friends were nice, but I felt so embarrassed even calling them. They say that they believed me, but deep down, I know they're probably laughing at me as I stand here."

"You can't think that way, Stacia. As long as you believe that there is something going wrong inside that house, then that's all that matters."

Stacia stood and studied Max for a few moments before asking, "Do you think I'm a nut?"

Max handed Stacia a blasé-type look, like he was telling her that her question was nonsense. "Stacia, you and I have known each other for years. Believe me, if I thought that of you then—

"No, Max, do you believe me?" Stacia urgently implored.

Max stood there in the hallway in front of Stacia with a vexed look on his face. Stacia could tell that he really didn't want to answer the question, and she really didn't want him to answer either.

"I'll give these folks a call." Stacia conceded before turning and walking out the door.

From there she found herself a cozy little spot next to some bushes and whipped out her cellphone. Stacia couldn't have pressed the numbers any faster.

"Good afternoon, this is the Broadview Lake Home. How can I help you?" A female voice said on the other end.

Stacia pulled the phone away from her ear for a second and frowned. The greeting wasn't exactly what she had expected.

"Uh, yes, I'm not sure if I have the right number or not. I was looking for a person by the name of Judy McFord."

"Is Judy a patient here?"

Once again, Stacia grimaced at the response. "I'm not sure really. I may have the wrong number. What place is this again?"

"This is Broadview Lake. Ma'am, if you want, I can look up Judy McFord."

"Okay…that would be fine." She apprehensively responded.

Stacia's brain couldn't help but to entertain a million and one thoughts all at once. She swore up and down that she had the wrong number.

"Hello?"

Snapping back, Stacia said, "I'm here."

"We do have a Judy McFord. She is under the care of Dr. Dick Worthy. Would you like for me to connect you with him?"

"Uh, please." Stacia stuttered.

The more minutes that passed by the more Stacia wanted to hang up. She didn't know what to expect next, a rational explanation or a stroke.

"Good afternoon, this Dr. Worthy." A light, male voice said.

"Uh, yes, my name is Stacia Taylor. Like I told the lady before you, I'm not sure if I have the right number. I was looking for a Judy McFord. I was given this number."

"Are you a family member of Ms. McFord?"

"Not exactly," Stacia grinned. "You see, Judy worked here at the warehouse where I'm employed, and I just had some questions for her."

A strong silence came upon the phone at that instant. For a moment, Stacia believed that the man had hung up.

"Just where exactly do you work?"

"I work at Crumbley Industries."

"Okay, I think we may have two different Judy McFord's here." Worthy sounded confused.

"I believe so, too. I don't know what I was thinking." Stacia chuckled to herself. "That poor old lady is probably somewhere at home."

"Hold on...old lady? Are we talking about Judith McFord? Ninety-three year old Judith McFord," Worthy questioned in a stale ramble.

"She was pretty old."

"We have only one Judith McFord here at this facility, and she has resided here since nineteen-seventy three."

"That's impossible," Stacia gulped, "we had a Judy McFord here as well. What kind of facility is this anyways?"

This is a psychiatric facility."

Stacia's mouth went completely dry right then. She tried in earnest to think up the most coherent thing to say at that second.

"Wait a minute, we have to be talking about two different people. Does your Judy McFord have long, grey hair and grey eyes to match?"

"Yes she does, I'm afraid."

"We had the same woman here a month ago. As a matter of fact, Judy has been seen all over this city working in other warehouses." Stacia adamantly stated.

"With all due respect, Judy McFord must have a very convincing twin, because she has been here at this facility since January of nineteen-seventy three."

"That's impossible; she was just here last month sweeping the floors, February ninth to be exact."

"Judy McFord was right here at this facility February ninth. As a matter of fact, I was taking her vitals that very morning. Judy McFord has been in a comatose state since nineteen-seventy three. Ms. McFord hasn't spoken in over forty years. Now, either we're talking about two different Judy McFord's, or she has an identical twin running around out there."

Without allowing another word to slip out from her mouth, Stacia pushed the "off" button on her phone and stood in place.

Suddenly, everything in front of her was transparent. Like a zombie, Stacia marched back into the building. Through throngs of workers heading back to their duties; straight through boxes that were placed on the floor in front of her. No one was there as far as she was concerned. To Stacia, she wasn't even inside her own body.

"Hey there, sexy thang," Young Jeremy smirked at Stacia as he walked beside her on his way back to the work area. "You ain't talked to me all day today. What's up with that, girl?"

Stacia did her best to ignore the fellow, but it seemed that the more she tried that was all the harder Jeremy made it for her.

Stepping directly in front of Stacia, Jeremy grinned, "Look, I got two tickets to the Laugh House for tomorrow. You get yourself all gussied up, and I'll roll by and pick you up. Whaddya say?"

All of the sudden, what was once unseen was gradually becoming visible right before her very eyes. With a trembling body, Stacia looked Jeremy straight in the face and growled, "Boy, if you don't get the fuck outta my face, I'm gonna stick my foot so far up your ass you'll be smelling my toe nails for a week."

Not only did Jeremy hear what was uttered, but also the rest of the workers within the vicinity. The entire area grew eerily quiet.

"You all get back to work, and if I hear one person say one more word you'll be going home early!" Stacia hollered before storming away and leaving everyone with hung jaws.

CHAPTER 26

Day 16
12:25 p.m.

"Where are the kids at?" Scott asked before sitting himself down at the kitchen table alongside Dee, Patrick and Stacia.

"There down a few houses with a couple of ladies watching DVD's." Stacia responded while sipping away at a glass full of soda.

"That's good, because we have some pretty shocking stuff to share with you." Patrick announced with a collection of papers in hand.

"But before he spills the beans, Stacia, how have you and the kids been doing since we last met?" Dee took a hold of Stacia's hand.

Humbly pressing her lips together, Stacia said, "We've been doing okay. Nothing out of the ordinary has happened here since you guys left. But...I did find out something pretty amazing back on Friday."

"What was that?" Patrick asked.

"It was about Judy, or I think it was about Judy."

"Speaking of Judy, we stumbled upon some pretty shocking stuff about her as well. Now, you mentioned that she worked at the same warehouse as you, right?"

"That's right."

"Well, we did a lot of research, and come to find out Judith McFord is actually at—

"At Broadview Lake," Stacia blurted out.

The gang of three all sat and studied each other with bamboozled stares on their youthful faces, apparently amazed that they were beaten to the punch.

"Yeah, she's been there since nineteen-seventy three." Patrick said before taking a photo and showing it to Stacia. "Would this be her by any chance?"

Stacia's stomach dropped. She placed her hand over her mouth as hard as she could while looking into Judy's decrepit face.

"What's the matter?" Dee asked.

Holding back tears, Stacia said, "I talked to those people back on Friday, and they told me she never left that place."

"But you say that she was there at your warehouse working, right?" Scott inquired.

Stacia just shook her head yes before dropping her hands to the table and exhaling. Everything after that was pointless.

"Well…we honestly don't know what to say." Patrick somberly said. "I mean, how is it possible that she could be at both your work place and—

"Pat, why don't you just tell Stacia what we found out," Dee impatiently implored.

"Okay, well, here goes. Someone didn't die in this house, Stacia, they were murdered." Patrick bluntly stated.

Stacia rolled her eyes clear to the back of her head before sitting up in her chair. "Fuck! My neighbor told me that someone died here, but he never once mentioned they were killed."

"Well, there was a guy who lived here by the name of Lucas McFord. He was beaten to death by four guys with baseball bats back in 1963. And it wasn't a pretty death either. They beat him literally from one corner of the house to the other.

He, uh… Lucas died in your bedroom. The police found the bloody bats down the alley the very next day."

Stacia caught the vomit that was gradually making its way up before getting up out of her seat and wandering around the kitchen.

"Judy and Lucas were brother and sister. But Lucas didn't live here in Lane, he was actually from Addington. We still don't know why he was here to begin with."

"From what we were able to gather, Judy remained in the house until nineteen-seventy three." Bruce mentioned. "It wasn't until January of that year that Broadview came here and dragged her away. She kept going on and on about how her brother was hurting her and wanting her to stay with him." "The press tried to talk to Judy, but she went into a sort of catatonic state as soon as she got to Broadview. She's been that way ever since." Patrick explained.

"So what does Lucas want with me and my grandkids?"

"It's a possibility he wants you all to leave." Dee beseeched. "Everything that's been happening is evidence that you guys aren't wanted here, especially the swastika."

"You all don't understand, you don't know where we just came from." Stacia pleaded. "We have nowhere else to go."

The kitchen became depressingly silent just then, like everyone gathered had nothing left to say to one another.

"What do you all think would or could happen to us while we're here?"

Patrick coughed, Dee rubbed her hands and Scott stretched. The response Stacia desired was taking its sweet time arriving.

"We're talking about ghosts here." Patrick clarified. "Till this day, Stacia, no one clearly understands them. Even mediums and the such still don't have a clue as to why ghosts even exist. The swastika, the Rebel flag that was downstairs, it's all evident that you three are on enemy territory."

"I…I don't know what to think or say." Stacia lost her breath. "I just wish you all were here that night when we saw that shadow cross in front of the TV, or heard that noise down in the basement. This shit doesn't happen to real people. I mean, I don't have the money to just up and find another house to live in."

Getting up to stand by her side, Dee said, "Stacia, we do understand. But…if all you say is true, then this could only be the beginning."

"Beginning of what?" Stacia's eyes opened wide.

"The beginning of the hauntings," Dee said. "It's a possibility that if whatever spirit is here, that the occurrences could only escalate."

Peering deep into Dee's eyes, Stacia asked, "Fuck Hollywood, has a ghost ever killed anyone before?"

Once more, the kitchen grew incredibly quiet while eyes shifted from one person to the next like everyone was waiting for the other to speak up first.

"There was one case way back in 1922 where a man was found dead inside his haunted home, and it wasn't a suicide either." Scott mentioned.

Both Dee and Patrick glanced at the man with scornful eyes, as though he had just told a terrible secret.

"What?" He hopelessly tossed up his hands. "Rather the truth than a lie."

Shaking his head, Patrick said, "Scott, why don't you gather all the cameras?"

"Ok." Scott soberly complied.

Turning back to Stacia, Dee said, "Look, would you like for us to stay here with you guys, until we at least try and get down to the bottom of all this?"

Stacia looked down at the grimy linoleum before raising her head and saying, "No, honey, you all have lives, too. I'm not going to inconvenience anyone else."

"It's no inconvenience, Stacia." Patrick said as he got up from out of his seat. "It's our occupation to figure out these things. Dee is right, this could only be the beginning, especially now that you know the history. We don't claim to be experts, but there is enough evidence out there in the world that makes the supernatural all too real."

Stacia glared on at the two before taking Dee by the hand and saying, "We'll be alright. It seems that my whole life has been one haunt after another. This just makes one more bump in the road."

Scott came back into the kitchen with all the cameras in hand. Once all of the equipment was gathered, Patrick, Dee and Scott left the house.

Stacia stood there at the front doorway like a permanent fixture. Everything that was said back in the kitchen had been ostensibly erased from her memory banks.

She was now aware that a human being had violently lost their life inside her home; all that was left by then was to let it all sink in as she stood face to face with not only her house, but the entity that saw her and her grandchildren as nuisances.

The Taylors had nowhere else to go, but Stacia wondered over and over just how to convey such an ardent message to someone she couldn't even see.

CHAPTER 27

9:51 p.m.

Patrick, Dee and Scott were all gathered inside their hotel room with TV monitors and bags of junk food surrounding them.

Both Patrick and Scott studied their papers in front of them while Dee stood in front of a monitor tinkering with various knobs.

"Babe, are you almost done with the re-linking?" Patrick asked.

"It's got about five more minutes, hun."

"Okay, while that's running I wanted to go over the Chamberlain case one more time, too."

"The Chamberlain case," Dee questioned with a frown. "What about the Taylors?"

"We'll get to them, too."

Pulling herself away from the monitor, Dee stood behind Patrick and said, "Don't you think Stacia's case is more important? We've seen what's been happening there at that house."

"We haven't seen anything yet." Scott said.

"He's right, sweetheart. So far, all we've seen is a huge swastika painted on a wall. I'm not calling Stacia a liar, but anyone could have put that there."

"Well, all we've seen at the Chamberlain's was a floating bed."

"But at least we saw something there. We didn't travel all the way from Columbus just to see a painted wall." Patrick insisted.

"Then you are calling Stacia a liar." Dee nudged at Patrick.

Patrick put down the papers that he was rifling through and turned around to Dee. "I'm not calling her a liar, I'm just saying that…we need more evidence."

"But she did have a point. How many African Americans encounter this?"

"What does race have to do with this?" Scott laughed out loud.

"It has a lot to do with it." Dee urged. "I don't know many blacks that cry ghost at the drop of a hat."

"Babe, I think you're getting emotionally involved here." Patrick caressed Dee's hand.

"Am I?" She pointed to herself surprised. "This is coming from the same guy who cried when he saw 'Up' for the first time."

Scott sniggered before Dee spun around and fiddled with the TV monitor. "You're movie is ready now." She said in a frustrated tone as she walked back to sit down in between Patrick and Scott.

Patrick and Scott glanced meekly at each other before Scott leaned forward and pressed the "play" button on the monitor in front of him.

"Ok, what we have here is the first night, 12:22 a.m.; the attic." Scot announced.

All three individuals sat, watched and waited for anything to occur. They sat and viewed for nearly an hour until the attic yielded no surprises.

"Ok, that was a complete waste of time." Scott sighed. "Next, we have the basement. 1:31 a.m."

Much like the attic before it, the basement stood absolutely still. The three students, who at first were hanging on to the edge of their separate seats, were all but exhausted by that point at watching nothing. For Dee, she really did want something to transpire; anything that would hopefully give Stacia at least a sense of coherence amongst a nest of cynics.

Patrick stretched his aching body before leaning forward and pressing the "off" button on the monitor. "I hate to say it, but I think we've stumbled upon another wild goose chase."

Dee sat back in her seat and crossed her arms in defeat while the two men beside her glanced on like she had just lost her best friend.

"We still have three more videos to see." Dee sat up and proclaimed.

"Ok," Patrick huffed, "you asked for it."

Scott cued up the next video before saying, "Dining room, 1:58 a.m. You know, we should start charging people for these out of city trips. Columbus isn't exactly right around the corner from here."

They sat and they watched. 1:58 dragged on into 2:22. Even by then, Dee herself was growing weary.

Stretching her tired arms, the young lady slouched her body and said, "I dunno, maybe we should just tell Stacia to—

But no sooner had she begun to speak, on the screen appeared a broad shouldered man that just casually walked into the dining room. The three sat up all in unison and held their breaths at what they were watching.

The man in the video stumbled about in the dark like he was lost before he eventually turned around and faced the camera that was at one time mounted upon the wall.

He was a white man, that much was evident, but beyond that, his facial features were distorted. The man neared closer and closer to the camera before he cracked a menacing smile and stood back.

Dee began to shiver in her seat while watching the strange person in the video carry on towards the wall behind him and ascend like a spider. He crawled about the walls and ceiling, back and forth before eventually dropping back down to the floor and moving towards the kitchen.

Dropping his head in disbelief, Patrick stammered, "Uh… that would explain the scratching noise on the floor that Stacia was hearing."

"Roll to the kitchen, quick!" Scott hastily fumbled.

Swiftly, Patrick switched screens. The video they were watching next was that of the man. He was blundering about in the kitchen, rummaging through the drawers before stopping and reaching into one of the cabinets.

From out of the cabinet he pulled a butcher knife and shined it at the camera that was perched on the wall above.

"The son of a bitch is showing off." Scott gulped without blinking.

The man with the knife moved out of range of the camera for a few moments before returning with a little black girl by his side.

"Oh God, is that Sidney?" Dee frantically jumped up from out of her seat.

"No, no, she's too small." Patrick tried to calm her down.

"Who is it then?"

"Honey, just wait," Patrick panted. "Just wait one second."

The man positioned the little girl in front of him before holding up his knife for the camera to see. He then lowered the blade and placed it against the girl's neck.

"What the fuck is this?" Scott hollered.

Just like that, the man sliced the child's neck. The little girl plummeted to the floor in a heap while blood oozed from her neck and onto the linoleum.

The three all stood up at once and watched with trembling bodies as the man in the video dropped the butcher knife and approached the camera. Then, like a flash of sudden lightening, the man's face struck across the screen before vanishing out of sight. All three students jumped and screamed before the TV monitors all went black at once.

"Did you all see that, too?" Patrick stuttered.

"Yeah...yeah, I did." Scott panted for air.

"Let's see if we can rewind it and get a closer glimpse of the bastard's face!" Patrick desperately said as he tried in earnest to replay the scene. But as many times as he rewound, the section which he wanted to view would not show up.

With tears in her eyes, Dee asked, "What's the matter? Why can't we see it again?"

Shaking his head in disbelief, Patrick continued to fiddle with the equipment. Soon, Scott joined in as well, trying fervently to aid his friend in the search.

"It's all gone." Scott sighed in defeat. "The data...it's all been erased."

"No, no, that's bullshit!" Patrick protested. "We've got backups! Check the rear mainframe!"

Before Scott could even turn around, the monitors and the rest of the electrical equipment in the room all sparked and fizzed until the televisions went up in smoke.

Dee screamed while both Patrick and Scott struggled to get their precious equipment out of the room in time.

They tripped over wires that were layering the floor, as well as bags of food and soda cans. Before long, the sprinkler system in the room went off, pouring down a torrent of cold water all over the floor and bed.

Patrick, Dee and Scott all made it outside the hotel room safe and sound. Most of their equipment, however, was unsalvageable. If not by electrical malfunction, then the sprinklers finished them off.

All three stood out in the dark of night with their mouths hanging wide open enough for all the air inside their lungs to escape.

All they could do was stand and watch as their room was being drenched more and more by the second.

"Anyone feel like sleeping tonight?" Patrick commented under his breath in a deadpan tone as he stared on and on at the saturated hotel room in front of him.

CHAPTER 28

3:47 a.m.

Stacia and Sidney snored peacefully away in the bed while Devon's eyes popped wide open. The little boy couldn't explain to himself why he awoke so suddenly, but inside his mind was a searing patch of fog that would not sift away. He could see everything in front of him, but his conscience was like mist that couldn't be erased.

Devon sat up in the bed and looked over at his sleeping grandmother and sister for a few moments before climbing out of the bed and creeping around to the locked door.

Ever so carefully Devon unlocked the hinge and twisted the knob. From there, he stepped out into the pitch black hallway and quietly shut the door behind him.

Down the silent hallway he skulked like a brazen thief. The boy trampled down the creaking steps and into the living room where the television abruptly came to life. Devon should have been alarmed by the sudden disturbance, but his fading conscience didn't seem to allow him to give it a second thought as he carried on past the set and into the dining room.

From the dining he came into the kitchen where six tall, red clad figures, all with pointy hoods covering their faces, stood in a circle.

Devon stopped short of the kitchen's threshold and just stood there with a blank, entranced stare on his face. It was a standoff of sorts, like everyone gathered was waiting for the other to make the first move.

Devon remained at the doorway for at least five whole minutes before a voice among the six whispered, "Come here, little nigger boy."

Devon did as ordered and slugged his diminutive carcass towards the six while one of the drawers beside the sink opened all by itself.

From out of the drawer levitated a butter knife that one of the hooded individuals took and held against Devon's neck. The child stood perfectly still while the blunt instrument was being pressed on his cold skin. Devon couldn't feel a thing; he couldn't even see shapes in front of him.

One of the hooded individuals then forced the boy down to his knees while keeping the knife against his still neck.

"Don't tell my grandma." Devon's tongue slurred.

The six then encircled the boy until he was no longer able to be seen. All that Devon could seem to view was darkness overlapped by even more darkness.

CHAPTER 29

Day 17

With a jittery right hand that was supporting a cigarette in between her lips, Stacia stood at the kitchen window watching Sidney ride her bike around the yard while Devon sat on the steps looking as miserable as an old man about to die.

She could hear Dee, Patrick and Scott behind her carry on, but Stacia just couldn't tear her eyes away from her poor little boy. He sat there with his hands holding up his loathsome head. She couldn't even tell if he was aware that his big sister was outside along with him.

"We would've called you last night, but we had a lot of explaining to do with the hotel's manager." Dee explained from the kitchen table.

Stacia turned around and sucked in a long drag before dashing the cigarette in an ashtray on the counter and aimlessly strolling around the kitchen. "Do you guys believe that we're in that much danger?"

"Stacia, I'll admit for both me and Scott, we really had our doubts at first." Patrick said. "That is until what we saw last night. We've never seen or experienced anything like that before. Forget the equipment that was destroyed, whatever is inside this house is conscious, and it's damn dangerous."

"Were you able to find out anything else about McFord?"

"We're still looking into him." Scott stated. "What makes McFord really interesting is that it seems there are some folks out there that want what took place here kept a secret. We can't even locate any other family either here or in Addington."

"And I think I speak for us all when I say that none of us wants to visit Addington anytime soon." Dee exhaled.

"Here, here." Patrick chimed in.

Stacia continued to ramble about the kitchen while taking quick glances outside at the children. "I know you all think I'm a damn fool for staying here." She sighed. "Just knowing that there's something crawling on the walls should have us packing up and running. But…this is it for us. I'm scared to death, and now I think the kids are starting to crack."

Dee got up from out of her seat and approached Stacia in the middle of her stroll. With a caring hand on her shoulder she said, "None of us will ever understand what you three went through in your last house, Stacia. We get that you have nowhere else to turn, but…we're scared to death for you three. Like Pat said, we've never seen anything like this before."

"She's right, Stacia." Scott stepped in. "We've read of hauntings that started out calm, and ended up escalating into something violent. Whether that was McFord in the video or not, something here in this house is malevolent. I'm not one of these people that goes around calling everything evil, you can ask Uncle Max, but even I know when I've stepped into something I shouldn't have."

Stacia looked on at three before her. She wanted so much for them to stay around and continue talking and explaining, anything that would keep her from being alone.

Getting up from the table, Patrick announced, "Well, we have to get going. We gotta make a stop back in Columbus and put in an order for new equipment."

Stacia and the three all headed into the living room and out the front door. Before following her cohorts, Dee turned and gave Stacia the tightest hug before fervidly mouthing the words, "Please…get out of here."

Stacia stood on the porch and watched as they all got into their van and drove away. It felt as though her own breath had left along with them.

Directly across the street was parked a U-Haul truck. Stanley was moving, and it didn't surprise Stacia one bit. A series of men were carrying out furniture and other belongings and loading them into the truck.

Stacia wanted to see Stanley at least one more time, but she was aware of the mood he had been drowning in ever since his mother's passing and the assault Dixon had laid down upon him. The last thing she wanted was to exacerbate the situation and embarrass herself.

Rather than stand for anymore, Stacia carried herself back into the house and upstairs to her bedroom. She lay down in the bed and watched as the gentle breeze waved the curtains in the window ahead of her back and forth.

Stacia held her pillows against her face and began wishing. She would wish to herself whenever life seemed overbearing. Stacia wished the proverbial "go back in time and change things." All of the sudden, the money that she had been saving all those years didn't seem all too important, and that thought alone caused the woman to cry.

Out of pulsating fury, Stacia pounded on the bed as hard as she could. She felt both trapped and isolated; like she was running down a dead end street and couldn't turn around.

The more she wept the more Stacia realized that her own decisions had betrayed her. No matter how much she cared for and thought of others before herself, it all came back to beat her across the face.

As Stacia sat up her bed, she wiped her eyes and almost immediately saw a dark figure standing behind the waving curtains. Frantically, she wiped her eyes some more and saw the silhouette spread its arms wide before running out from behind the confines of the curtains and jumping onto both her and the bed.

Stacia screamed her lungs out while the blackened figure restrained her arms. Stacia kicked, spat and yelled as hard as she could, but no matter what, the invader would not release her.

With all the fight that she was putting up, Stacia couldn't see its face, but she could hear it. It was grunting like an angry dog. It had a scent of something old and musty.

With every attempt to free herself, Stacia's body was pushed right back down onto the bed with such a force that it hurt her head. Stacia then saw her legs being stretched wide open. She tried in vain to keep them closed, but no matter what, her captor was entirely too strong.

From there, her pants began to unzip and drop down her legs. Stacia wept and hollered for all she was worth. At that point, even if the kids had seen what she was going through, at least it would have possibly given her a chance for escape.

"Millie." A feeble voice uttered into her face.

Stacia heard it, but she was entirely too enthralled in battle to pay any attention. Before long, even her panties were being slipped off.

Stacia screamed…and that was all that was left.

CHAPTER 30

Day 18

Stacia Taylor sat in her car and stared on endlessly at the large building ahead of her. Her mouth was hanging slightly ajar while a whiff of lemon from the deodorizer that dangled from the rearview mirror whistled into her nostrils.

Only hours removed and she could still feel its hands all over her body as though the incident had just taken place moments ago. She did a wonderful job in keeping her distance from the children since the event; she had absolutely nothing to say to them or anyone else.

Stacia was aware that eight o' clock was right around the corner, and yet, the will to climb out of her car was subdued, like something was holding her in place.

She watched with lethargic eyes the lagers that shuffled inside the building before she pulled her sore carcass out of her car and dragged on towards the entrance. With every step she made it felt like scorching fire in between her legs. Her entire body from head to toe was reeling in agonizing pain. It felt as though she had just finished doing five thousand jumping jacks nonstop.

Like a cripple, Stacia limped inside and past the two security guards who inquired of her apparent condition. Stacia only ignored the men and carried on through the loud warehouse where various people greeted her with the usual "good morning", and "how you doing, Stacia?" Stacia continued on tight-lipped; too ashamed and startled to utter a word.

The alarm that signified that it was eight on the dot blared out loud enough throughout the warehouse to astound even the most dead individual, but Stacia remained comatose. She didn't even budge in her limp that only grew slower with every turn she made down one aisle after on her way to the her own work area.

The second she arrived at her section, Stacia caught sight of Max who was delivering his daily work detail to the others. She stopped short of one of the shelves and leaned up against its hard steel.

Stacia stood and watched, and that was all she did. The words that Max was saying went into one ear and out the other like wind through a tunnel.

"Okay, gang, let's get to It," Max loudly announced before making his way over to Stacia.

Among all the workers, Stacia saw Max's large girth coming towards her like a cloud above the masses. She immediately pulled herself from off the shelf and pretended to go about her business.

"Hey there," Max said. "You just get in?"

Without even glancing at the man, Stacia replied, "Uh, yeah, had a hard time with the kids today."

Following in behind her, Max asked, "Were you able to get the rest of the orders from—

Stacia paused at that very moment to see why Max had suddenly stopped talking. When she noticed the concerned look on his face, she right away knew that it was time to conjure up a story and quick.

With a blasé grin, Stacia said, "Look, I know what you're thinking, and believe me, it's nothing serious. I just fell down the basement steps last night."

"Oh really," Max's eyes lit up. "You falling down didn't have anything to do with what's happening there, did it?"

Stacia shook her head no before saying, "It was a simple slip, that's all. Now, what were you gonna say?"

Max stared on a little while longer at Stacia before asking, "Were you able to get the rest of the orders from the Cincinnati hub?"

"No, not yet, they're still waiting on the overnight shipment from Kentucky."

Max just couldn't seem to take his worried eyes off of Stacia, which in turn only caused her to become even more agitated.

"Max," she moaned, "I told you I'm fine."

"No you're not." Max replied in a grunt. "What happened to your neck, Stacia? Were you bit?"

Stacia concealed the wound with her right hand before limping past Max in a spiteful manner on her way over to the her assigned work area.

Stacia figured to herself that she must have been wearing the single most disgusted frown on her face considering that just about everyone did their best to steer clear of her. Even her own to friends saw fit to remain at their assigned stations rather than approach Stacia with their concerns.

Stacia went about her duty, filling empty boxes with product and writing out work orders while keeping her eyes away from those she was forced to work amongst.

"Stacia," a young, handsome white man said a' loud as he came down the aisle where she was working.

Stacia spun around, seemingly forgetting that she was in pain, and faced the man with a determined purpose.

"Just wanted to see if you got that order out yet," the man said.

"I just told Max that we had to wait for the Cincinnati hub because they themselves are waiting for word from Kentucky."

"Are you serious?" The man gasped. "Look, it's your job to make sure these people stay on their toes."

Stacia continued to gaze on at the man as if she wanted to rip out his throat. "I'll get on it right away, Peter." She calmly stated.

"You do that, and also make sure we get the Toledo orders out by noon, or else all of our asses are on the line."

Stacia watched as Peter turned and switched his pretty little self away before she dropped the papers she had in her hands down to the floor and stormed away in the opposite direction.

She hobbled like an old cripple down the cement floor until she reached the women's bathroom. Once inside, she immediately went for the very first empty stall and slammed it shut behind her before securing the latch.

Stacia sat down on the toilet seat and covered her head with her hands as though she were trying to shut out the screaming world.

All the rampant walking only caused Stacia to remember that she was in pain. Ever so gradually she unzipped her pants and pulled down her panties enough to where she could see the black and blue bruises that were layered up and down on the left side of her midsection.

Just looking at the wound caused Stacia to burst out into tears and recall the hands that wouldn't let go. Its presence hung all over her body like a hot, itchy blanket. She couldn't even recall what took place after so long due to the fact that she had passed out during the inexhaustible supernatural experience.

Stacia pulled up her pants before reaching into her right shoe and slipping out a switchblade. The woman was tired, so much so that the thought of moving forward drained her beyond belief.

Stacia put the blade to her right wrist and pressed down without allowing the sharp end to sear her skin. She wanted it, but the nerve to do so was hanging on to a thread.

"Stacia," one of her friends called out as they entered the bathroom.

Right away, Stacia put her blade into her pants pocket and wiped her eyes clean before getting up, flushing the toilet and stepping out of the stall.

"Hey ya'll, what's up?" Stacia sighed while straitening her ball cap.

Both Veena and Lucinda stood and looked at Stacia like they had never laid eyes upon the woman before. Stacia stared back at them both, fully aware of what was on their individual minds.

Giggling, Stacia said, "Let me get my crazy butt to work before Peter comes back and throws another bitch fit."

Before Stacia could even take one step Veena took her by the hand and stopped her, while Lucinda came up behind Stacia and wrapped her arms around her waist.

Like someone had just knocked her down, Stacia dropped to the floor in a heap and wept in both ladies arms.

Without a word uttered amongst them, all three women held on to each other like they were falling from out of an airplane.

CHAPTER 31

3:25 p.m.

"Grandma is gonna whoop us when she finds out that we left school early." Little Devon warned as both he and Sidney got off the city bus and began walking down the sidewalk side by side.

Securing her bookbag tightly on her back, Sidney rolled her eyes and said, "That's why she's not gonna find out, Devon. You have to keep your mouth shut about it."

"Why did you and Tracey throw that paint at everyone?"

"We didn't mean to, we were just playing around. I just hope Mrs. Andrews doesn't give us detention again. Grandma said that if I get another detention then she won't let me go over to Tracey's birthday party."

"But grandma said that we're not 'posed to go into the house all by ourselves. What if the ghost gets us?"

Sidney twisted her lips while looking down at her brother. "Mrs. Andrews said that ghosts aren't for real."

There settled between the children a momentary hush that lasted for at least two whole minutes as they trekked along the rugged sidewalk that led to their neighborhood.

"Why did grandma sleep on the floor last night?" Devon asked.

"I dunno, maybe she wasn't feeling good." Sidney shrugged.

"I wasn't feeling good, too." Devon sighed.

Sidney gawked down at the boy and asked, "What's the matter?"

"I dunno, I keep on having dreams about these men in the kitchen. They got these red clothes on, and masks, too. It makes me sad."

"It's only a dream. Is that why you didn't want to play yesterday?"

"Yes." Devon despondently replied.

Sidney patted her brother on the back and said, "Maybe one day grandma will find us another house to live in. I don't like living there anymore."

"Me, too, it scares me there."

"Don't worry, maybe Dixon will get us some pizza and take us away."

"Why won't grandma let us stay at Dixon's house? Does his house have ghosts, too?"

"I dunno, maybe he doesn't have a house."

"I hope we all get to live with each other one day, so we can have a granddaddy."

Sidney only smirked before she and her brother turned down a corner. "Grandma didn't say good morning or I love you to us today when she dropped us off at school." Sidney commented in a melancholy sort of way.

"Maybe she's sick."

"Yeah, maybe so," Sidney sighed. "Tracey said that the last time her mom got sick she found out that she was gonna have a baby."

"Is grandma gonna have a baby, too?" Devon looked up surprised.

"I dunno, maybe so."

Five or so minutes later the kids at last arrived at their forlorn looking house. The second Sidney saw that her grandmother's car was parked in front she immediately broke out into a feverish sweat.

"What's she doing here already?" Sidney gasped while gripping her bookbag's straps.

"I dunno, maybe she came home from work sick."

Sidney gawked all around the neighborhood before sneaking around to the backyard to find her grandmother standing directly in the middle of the grass smoking a cigarette.

The girl then turned to her brother and whispered, "Okay listen, you and me are gonna go inside."

"But grandma said not to be inside the house all by ourselves."

"Shut up and listen." Sidney scolded the boy. "I'm just gonna take a quick shower so I can clean this paint off of me and then we'll leave and go down to that corner store and hang out until it's really time for us to come home."

Devon wore a peculiar, if not worrisome glare upon his face. All Sidney could think of was how angry her grandmother would be if she found out about her indiscretion at school; conjuring a more rational plan didn't exactly cross her mind at that painstaking juncture.

Both children ran back around to the front of the house. Sidney then took out her house key and unlocked the door.

"Okay, come upstairs and go into your bedroom." Sidney ordered.

"But grandma said—

"I know what grandma said, but I'm only gonna be taking a shower for a few minutes. She won't find out as long as she's outside."

The children raced upstairs. As commanded, Devon went into his room while Sidney barricaded herself inside the bathroom.

The girl took off her jacket and looked at her once white uniform shirt that was plastered in red and blue paint all over. She unbuttoned the shirt and took it off before reliving herself of the rest of her clothing. Sidney then hopped into the shower and watched as the paint smeared off of her body and down into the drain.

She scrubbed herself vigorously enough to where it hurt, making sure not to miss a single spot on her body.

After a few minutes, Sidney began hearing what sounded like heavy footsteps walking across the hallway outside. She poked her head out the shower curtain and listened as the footsteps carried on back and forth.

"Devon, is that you?" She whispered strongly.

When she received no answer, Sidney went back to her bathing detail, scrubbing from head to toe and hoping her brother would be right where she last left him.

However, just as soon as she was nearly done, Sidney began hearing the doorknob twist and wrestle back and forth. The girl once more peeked outside the curtain. "Devon, get away from the door."

But no answer was given. The doorknob continued to turn. Believing it was her nosey brother, Sidney climbed out of the shower and opened the door to find no one on the other end.

Sidney stared all around the hallway before catching sight of a dark, hulking figure turn down the corner and stand clear at the other end of the hallway. Sidney screamed for all she was worth before the figure wailed out its own yell and came racing down towards the girl.

Sidney shut the bathroom door and squealed for her grandmother. Without little effort, the door swung wide open. Sidney jumped right back into the warm shower before having her arms snatched up by an invisible force. She then saw her entire body being dragged out of the bathroom and down the stairs.

The child kicked and screamed to the point where even her heels began to bleed as they bumped against the wood steps. Sidney looked up and all around but could see absolutely no one, but she was well aware that something had her.

She then gawked up to see the front door open wide. Like she was yesterday's trash, Sidney's naked body was flung outside on the porch. The girl got to her feet as fast as she could, but not fast enough, the door shut right in her face, leaving her outside bare to the world.

The girl screamed, banged on the door and cried as loud as she could before Stacia, along with Devon, came running around to the front.

Without a asking a single question, Stacia quickly took off her jacket and wrapped it around Sidney's still wet and naked body before gathering her grandkids and shuffling them off to the car.

Still yelling like a frightened puppy in the backseat, Sidney watched as her grandmother turned on the car and pulled away as fast as she could down the road.

"Sid, baby, it's gonna be okay!" Stacia frantically assured the child as she veered from one lane to the other.

Devon in the backseat with his sister tried to console her the best he could by patting her on the shoulder, but the girl just couldn't be brought down, she persisted in her yelping like she was still being assaulted.

After so long, Stacia eventually pulled the car to the side of the road and climbed in the backseat alongside Sidney. She rocked the little girl in her arms back and forth while whispering soft words in her ear.

The more Stacia spoke kindly to her that was all more Sidney began to calm down. Before too long, there was nothing but whimpering inside the car from all three individuals as they held on to each other in such a painful way that not a thing in the world could separate them.

CHAPTER 32

S tacia tooled around Lane until the afternoon sky gave way to the stars and darkness of twilight. She had no particular place in mind to stop; just as long as she was driving she seemed content.

In the backseat both Sidney and Devon snored away like two babies. Every so often Stacia would hear Sidney sniffle and sigh in her sleep, remains of her tirade from hours earlier.

Stacia didn't want to ask the girl what had taken place inside the house for a whole host of reasons; one being that it would only invoke even more insidious recollections of what she herself endured at the hands of the beast that dwelled inside the home. She thanked God that she had passed out during the assault, or else she would have possibly died from sheer fright.

Stacia drove on until the steady rain began pelting the car. She cut on the windshield wipers and pulled down one lane after another until she came across an all too familiar sign up ahead. The sign read "Junction Five." Stacia sighed inside her stomach before stopping at a traffic light and shutting her eyes. The woman then rested her head on the steering wheel and bit down on her bottom lip in a sort of gentle way as not to break flesh.

The rain only beat upon the car all the harder at that point as she sat there at the lonely intersection. All she could seem to ponder on was what awaited her just around the corner from the traffic light. Suddenly, all that had taken place earlier back at 833 Husk Drive had drifted from her memory for the time being.

A honking horn behind her awakened Stacia so violently that her own forehead bumped against the steering wheel. The woman regained her bearings and pushed along around a bend and down a wooded, narrow lane that before long turned into what appeared to be a driveway and a steel, black gate.

Stacia looked on in dreaded expectation as the gate lifted ever so slowly. The long, grinding racket that the gate made as it raised caused a bitter cold to slither down her back.

Without putting much weight down on the gas, she pushed along into the parking lot and stopped right next to a white van. The rain that was coming down hard and torrential moments earlier only seemed to pour down even more rigid as Stacia sat there in her car. She stared intently at the brightly lit, one floor building ahead with lazy, unenthused eyes that looked like they could have fallen asleep at a moment's notice.

Stacia put her hands on the steering wheel and gripped as tight as she possibly could before turning around and patting the kids on their legs.

"Hey, guys, c'mon and wake up."

Gradually, both Devon and Sidney awoke from their hostile slumber and looked all around them like they had just awakened in another world.

"Are we home, grandma?" Devon yawned.

"No, baby, we're not home." Stacia muttered. "Let's hurry and run so we won't get too wet."

Wiping her eyes, Sidney whimpered, "But I don't have on my clothes, grandma."

"I know, baby. They have clothes in here for you."

Stacia grabbed both her keys and purse before getting out of the car and opening the door for the children to get out. All three ran for the building and its two automatic doors that slid apart the very moment the Taylors came within sensors' range.

"Good evening." A young black lady that sat at the front desk greeted in a salty manner. "How can I help you?"

Shaking off the rain that covered her bare head, Stacia replied, "I need clothes for my granddaughter, and we need a place to stay for a while."

The young woman viewed all three individuals that stood in front of her before getting up out of her seat and walking around her desk.

"Okay, before we do that, I need for you to fill out some forms, and—

Before the woman could utter another word, from behind an adjacent door appeared a homely looking, middle-aged white woman who started to pass by all three Taylors, that is until she caught sudden sight of Stacia.

Stacia tried her best to conceal her wet face away from the woman, but it was almost impossible as the woman kept ogling her up and down like a famous statue.

"Stacia," the woman marveled, nearly dropping her purse to the floor. "Stacia Taylor, is that you, sweetheart?"

Once more, Stacia bit down on her bottom lip before raising her head. "Hello, Val." She humbly muttered.

Val stood in the middle of the floor seemingly flabbergasted at the sight she was beholding. Stacia again tried to divert her attention elsewhere, but Val was ever so persistent.

"Stacia…I…I didn't expect to see you here." Val stammered with a jittery smile.

"Well," Stacia grinned with a blush," neither did I, but my granddaughter needs some clothes, please."

"Granddaughter…okay, we'll take care of her." Val instantly snapped to. "Tyeshia, take the children to the clothing area and make sure they get something to eat. We can forgo the paperwork for the time being."

"Grandma, I wanna stay with you." Sidney whined while holding onto her grandmother's hand.

Stacia secured her jacket tighter around Sidney's body before saying, "It's okay, these people are gonna take care of us. They're gonna give us food and some new clothes. Everything is gonna be alright."

Stacia stood back up and watched as Tyeshia led a frightened Sidney and Devon down a well-lit corridor and behind a door. Once they were out of sight that left only her and Val.

Stacia stood there in the main hallway at a loss for words as both she and Val glanced at each other and the walls behind them in nervous anticipation at what would or could be said next.

"Well, I'm glad you guys showed up when you did." Val beamed. "I was on my way out the door for the night."

Beaming right back, Stacia remarked, "Right, I'm glad, too."

Once more, a nervous, if not agitated pause took prevalence between the two women. Stacia could tell right off the bat just what was on Val's mind at that instant. Not only was she soaking wet from the rain, but there was also the matter of the bruise on her neck, as well as the noticeable limp.

"Well," Val sighed, "while the children are being attended to, why don't you and I go into my office and talk?"

Stacia followed Val behind a door that led down a hallway. On the walls were framed pictures of various women and their children, all laughing and carrying on in ways that made the establishment seem inviting to both its current and future residents. Stacia just couldn't seem to take her eyes off of the walls; in a way, they held a powerful spell over her.

Val then unlocked an office door and cut on a light. "Do you want to get yourself a new change of clothes?" Val asked as she sat down behind her desk.

"No thank you." Stacia waved as she sat down in the seat opposite the desk. "I'll be ok."

"Well, I can't believe it's you again after all these years." Val carried on. "How is Deontae these days?"

"He's fine." Stacia immediately and defiantly replied as though the answer were on the tip of her tongue. "He's just fine."

Val sat and blushed before clutching her hands together and saying, "It's funny, you look the same, even though you've grown up."

Humbly smirking, Stacia stated, "It's good old me, alright."

"I sure do wish you would give me the secret to how to age well." Val laughed out loud. "You honestly don't look a day over twenty-five if you ask me."

Stacia herself blushed and said, "Girl, please, I'm forty-three years old, and I feel like I'm seventy-three sometimes."

"You look very well, Stacia." Val quietly commented.

Stacia sat glued to her seat while listening to the overbearing rain outside the window beat down upon the building like it were trying to break it apart. She couldn't tell if the wetness on her brow was from the rain or just plain sweat, she was so tense.

"So, you have grandchildren?" Val asked.

"Yep, Sidney is nine and Devon is seven."

"I bet they're angels."

"They're spoiled rotten." Stacia smirked.

"I remember when Deontae was here, and—"

"Val, I need for you to understand something." Stacia right away cut in. "I know what you see before you is...strange, but I assure you, I'm not that same loud-mouthed girl you once knew. I'm a long way from that. I know you have a lot of questions you wanna ask me, but instead, I need for you to trust me. We've had some very strange things happen to us lately, and all we need is a place to stay for a few days, nothing more. Please, I need you to trust me."

Val stared pensively into Stacia's eyes as though she were trying to read the woman's thoughts. Stacia expected it, she also expected Val to recognize distress when she saw it, it was her job.

"Stacia...I, I just want you to know that nothing here has changed. And when I say nothing here, I mean nothing between you and I. We've had our tussles in the past, but I've always been able to trust you. And I know that if you've showed up here after all these years, then it has to be for a very good reason."

"Believe me...there's nothing good about any of this." Stacia earnestly declared.

Reaching across the desk, Val said, "We'll get you guys situated as quickly as possible."

Stacia leaned forward and took Val's hands into her own. The two ladies held on, and held on some more.

***

Clothed in a pair of light blue pajama pants and matching top, Stacia shut the door to the small room that she and the children called a temporary shelter.

Lying in a bed right next to hers was Sidney and Devon, who were wearing their own set of pajamas. Outside the door Stacia could hear other children screaming and crying, while their mothers yelled for them to either shut up or quit running down the hallway. To Stacia, it was all removable racket.

As Stacia sat down on her bed, Sidney immediately raised her head and asked, "What is this place, grandma?"

"It's a shelter, sweetheart. Your daddy and I came here a long time ago, when he was a little boy himself. These people help women and children in need."

"Why can't we go to the hotel again?" Devin questioned.

"Because, son, I don't get paid till Friday, and even then, I have a ton of bills that need taken care of. This is our only option for now."

"Are there any ghosts here, grandma?" Sidney sniveled.

Stacia immediately got up and went over to the kids' bed where she cradled the girl in her arms. "No, baby, no ghosts here," she tried to hold back tears.

"I don't ever wanna go back to that house again." Sidney rattled on. "I saw him, grandma. I saw the man in the hallway. He ran at me—

"Be quiet, baby." Stacia gently patted the child on the face. "Just be quiet. Everything is alright now. We're as far away from that place as possible."

Devon reached his arm around his grandmother's neck before asking, "Grandma, are you gonna have a baby?"

Stacia nearly snapped her neck looking over at the boy. "What on earth makes you ask that, child?" She couldn't help but giggle.

"He knows that you haven't been feeling good lately." Sidney responded.

Stacia took the boy into her bosom and said, "My love, no more kids will be coming out of me. My baby making days are long over. I'll be just fine. We'll all be just fine."

Stacia then reached over and attempted to cut off the lamplight, only to have Sidney catch her hand and beseech, "Please…leave it on."

Stacia rested her exhausted body on the bed with her grandchildren snug beside her. She had hoped that they wanted the light to stay on; Stacia was tired of being the hero for the day.

***

Much like the military, the shelter, too, had its own wake up time. Seven a.m. rolled around far too quickly for Stacia's liking, even though she was all too used to it. She wanted at least another hour of rest from the punishment that had been laid down upon her.

As usual, Stacia attended to the children while taking care of herself along the way. Teeth had to be brushed, hair had to be combed, and the usual pep talk of "no discussing ghosts with others" had to be drilled into two little minds before venturing out into the new accommodations.

Stacia led the kids and herself into the main cafeteria where women of various backgrounds and ages along with their children were all eating and conversing.

The Taylors felt like aliens on a strange, new planet as they set foot inside the eating area. Everyone gathered stared at them like they themselves had never looked in a mirror before.

Stacia and the children carried on until they found an empty section clear on the other side of the cafeteria. On the table before them were four covered plates. Stacia handed the children their meals before lifting her lid to find scrambled eggs, two sausage links, two pieces of toast, an orange and miniature cartons of milk and orange juice. The woman was far from hungry, which was why she had no problem shoving her plate over to the kids.

"Are we going to school today, grandma?" Devon asked as he drank his orange juice.

Stacia sat and pondered for a second or two before saying, "I don't know, honey. Just give grandma a moment to think things over."

While the children ate, Stacia took time to gloss over her surroundings that after twenty some odd years seemed a lot smaller than she remembered.

"You all gonna eat that plate?" A young, scraggly looking white woman asked as she and her three kids all stood by her side.

Stacia looked up at the woman and said, "No, you can have it, and this other plate, too."

Without a thank you, the woman gathered both Stacia's uneaten plate and the fourth plate before shuffling off in the other direction.

"Fuck that, that was my fucking plate, bitch!" A big, black woman raged as she came racing towards the white woman.

Everyone inside the cafeteria came to a pause and watched as the black lady snatched the plates from out of the white woman's hands before wrestling the woman down to the floor. Before too long, two other women, one black and the other white, joined in the fray.

Dishes, chairs and cutlery were thrown from one end of the cafeteria to the other while racist insults and curse words blared loudly in the air.

"That honkey bitch stole my fucking plate!"

"So, you stole the money I had in my duffle bag two nights ago, you fuckin' nigger bitch!"

Soon enough, two male guards came rushing into the cafeteria and pulled all four women apart before a plate came hurtling at Devon, just missing the boy's head by mere inches.

"I'm gonna fuckin' kill that nigger when I get back here! I swear I'll kill her black ass!"

"Fuck you, you piece of white trash!"

Children screamed and cried while the four women continued to kick and scrap while being carried out of the wrecked cafeteria.

Stacia looked down at Devon's scared little face before taking both children by the hand and tearing out of the cafeteria on her way out of the building.

As soon as they reached the car, Stacia couldn't get the keys inside the lock fast enough. Like she was gathering cattle into a stable, she hurried Sidney and Devon inside before getting herself in and ripping out of the parking lot.

In her frazzled state of mind, Stacia couldn't explain to the children just what took place back inside, and that was exactly the way she wanted it to remain.

CHAPTER 33

The rain dragged on, much like the morning that the Taylors found themselves lingering in. From one end of town to the other Stacia carried on. There was no particular direction she was headed, just aimless driving and stopping whenever a traffic light appeared in front of her.

Every so often, Stacia would glance back at the children who were either dozing off asleep or gawking out the window with lackluster eyes at the passing scenery. She didn't even once entertain the notion of sending them off to school that day; she realized that their pitiful little souls were in no condition for such a grueling task as putting up with other people that day.

Stacia herself was a picture of absolute exhaustion; the woman could hardly keep her eyes open. She must have skipped at least three or four traffic lights here and there while driving, and at that point, if the police happened to pull her over then it would have been a welcomed reprieve.

Her wretched house never once left her psyche. Stacia was aware that no matter how much she tried to forget or how long she lived, all that took place inside would stay with her for an eternity.

The hopelessness that she was trapped in made her feel as though even Mars wasn't too far away from 833. No matter where she turned, every dilapidated house that she may have passed along the way reminded her of her own home.

Stacia turned down one road after another before coming to a complete stop in front of a well-built black and white, two story house brick house that was located in a well-established community.

Stacia looked at the clock on the dashboard that read 11:21 a.m. She then turned her lazy head to her immediate left and stared forever at the house.

"Whose house is this, grandma?" Devon rubbed his sleepy eyes.

Stacia didn't reply, she just pulled the keys out of the ignition and got out. From there, she opened the backdoor and watched as the children climbed out and onto the wet pavement.

Taking them both by the hand, Stacia ventured towards the front door of the home and knocked repeatedly. After three whole minutes the knob on the other end of the door could be heard twisting and turning. From behind the door appeared an older, black lady, somewhere in her early to mid-sixties. At first glance she appeared upset, but it seemed that once she laid eyes on Stacia, her mood instantly changed from belligerent to subtle astonishment, like the woman was somewhat surprised by her visitors.

Swallowing hard, Stacia said, "Good morning, mama."

The woman stood at the doorway with a haughty glare on her face before saying, "Good morning. And what do we have here?" She pointed at the children.

Blinking rapidly, Stacia answered, "This here is Devon, and this little lady is Sidney."

"Sidney?" Stacia's mother remarked with a tone of restrained shock. "Well, at least she doesn't have one of those God-awful ghetto names."

Stacia pressed her lips tightly before saying, "Mama, can we come in for a while."

Stacia's mother stood steadfast at the doorway while the saturating rain plastered Stacia and the kids. Then, without so much as a verbal response, she stepped aside and allowed the three to enter.

The very moment Stacia stepped through the threshold, her breath immediately escaped her. She shook the wetness off of her shoulders before attending to the children by taking off their jackets.

"You can leave their coats on the floor by the door." Stacia's mother said as she shut the door behind her and began for the living room.

Stacia did as told and laid the jackets down onto the floor. From there, she led the children into the spacious and modestly comfortable living room where various paintings of African art and pictures of family members hung on the walls. Stacia looked high and low, but could spot not one picture of herself hanging around.

"Take off those shoes; this isn't one of your usual flop houses." The woman scolded.

Taken aback by the cold reception, Stacia took off her shoes, as did the kids, before placing them back at the front door.

"I see the place hasn't changed all too much." Stacia commented as she strolled about the living room.

Sitting herself down onto a plush couch, Stacia's mother asked with a turned up nose, "Why on earth would anything change? Some things are best left alone."

Stacia ignored her mother's remark while continuing to take a tour of the home. All along the mantle were placed pictures of family members, both young and old, but not one of any she expected or wanted to see. It really didn't surprise her all too much, in fact, it would have blown her away if she had seen at least one tiny picture of herself anywhere in the living room; even one where she would have been buried somewhere in the back of the photo.

Sighing, Stacia's mother said, "So, this is them, I see."

Stacia turned around and stood behind Sidney and Devon. "Yep, my little ones," she proudly proclaimed.

Stacia's mother glared smugly at both children like they were mere scraps from off the street. "Good Lord, can't you clothe them better than that, child?"

"Well, we sorta had a little problem at our house, and we didn't exactly have time to get decent clothes on the way out."

"A house," Stacia's mother lifted her head. "So, we're moving up in the world, huh? No more Section Eight or shacking up with someone?"

Stacia held on to Sidney and Devon's shoulders tightly while saying, "That's right, we got us our own house."

"I see." The woman twisted her lips before taking a few moments to sit still and stare even harder at the children before her. "At least these two seem to be more well-mannered than their dad was at that age…or their grandmother for that matter. How did you get them to be so well behaved?"

Swallowing once again, Stacia replied, "It takes a lot of practice."

"I see." The woman said under her breath. "I knew about the girl, but the boy is a surprise. What, did Deontae just accidentally squirt him out under your nose?"

Inside of Stacia was a driving car, before stepping inside the house, the car was cruising down the road at a well maintained pace, but upon listening to her mother's ongoing commentary, the vehicle was ramping up its speed.

Stacia walked around and in front of the children before standing in front of her mother. "Devon is as much a blessing as his sister." Stacia boldly, yet, reverently replied to her mother.

The woman sat in her seat while handing Stacia a caustic stare. "Why did you come here, Stacia?" She asked with a grunt in her voice.

"Mama…I need to talk to you in the kitchen, please."

"I don't have any money for you." The woman defensively stated.

"I never asked for money, mama."

Stacia's mother sat and stared on a bit longer before rolling her eyes and getting up to walk straight into the kitchen.

Stacia turned to the children and knelt down before saying, "Okay, you two have a seat while I got talk to your great-grandmother for a second, okay?"

"Yes, ma'am," they said unison before planting themselves down onto a couch.

Stacia then took herself into the wide open kitchen to find her mother standing over the sink peeling onions.

"I see you're still doing that after all these years." Stacia stood next to her mother.

Without taking her eyes off her duty, Stacia's mother said, "Well, not many folks down at the church enjoy being around onions all too much, but of course, no one ever seems to mind eating them whenever revival comes around."

"They're still doing revival after all these years? I thought that—

"Why are you really here, Stacia?" The woman suddenly spun around.

Taken completely off guard by her mother's abruptness, Stacia reclaimed her breath and replied, "I…the kids need somewhere to stay for a few days."

Stacia's mother stood by the sink with her small knife in hand and a scathing glaze in her eyes that caused Stacia's heart to beat all the faster.

"A place to stay, huh," the woman cracked a smile. "What, did you lose yet another place?"

"No, mama, we just had some problems at our place, and we just need a few days away."

"Why kind of problems, Stacia?" Her mother adamantly questioned.

Stacia relented at first before eventually coming around and saying, "The house we have isn't exactly what we expected."

"Not what you expected." Stacia's mother turned away. "Well, life isn't always what we expect it to be either. Believe me, I should know."

"I should know, too. But believe me, mama, you know I wouldn't be here if I didn't have to be. What have I asked you for in the past eight years?"

Stacia's mother resumed her peeling detail, not once taking her eyes away. Stacia stood defiantly next to the woman, awaiting a response.

With a bitter quietness in her tone, Stacia said, "You know full well that I'm not the same woman I was back then. Don't treat me like I'm a piece of garbage all over again."

"Don't you dare stand there and tell me how to treat you!" The woman barked into Stacia's face. "No one on this planet knows you better than I do!"

Every fiber in Stacia's being wanted to fight back; the car that was traveling at a steady pace before was firing up for a full blown assault down the highway at that point. But no matter what, Stacia remained in neutral. It hurt her like hell, but she held on for dear life like a climber at the edge of a mountain.

"I don't know what you have going on in your life, and frankly I don't care! But I'm not going to have you bring your hell down on my head again! I went through that once before, I won't do it again!"

Stacia gripped the side of the sink with her left hand while watching the redness in her mother's face grow darker by the second.

Shaking from head to toe, Stacia said, "All I ask is for a few days, nothing more. No money, no possessions, just a few days for my babies."

Stacia's mother stood breathing in and out like she was on the verge of an asthma attack. Then, after so much standing and staring, the woman placed her knife down onto the counter before taking a towel and wiping her hands.

"Have they been fed today?"

Somewhat surprised by the question, Stacia replied, "Not really, but I can go and—

"I still have some pancake mix in the refrigerator; they can have that this morning."

Stacia watched as her mother went for the refrigerator and began rooting about inside. The gesture should have caused Stacia to break down and weep, but she was standing on pins and needles; from then on out, every move her mother would make would be suspect.

Stacia walked past her mother on her way into the living room to find Sidney and Devon still seated on the couch where she left them earlier.

Stacia sat down in between them both and pulled them close to her. "Okay, I want you both to listen and listen carefully. You're going to stay here for a while. Your great-grandmother is gonna take care of you two while I'm away."

"Where are you going?" Sidney asked with watery eyes.

Gulping, Stacia said, "I'm going to do some things, but I'll be back."

"Why can't we come with you?" Devon asked.

"Because, honey…I just need to take care of some stuff. But you two will be just fine here, I promise."

"You two come in here and get some breakfast…now!" Stacia's mother strongly commanded from the kitchen.

Wiping their wet faces, Stacia kissed Devon and Sidney on the cheek before giving them both hugs and storming out the front door.

Not once did Stacia look back at the house, she just ran out to her car and tore away like a madwoman while trying her best to keep the blinding tears she was crying away from her eyes so she wouldn't crash into something or someone.

CHAPTER 34

Much like she had been doing the night before, as well as in the morning hours, Stacia aimlessly drove from one end of Lane, Ohio to the other in a fashion that would have one believing she was either new in town or just plain bored.

Still, the rain persisted, so much so that certain areas saw rampant flooding. Stacia, in her comatose state, would drive straight through heavily flooded patches without giving much consideration to her car that could have been damaged in the high water she treaded through.

Just seeing her mother, let along having to hold a conversation with the woman, caused a sourness to stir in Stacia's belly. But having to leave her grandchildren behind only made her want to vomit all over herself. Verbally, Stacia said only a few days, but even she didn't know if she would ever return again. Return to her kids, her mother or a tormenting house that was home? All Stacia wanted was to forget, but even that task seemed at best grueling.

Soon, one p.m. turned into four p.m., and four p.m. into eight p.m. As soon as Stacia realized that darkness was drowning the wet city, she found it in herself to pull down a street and park right in front of a house where a flickering street lamp shined down upon her.

From out of her pocket she pulled her cellphone. She had countless messages from friends at work, Dee, Ashley and Tammy, and even her mother. Not one of them seemed important enough to Stacia. Without much thought, she simply dropped the phone onto the seat next to her before getting out of the car and walking in the rain down the sidewalk.

She plodded past one shabby house after another before turning left and walking onto the brown, half lawn that connected to a small, white house that looked like it hadn't been lived in in years.

Wiping the rain away from her eyes, Stacia knocked on the door and waited. She could hear the loud music on the other end of the door thump and rattle. She didn't even want to turn around to see if anyone was walking about the neighborhood, Stacia just kept on knocking until the door finally opened, behind the door was none other than Dixon.

Stacia lifted her shameful head to see the man who himself was wearing a disgraceful grimace on his face. Without saying a word, the man stepped aside. Stacia stepped into the house that reeked of skunk weed from top to bottom; all a person had to do was stay inside for two minutes and they were instantly lifted.

Stacia took off her jacket and handed it to Dixon. Within the dining room at the table were seated all three of Dixon's nephews who were rolling up weed and counting money. They all looked at Stacia and their uncle like the world they were living in had suddenly collapsed before them.

Dixon simply took his left hand and patted it in the air, as to say that everything was ok, before taking Stacia by the hand and leading her down a hallway.

***

It was late, that much was for sure. The music at that juncture was louder than it was before earlier in the evening, but inside Stacia's blazed head, *Drake's, 'Worst Behavior,'* both sounded and felt as soothing as warm bath water oozing all over her completely naked body as she laid in bed, wallowing back and forth against Dixon's equally nude frame.

Every so often, she would reach over and kiss the man on the lips while stroking his dick in her hand. Sprawled out on the floor were Dixon's nephews, who were clothed only in tank top shirts and no pants. They, much like Stacia and Dixon, were as high as clouds and not caring one ounce about the world.

Out of Stacia's mouth came fruitless, non-coherent babblings, the kind that even her companions didn't seem to give much attention to.

Her entire body felt as loose as a strand of spaghetti. Stacia couldn't even maintain a proper balance as she all of the sudden stood to her feet on the wobbly bed above Dixon.

Taking a mammoth slug from her joint, Stacia stood and slurred, "Do ya'll remember that one show…that one show where it had that ugly ass *Roger*, and that fat ass *Rerun*? And they would always be in that bar or whatever, talkin' and shit?"

Every male inside the compact room laid back and watched as Stacia swayed about before she eventually lost what little balance she had and crashed right back down onto the bed face first. The woman just laughed it off before dropping herself down onto the floor and crawling towards one of the young men like a lioness on the hunt.

With a devious smile on her face, she grabbed a hold of the man's dick and began sucking. One of the other young men put his dick next to Stacia's face in the hopes that she would pleasure him equally. Stacia gladly complied by taking the man's member and sucking on him.

Before long, Dixon came up behind Stacia and easily inserted his penis into her vagina. Stacia moaned in ecstasy as the man went in and out of her while smacking her rear end like a disobedient child. The pain that she would usually feel whenever Dixon would slap her backside was nowhere to be found, she was too ripped in the head to even notice that she was in agony.

Soon, Stacia could feel her own asshole being widened. When she could no longer see the third nephew, she knew right away what was taking place. But rather than become alarmed, she allowed herself to become immersed in the event, back and forth sucking on two dicks while having two other men behind her.

"Ride that ass, nigga!" Stacia heard one man say out loud.

"We some motherfuckin' ridas up in here," she heard Dixon holler out in glee. "Motherfuckin' Fort Greene up in this piece!"

Drake rapped on and on, seemingly repeatedly as the orgy raged on like a war that never wanted to end.

CHAPTER 35

I'm awake; I know that much for sure. I can see this cute little black girl across the street selling those big daisies so she can buy some new shoes for herself.

It's so bright outside, so bright that I can't see anything but the car that I'm sitting in. I know it's my car, I can smell the cigarette smoke. But there's something different here, oh yeah, Deontae is right beside me.

I can see my baby, not wearing a shirt, as usual. He always hated it whenever I got on him about not wearing his shirt.

For some reason or another, he's not saying anything to me. He's probably mad at me for something, again. But no matter, I still love seeing his sweet face. Sometimes I can't believe how much he's grown. It just seems like yesterday he was running around in diapers. Now, he's a teenager.

I want to reach out and touch him so bad, but I can't move my arms or hands, it's like something has them strapped down, as well as the rest of my body.

Why can't I touch my baby?

"Because, it's not for you to touch me, mother."

What the hell? Was that my son speaking that way? Mother? No, this can't be my son.

"It's me, mother. I tried to tell you."

Tell me what?"

"About that man."

What man?

But he won't turn his head. I know what man he's talking about. Maybe I just don't want to admit it to myself.

"Get away from him; get away from them both."

Both? Wait a minute, who's the other man?

But no matter what, Deontae won't turn his head. He just opens the door, gets out and walks away into the stinging brightness.

I want to reach out and scream for him to come back, but I can't. No matter how hard I try, I just can't seem to bring myself to open my mouth or lift a single finger.

Perhaps that's the whole point…maybe I'm supposed to reach out for something else.

Day 20

Stacia awoke inside her car, fully clothed. It was morning, and the rain had at last ceased pouring. Like a paranoid lunatic she gawked all around the car before she finally came to the realization that she was the only person inside, much to her chagrin.

She then wiped the foggy windows and looked at the neighborhood that she was surrounded by. Just a few houses down sat Dixon's home. Why and how she managed to be inside her car rather than beside Dixon was beyond her. At that point in the morning Stacia felt like a 138 pound sponge.

Her aching head caused her to drop back in her seat and close her eyes. The moment she opened them again, she noticed her burned out reflection in the rearview mirror. Her eyes were completely bloodshot, and there were scant traces of a dried up, white substance around her mouth and chin.

Right then and there Stacia's body began to shake. All she could think of at that instant was Sidney and Devon, and how she wanted ever so much to hold them in her arms again.

Without giving much concern to her personal appearance Stacia started the car and pulled away, not even giving a glance at Dixon's house that she sped by.

***

It didn't take too long for Stacia to reach her mother's house, in fact, on any other occasion, the travel would have been a half an hour at best, but on that morning, it took no longer than ten to fifteen minutes, a new record.

Feeling soaking wet, Stacia got out of the car with a hell-bent determination and rampaged towards her mother's house. Like a furious warlord she banged on the door as hard as she could and waited for someone to answer.

"Well, look at this." Stacia's mother stood back with her sanctimonious hands on her hips.

Stacia ignored the woman and blasted her way inside. From one room to the next she ventured until she found both children at the kitchen table eating breakfast.

"C'mon, you two, we're leaving."

"I see," the woman conceitedly stated as she stepped up behind Stacia. "You had some things to take care of, huh?"

"Get your coats on and let's go." Stacia said to the children as she shuffled them into action.

"I remember that smell all too well." Stacia's mother ranted as she followed the three into the living room. "You're sorry ass is back at it again. It just goes to show, you can't turn a hoe into a housewife!"

Stacia continued to ignore her mother while helping both kids into their jackets. As far as Stacia was concerned, her mother was dead.

"Is that where you went yesterday, to be a hoe all over again? You can't change, Stacia, you're too set in your ways. Hell, even your own daddy gave up on your ass. You can't take care of yourself, you can't take care of your kids! That's exactly why Deontae's ass was gunned down in the street!"

It was like someone had fired off a gun right in Stacia's face. With the children huddled behind her, Stacia stood before her mother. There were so many words that she wanted to use to describe the kind of woman that her mother was. There was so much hatred that wanted to spill out.

Stacia looked at her mother who for the first time since knowing the woman had the most startled frown on her face. Her mother was scared, and that alone was all Stacia required.

Stacia, with her grandchildren, went right back out to the still running car and flew away down the road.

"Grandma, are we gonna go to Dixon's house now?" Devon desperately asked.

Stacia didn't respond, she just kept on driving along as though her next destination was that of life and death.

"I didn't like her, grandma," Sidney whined, "she made us read books and told us to always sit down and be quiet."

Still, Stacia had absolutely nothing to say. She was ignoring the children for a reason, she had a purpose, and it didn't involve answering frivolous questions.

Upon noticing that their grandmother wasn't replying to their inquiries, Sidney and Devon sat back and held on.

***

From her mother's house all the way back to 833 took a mere eleven minutes. As though she was learning to drive for the very first time, Stacia careened the car up onto the curb before taking out her keys, getting out of the car and opening the door for the children.

"But, grandma, I don't wanna go back in there no more!" Sidney wailed for mercy.

But Stacia would not relent, she dragged both children kicking and screaming into the house and up the stairs.

As soon as they reached the second floor, Stacia, with the kids locked to her, went straight for her bedroom and locked the door behind her.

"Grandma, can't we go back to the hotel, please?" Devon cried like a baby.

All three individuals climbed onto the bed and held each other for ceaseless minutes before footsteps came blasting up the stairs and towards the bedroom.

"The ghost is coming for us!" Sidney screamed out in terror.

Stacia covered both her and Devon's mouths before she looked at the door and yelled, "This is our fucking house! Leave us alone!"

The loud, animal-like sounds that everyone heard nights earlier in the basement bellowed beyond the bedroom door. Stacia could tell that it was mad, possibly angrier than it had been before, but she would not back down, no matter how much her children cried and fought, Stacia fought all the harder.

Soon, the screaming from outside turned into pounding against the door, pounding that nearly knocked the door down.

Devon kicked like a stubborn mule, trying his best to holler out loud, but his grandmother managed to hold him down with all her might.

"Leave us alone! This is our house now! We live here! Go away!" Stacia shouted at the top of her lungs until she could no longer do so.

But the beating at the door persisted. It sounded like the entity on the other end was not only knocking but kicking as well. Stacia sweated like a farm animal as she wrestled about in the bed with her frightened grandchildren that only wanted to jump out the nearest window and away from the house.

"We're not leaving! Get away from us! We've never done anything to you!"

Five more beatings at the door, and just like that, the assault ceased. Stacia could hear the being on the other end breathe like a fuming horse before it eventually walked back down the steps and out of earshot.

Stacia held the children down for a few minutes more before relinquishing her grip on them and sitting up on the bed. She listened hard at the stillness of the house before wiping the sweat away from her brow.

"Is the ghost gone, grandma?" Devon shivered underneath the covers.

Stacia placed her hand on the boy's head before taking Sidney by the hand. She then looked down at the children whose faces were drenched in tears.

Stacia wasn't sure what she had accomplished, or even if she accomplished anything all, but they were home, and away from the world.

CHAPTER 36

Day 21
1:22 a.m.

Something within 833 stirred, like a stiff, cold breeze on a sweltering, hot day. It began clear down in the basement. From the basement it ventured into the kitchen where the cabinet doors swung open, which in turn allowed dishes to fly out and onto the floor.

From the kitchen, the force went next to the dining room, and eventually into the living room where the television came on. The TV was showing *The Walking Dead*. The volume was raised to its highest point before the force carried on upstairs.

Sidney's bedroom was visited first. The girl's comb, as well as the vanity mirror was knocked onto the floor before her poster of *Kanye West* was ripped right down from off the wall.

The entity then went for Devon's room where his collection of wrestling figures were all scattered about like they were useless rubbish.

The bathroom took on its own life as the shower came on and the toilet flushed repeatedly. That left only one more room. The entity unlocked Stacia's bedroom door and allowed itself inside. Lying in the bed were all three Taylors fast asleep.

At first, they all slumbered peacefully away before Sidney began to talk in her sleep, which in turn caused her brother to do the same.

Stacia wallowed about in the bed, nearly knocking Sidney out and onto the floor. The woman's body seemed uncontrollably restless. She grabbed a hold of the covers and gripped them tightly while reaching out with her other hand at the air that she was breathing.

"You fucking black bitch!" She yelled in her sleep.

Sidney sat up in the bed with her eyes shut while Devon responded in kind. Both children sat perfectly still before the bed began levitating no more than six inches off the floor. It remained in mid-air for at least ten whole minutes before coming back down gently.

Stacia rested her arm back down onto the bed before tossing and turning once more. There were faint whispers that came hurtling out of her opened mouth.

The bed then scooted all by itself closer to the window ahead. All three Taylors slept in their various positions as the uncanny disturbance lingered on in the early morning hour.

CHAPTER 37

8:37 a.m.

Stacia's eyelids slowly creaked open that morning. The second they were wide, the first thing she saw was the long dresser that sat to the right side of the bed.

The sound of old raindrops plopping down from off the gutters outside could be heard from within the bedroom, as well as the birds chirping about.

Stacia's entire body felt like a dried up rag that had been laid out in the sun for days. Just stretching one limb seemed like breaking an arm rather than an everyday, ordinary movement.

She raised her body up to see Devon seated on the edge of the bed with his head pointed down to the floor. Behind Stacia was Sidney, who as well was sitting on the other end of the bed, but instead of her little head down, it was facing the wall in front of her.

Neither child was saying a word; Stacia could hardly even hear them breathe. But for the oddest, more unreal reason, the woman couldn't find it within herself to even care as to why they both were sitting on the sides of the bed the way they were.

Stacia sat all the way up and allowed her ears to take in even more sounds that were becoming clearer by the moment. In the distance she could hear running water, while downstairs, the sound of women screaming made it seem like they were inside the house along with her and the grandchildren.

Stacia's head was like a fishbowl, even her eyesight was watery. All she could see was a dull mist. Her eyesight was there, but it wasn't her own.

Then, without uttering a single word, both Sidney and Devon got up from off the bed and simply dragged their individual carcasses out of the bedroom.

Stacia didn't seem to have a care in her as to where they would have gone to. She sat on the edge of the bed for at least ten minutes more before eventually standing up and methodically carrying herself out of the room and into the hallway.

The sound of the running water was coming from the bathroom. Appearing as though it were the most unimpressive matter in the world, Stacia stepped down and into the bathroom to twist the shower water off. The entire bathroom was a foggy cauldron of heat; if the room wasn't so small Stacia would have become lost within.

From the bathroom Stacia meandered back down the hallway and downstairs to find the children seated on the couch watching the loud television. The second her feet hit the living room floor, Stacia saw that they were watching *The Walking Dead,* a show that she forbid them both from ever viewing.

She stood by and watched as they both sat and stared endlessly at the TV. People shooting, stabbing and blowing up zombies left and right didn't seem to neither amuse nor disgust the kids, they both appeared amazingly hushed and oblivious to all the carnage.

With dull eyes, Stacia stood by a bit more before taking herself into the kitchen to find the floor littered with broken dishes and cutlery. With only her socks covering her feet she stepped over the shards of silverware before coming to a stop at the sink.

She peered out the window for a second or two before grabbing her head in pain and squeezing as tight as she could. It was a headache, as sharp as one Stacia could ever recall. Never before had any of her headaches been so nauseating to where she wanted to vomit. But sure enough, standing over the sink, she just happened to be in the right place at the right time.

Suddenly, someone knocked at the front door. Stacia immediately pulled away from the sink and charged back into the living room. As soon as she opened the door, standing before her was Ashley and Tammy with troubled looks on their separate faces.

"Good morning." Tammy's eyes lit up. "How is everything?"

Stacia heard the woman just fine, but opening her mouth to respond right away didn't seem to register in her head.

Allowing themselves inside, Tammy and Ashley stepped into the living room and quickly noticed what the children were watching on the television.

"Wow," Ashley smirked, "I forgot *AMC* had that marathon on today. Oh well, we got all the seasons on DVD anyways."

Stacia only stood by the couch where the kids were seated and examined both women like she were trying to figure out just who they were.

"When we saw you guys running away the other day we didn't know what to think." Tammy said. "We thought there was something or someone in here with you."

"Yeah, all we heard was poor Sidney screaming, and then your car screeching away. Is everything alright?"

"Yeah," Stacia droned on as if speaking hurt her vocal cords. "Everything is just fine now."

"Good, you guys have been through enough as it is; the last thing you need is yet another calamity on your hands." Ashley exhaled.

"Yes…another calamity." Stacia sneered at both women. "Tell me something, when was the last time you two ate out?"

"It's funny you should ask that, because we just had Chinese from the deli down on Seventh Street last night. They've got some really great dumplings, too." Tammy answered.

"No, I don't mean that, I mean, when did you two eat out?"

Ashley and Tammy glanced strangely at one another before turning back to Stacia. "Uh…Tammy just told you." Ashley looked around sort of confused.

"Did it taste good?"

"Uh, yeah, you should try it out sometime." Ashley strangely squared her eyes.

Smiling from ear to ear, Stacia stepped forward, just enough to smell both women's breaths. "Does it taste good every time you vaginatarians go at it?"

"Vaginatarians," Tammy blurted out in laughter. "That's a new one I haven't even heard yet. Where did you hear it from?"

Stacia only stood back and leaned against the arm of the couch. She then folded her arms and pointed her drowsy eyes at the ladies like she was sizing them up for a meal of sorts.

"Are you okay, Stacia?" Ashley asked in a tense manner.

Stacia stood at a hush for a second before saying, "Why don't you two get out of here before something happens."

As if someone had devastated their entire world, both Ashley and Tammy stood back stunned at what was spoken.

"Get out of here?" Tammy said in shock. "Wait a minute, we just stopped by to see how you guys were doing. Did we do or say something that—

"Just leave." Stacia cut in.

Ashley and Tammy looked at each other before turning and heading back for the door. "We'll check in on you guys another time. It looks like you three have been through a lot." Tammy said.

"Do us a favor, just leave."

At that, Stacia slammed the door right in their faces before turning around and saying to the children, "Do you two see that? Those faggots traipsing around infecting the world with their evil cunts?"

Sidney and Devon never once allowed their faces to turn away from the TV; it was as if they were totally mesmerized with the visuals they were taking in.

"Go and get ready for school…now."

It took a moment, but eventually the kids slowly turned their heads to their grandmother before getting up from off the couch and carting themselves up the stairs.

Stacia stood there in front of the television as zombies ate away at human flesh in reckless abandon. Blood and guts went flying to and fro. Men, women and children either fled for their lives or used whatever weapons they had in their arsenal to dispatch all sorts of violence and mayhem upon the torment their world was imprisoned in.

Stacia just couldn't seem to budge an inch as she took in all of the butchery at once. At that instant, she wasn't concerned on how the TV show may have affected the children, all Stacia could seem to focus on was the bullets that ripped through heads, and the truck that ran over dozens of zombies like bowling pins.

It all soaked inside of her to where in only a span of ten minutes Stacia became oblivious and numb.

CHAPTER 38

11:43 a.m.

Inside the school library was a menagerie of children of varying races, all ranging between the ages of six and eleven.

From one end of the spacious room to the other young ones went about their regular routines of reading, being read to, carrying books from one shelf to the other or sitting at the numerous computers and playing games or working.

Teachers and the three librarians all did their best tending to their students or helping kids check out books. It was a busy hustle that carried on all day from Monday thru Friday.

However, in a secluded corner of the library, seated by each other, was Sidney and Devon. Much like they were back at home, they sat dead silent, but in front of a computer screen.

Devon had his little hand on the mouse. Without the slightest movement in his eyes, the boy scrolled through numerous webpages, links and photos of disturbing images, the kind that were to be banned from the sight of anyone under the age of fifteen.

The images were those of murders; the hangings in Shubuta, Mississippi, Ku Klux Klan rallies, policemen and their dogs mauling blacks in the middle of the street, African slaves being whipped or beheaded by their white masters for escaping their plantations.

When they came upon pictures of Emmett Till, they stopped. Devon's hand ever so gradually scrolled downwards until photos of the late boy's gruesome mutilation came into view.

One by one, pictures of Till's beaten and broken face came upon the screen, as well as the white men that were acquitted for his murder. But the very moment images of Emmett's body lying in his casket came up, on the faces of Devon and Sidney appeared subtle grins that were soon followed by tingles in their stomachs.

"Eww, what is that?" A little Hispanic boy gasped behind the two Taylors.

Unfazed by the boy's disgust, Devon closed the webpage before taking his sister by the hand and getting up from out of their seats.

"Hey, Devon, are you gonna still trade me your Undertaker toy?" The boy eagerly asked as he walked in behind the siblings.

Both Sidney and Devon carried on as though the child behind them didn't even exist. But the boy persisted in his fervor.

"C'mon, Devon, my brother said that he could ask my mom for another Dolph Ziggler if you would let me have your Undertaker action man."

Sidney then stopped before spinning around and facing the boy, boldly saying, "We don't have anything to do with fence jumpers."

The little boy stared awkwardly at both Taylors before directing his attention back on Devon. "How did you know me and Miguel jumped Mr. Henderson's fence yesterday? We only went to get our ball."

"Go mow a lawn, spic." Devon said right into the child's face before pushing him to the floor and going down to beat the boy in the face with his fists over and over again.

It was as if an alarm had gone off, because at that moment, every child in the library all descended at once to see Devon Taylor beat the little boy within an inch of his life. Soon, blood began to splatter all over the carpet and onto some of the student's shoes.

"Get up and stop!" A white female teacher screamed as she struggled to pull Devon off of the child he was laying waste to.

"You fuckin' spic fucker!" Devon spat and cursed like a mad dog, kicking along the way out of the library and down the hallway.

"Get off my brother, you goombah!" Sidney yelled as she tried to yank her brother away from the already overwhelmed teacher.

It took a large black man to come up behind the girl and restrain her as he followed the teacher and a still raging Devon down the hallway and out of sight.

CHAPTER 39

12:58 p.m.

Stacia sat in the frigid principal's office shaking her right leg that was overlapped onto the other. There was a lackadaisical presence written all over her face that would have suggested that her so called valuable time was being wasted.

The woman wanted to be anywhere but at the school. She had a vicious hungering inside of her to masturbate, more so then than she could ever remember. The urging gnawed away at her so much that keeping her legs locked as tight as they were wasn't helping as much as she desired.

Stacia wasn't quite sure why she was summoned to the school so abruptly, but rather than have the worry that would be attached to being called to her grandchildren's school, she instead chose to ponder on having her dildo inserted in between her legs for the rest of the day.

"We're sorry for keeping you so long, Ms. Taylor." Mr. Ayers, the black principal said as both he and a dark haired white lady rushed into the office. "We were having some trouble with Sidney just a moment ago."

Stacia sat and watched as Ayers planted himself behind his desk, while the white lady sat herself in a chair next to where Stacia was already seated.

Sitting up in her seat, Stacia asked, "So, what is this all about?"

Exhaling, Ayers explained, "Well, to put it simply, Devon got into a fight today. And Sidney attacked Mrs. Belini here."

Stacia glanced over at Mrs. Belini for a second before redirecting her fading attention back to Ayers and sighing, "Okay, just go ahead and suspend them, and I'll take care of them when we get home."

Both Ayers and Belini gave one another the most confounded grimaces before Ayers turned back to Stacia and said, "Ms. Taylor, did you hear what I just said?"

"Yeah, I heard you, and like I said, just suspend them and we'll be on our way."

"Ms. Taylor, you don't understand," Mrs. Belini cut in, "Devon got into a fight with Rodrigo Torres today."

Stacia stared at Mrs. Belini for a moment before sitting back in her seat. "You mean the little Mexican boy?"

Cocking her head and batting her eyelashes, Belini replied, "Yes, Ms. Taylor…Rodrigo."

Nonchalantly waving her hand in the air, Stacia said, "Oh, that's it? Boys will be boys."

"Ms. Taylor, Devon said some things today that causes us to wonder if there was something wrong between the two boys. Devon made a racist remark at Rodrigo."

"What kind of remark?"

Mrs. Belini hesitantly glanced at Ayers before turning to Stacia and responding, "He called Rodrigo a spic."

Stacia's eyes at that instant brightened. It was like a light bulb had suddenly been turned on inside of her head.

"Oh really," Stacia asked in passive awe.

"I'm afraid so, Ms. Taylor."

"Well, I'm sure Rodrigo said something to Devon that caused my child to break off on him."

"That's what we're trying to figure out. I mean, Devon and Rodrigo are like twin brothers. With all due respect,

Ms. Taylor, those two go to the bathroom together. They're practically inseparable, "Mrs. Belini ardently clarified.

"Once again, I'm sure the other boy did or said something that set Devon off. Hell, how do you know that Rodrigo didn't call Devon a nigger?"

"We don't know that, Ms. Taylor."

"Then there is the issue of Sidney." Mr. Ayers jumped in.

Turning to the man, Stacia exhaled, "What did she do now?"

"She not only stood back and watched her brother beat Rodrigo, but she also made a racist comment towards Mrs. Belini."

"What did she call her?"

"She called me a goombah."

Stacia sniggered at first before asking, "I'm sorry...a what?"

"It's a racist slur used towards my people. Believe me, Ms. Taylor, I've heard it before."

Like a teenager, Stacia slumped down in her chair and covered her face with her hand as though she were weary on the whole situation.

"Ms. Taylor, do you somehow find this to be amusing?" Ayers questioned.

"I never said it was funny, but...their kids for God's sake. Kids do and say stupid things."

"But kids don't always use racist slurs, Ms. Taylor. To be honest, I haven't heard the word goombah since I was a little girl way back in the seventies. Sidney must have heard that from somewhere."

"So are you blaming me?" Stacia arrogantly pointed at herself.

"No one is blaming anyone, Ms. Taylor; we just want to get to the bottom of this."

"Mrs. Belini, can I have a moment with Ms. Taylor, please?" Ayers requested.

"Gladly," Mrs. Belini spitefully said under her breath before getting up out of her seat and walking out the door.

Stacia only rolled her blurry eyes at the woman and twisted her lips before turning to Ayers and watching a troubled pout cross his face.

"Ms. Taylor, is there something going on at home we need to know about?"

Stacia rolled her eyes again before saying, "Look, I didn't come here to be analyzed over a stupid fight."

"Ms. Taylor, this wasn't just a fight; Devon not only knocked out two of Rodrigo's teeth, he also broke the boy's jaw. That wasn't a fight, that was a mauling." Ayers strongly clarified. "What took place today wasn't normal, this was—

"Don't sit there and talk to me about normal!" Stacia sat up in her chair. "Ain't nothing normal happened to us in years!"

"Ms. Taylor, why are you getting so defensive," Ayers sat back.

"Because I can see just where this whole conversation is going," Stacia retaliated. "I went through it as a child; I had to go through with it with my own son, and now my grandchildren!"

"Ms. Taylor, I have to believe that there is something taking place within the home that is causing Devon and Sidney's erratic behavior. For the past few weeks they both have been going on about a supposed haunted house. For one child to bring up such a story is one thing, but two children is cause for concern."

"I told them both not to bring that shit up." Stacia bit down on her bottom lip.

"Ms. Taylor, I remember the mountain you had to climb just to get your grandchildren into this school. And ever since Devon and Sidney have been here, they both have been an absolute delight. But something very bizarre took place here today. Mrs. Belini took a look at some of the websites that they were viewing right before the incident occurred, and to be honest, they were quite disturbing."

"Were they porn sites?"

"Well…no. But—

"Then what do you want me to do? Tell them not to go on the internet anymore?" Stacia shrugged. "You sit there and say that they've been such a delight to have here, well then, go ahead and reprimand them, and we can forget this entire thing took place."

Mr. Ayers sat back in his chair and folded his hands. "Ms. Taylor, I have no other alternative but to expel both Sidney and Devon from this school."

Stacia batted her eyelashes at the man and looked at him like he had just lost his mind. "Wait a second, you drag me all the way down here to this place? Have me sit in this freezing cold office for nearly twenty minutes, just to tell me that you're kicking my kids out of this school? Hell, if that's the case, you should've just left their asses outside on the front steps and I would've just scooped them up right there!"

"Ms. Taylor, you know of our zero tolerance policy here. Violent aggression of any kind will not be accepted."

Stacia nearly fell over onto the floor just trying to get up out of her seat. She then wrapped her purse around her right shoulder and said to Ayers, "Yeah, I know of your little zero tolerance policy. Tell me something, how long do you think this little government run school will put up with you, sunshine?"

"I beg your pardon?" Ayers squinted.

"You know exactly what I mean. Watch your back, when they don't need an Uncle Remus anymore, I'll be sure to put in a good word for you down at the warehouse…brother."

Stacia turned and stormed out of the office. Seated out in the waiting area was both Sidney and Devon. Without saying a word, she pointed to the children, and like obedient dogs they followed their grandmother out of the building and out to the car in the parking lot.

"This place can kiss my fuckin' black ass!" Stacia sternly growled before turning on the car and bolting away, leaving only a cloud of dust in her enraged wake.

CHAPTER 40

Day 22
4:22 p.m.

"I keep on telling you guys, the hauntings have ended. There's nothing going on here anymore." Stacia said in a blasé tone while sitting at the kitchen table alongside Sidney and Devon who were eating away at separate bowls of cereal.

"I don't know, I'm getting readings that are far more critical than before." Scott mentioned while keeping his erratic EVP meter against the kitchen's walls.

"If Scott is getting stronger readings, then that possibly means you guys are in the calm of the storm." Patrick said while punching away at his laptop on the counter.

"The calm of the storm," Stacia questioned.

"Usually in hauntings, they start out slow and subtle, then they ramp up. After considerable damage has been caused, the disturbances subside for a spell before starting back up all over again. That's not the case in every haunting, but Scott's readings, along with the static I'm getting on my computer would suggest that you three are in the middle of something bigger."

Stacia happened to look over at Dee who had the most distressed sulk on her face, as though she herself were facing the torment along with the Taylors.

"What's the matter, little girl?" Stacia grinned at Dee.

"I, uh…I just can't believe you guys haven't left this house yet. I mean, we don't want to scare you, but Pat may be right about all of this."

Sighing, Stacia leaned back in her chair and said, "Look, if something terrible were still happening here, believe me we would have left a long time ago. All that haunting stuff, it's just fairy tale."

"How can you say that, Stacia? Especially after all that you three have been through since being here?" Dee gasped.

"Because she can; she's not crazy." Sidney out of nowhere stepped in between spoonful's of cereal.

Dee sat back for a second, seemingly bowled over at the nonchalant approach in which the Taylors were taking the situation.

"Hold on, everyone." Scott announced while standing next to the backdoor. "I'm getting something very weird here."

Both Patrick and Dee stood behind Scott and studied the readings that were on the EVP, while Stacia and the children all sat still at the table and casually observed their curious visitors.

"I've never seen anything like that before." Patrick gulped before turning around and staring hard at the Taylors. "Stacia, are you for sure that nothing else has taken place here lately? Because according to these findings, we're reading that something pretty dramatic took place inside this house just recently."

"You don't say, sunshine." Devon uttered in a totally unfamiliar male voice all of the sudden.

Standing up from the table, Stacia said, "Look, if we're okay, then everything here is okay. You don't see the three of us running for our lives do you?"

"Well, no, but that doesn't mean that the hauntings have ended." Dee said.

"My goodness, Scott, how can you stand to work with these two?" Stacia sighed.

Without taking his eyes off of his EVP meter, Scott replied, "It's nothing; they keep me on my toes."

"I don't mean that, I mean, how can you stand to be around two totally different people?"

Scott suddenly took his attention off of his meter to turn and face Stacia. "How…how do you mean?"

"She means, how can someone as pure as yourself, be cooped up with such a mitch-matched couple of people?" Sidney spoke up.

At that moment, the kitchen came to a complete hush. Only the dripping sink and the clicks on Scott's EVP meter were the only things audible.

"Cat got your tongue?" Stacia grinned at Scott. "Wise up, son, if these two are sick enough to get married, just think what kind of poison they'll inject in you."

"Whoa, whoa, whoa," Patrick held up his hands. "What's going on here?"

With her hands out to Scott, Stacia continued, "Scott, can you imagine what their children will look like? Half darkie, half with their eyes slanted?"

"Stacia, what are you saying?" Dee stood back flabbergasted.

"I'm saying get the fuck out of our house before I finish the job the bomb should have!"

"Hold on, dammit." Patrick stepped in front of Stacia. "You called us! We're only trying to help you guys!"

"I never called you all, Max did!"

"It doesn't matter! You don't talk that way to my fiancée!"

"Your fiancée," Devon chimed in. "What, didn't your parents ever teach you to stay with your own kind, boy?"

"Okay, okay, just hold on, everyone." Dee forced her way in between Stacia and Patrick. "I think we all just need to cool down and—

"Fuck cooling down," Stacia fired back. "I want this little rainbow coalition out of my damn house, and now! All three of you need to go and get real jobs and stop all this ghost bullshit!"

"That's it, we're leaving!" Patrick yelled before gathering his laptop and other belongings, including Dee, and heading for the front door.

Both Sidney and Devon gave simultaneous, devilish smiles as their unwanted guests stormed away.

"And don't expect me to pay you, because it aint gonna happen!" Stacia hollered behind the three.

"We never once asked you for a single penny!" Patrick screamed back.

With tears in her eyes, Dee stopped and turned around to face Stacia. "What did we do?"

With a straight face, Stacia stared cold at Dee before turning to Scott and saying, "Do the right thing, get away from these two and quick. They're a bad influence. Next thing you know, you'll be bumping uglies with an Arab of all things."

"C'mon, man, let's go!" Patrick roared as he dragged Dee out of the house, with Scott right in behind them both.

Stacia slammed the door as hard as she could before dropping herself down onto the couch and turning on the television set to see none other than *Sylvester Stallone* shoot arrows through a man's chest before using a grenade to blow up a hut full of "bad guys."

Sidney and Devon came into the living room and sat themselves down on the floor in front of the couch. They, much like their grandmother, remained glued to TV, seemingly enthralled with all the bloodshed that Hollywood could dish out in less than ninety minutes.

Stacia's sullen eyes never left the television. She wasn't even concerned that the children seemed to be enjoying what she herself considered nonsense. All that mattered to her was the killings. The more people that died, the lazier she became.

CHAPTER 41

Day 24
8:41 a.m.

Like a shameless fool, Stacia strolled into the warehouse that morning like she hadn't a care in the world.

The security guards, two of the three that were white, she simply nodded at, while the other she ignored. The same treatment was handed to other employees that she passed on her way back to her section of the warehouse.

As arrogant as her stride was, it was just as determined. Stacia seemed to have a purpose that morning, and it didn't have anything to do with work. In fact, lifting and sorting boxes that morning was the furthest thing from her mind, the entire concept only sickened her.

The very instant she reached her section, every worker was already busy at their individual duties. Some of the employees gave Stacia their usual morning greetings, Stacia, however remained aloof, not even wanting to make eye contact with anyone.

Before she could even settle herself in her station, right beside her was Lucinda who came up and asked, "Hey, how have you been lately? Kohler has been raising holy hell wondering where you were."

Without even looking in the woman's direction, Stacia asked, "Tell me something, what do you call a black woman who gets an abortion?"

Lucinda scrounged up her face before saying, "I…I don't have a clue."

"A member of Crime stoppers of America." Stacia replied while looking down at her duty roster.

"Okay…where did that come from?" Lucinda sheepishly asked.

"I don't know, I just thought it would brighten your day."

"Uh, Stacia," Jeremy skittishly approached.

Still studying her roster, Stacia said, "What can I do for you, son?"

"I can't seem to find row 21B. I looked all over this section, but I think they moved it."

Groaning, Lucinda said, "Jeremy, Veena told you that all they did was remove the sticker. 21B is still—

"I got it, Lucinda." Stacia took Jeremy by the hand. "You can't trust everything people like Veena say."

Stacia lead Jeremy down a dark and lonely corridor full of boxes. As soon as the corridor dead ended, Stacia dropped down to her knees, unzipped Jeremy's sagging jeans and pulled out his dick. From there, she sucked and licked on the boy's rod.

Jeremy, apparently at a loss for words, held on for dear life against the shelves, nearly knocking over some of the boxes that were stored on top.

After nearly two whole minutes, the young, bewildered and elated man, came all over Stacia's face to where his semen even got into her hair.

"Who is that down there?" Veena called out from the other end of the corridor.

Immediately, Stacia took her own shirt to clean off her face before getting up and facing the woman that was making her way towards her and Jeremy.

"What are you two doing all the way down here?" Veena questioned.

Still trying to clean his dick off and quickly stuff it back into his pants, Jeremy stared at Stacia. Stacia, on the other hand, gave Veena a conceited frown before brushing by her on her way down the other end.

"Hey, girl, what were you two doin' down here?" Veena caught Stacia by the arm.

Stacia handed Veena the most maniacal stare before snatching her arm away and continuing on towards the work area.

"Stacia, you still have some of that shit in your hair!"

Stacia stopped and slowly turned around. It was dark in the corridor, dark enough to where only outlines of a body could be seen. Stacia stood there in the shadows and said, "Gal, do I look like I care?"

From there, Stacia continued on until she came out into the light of the work area. As she swaggered through the throngs of workers, even she couldn't help but to take notice of those who stopped and stared at her as if she were growing a tail. It seemed that the entire assembly came to a screeching halt all of the sudden.

Stacia stopped just short of her work station and yelled out, "Is there a fucking problem here?"

Everyone gathered either glanced at her or each other before going back to their various duties. But before Stacia could even resume her own detail, Veena came rushing up beside her.

"Do you know what you have on your face, girl?"

Stacia stopped what she was doing and began to wipe her face with her hand. When she looked down at her right hand she noticed a glob of semen that she had missed earlier. The woman simply wiped the mess on her jeans and went about her work.

Grabbing Stacia by the arm, Veena stared into her eyes and forcefully said, "Girl, you need to excuse yourself before—

"You need to get your black ass off of me before I knock the shit out of you!"

"What the fuck is your problem?" Veena screamed.

"You're my fucking problem!" Stacia angrily hollered before tearing her arm away from Veena and walking away.

"Don't you walk away from me, bitch! Not after all I've done for you!" Veena snapped as she attempted to grab Stacia by the arm once more.

The attempt, however, was all Stacia could stand before she spun around and slapped Veena across her chubby face. Once again, every worker halted what they were doing to see the spectacle unfold before them.

"Bitch done gone and hit me!" Veena squealed before rushing Stacia into one of the conveyor belts.

Stacia fought back against the hefty woman, pounding on her back while cursing a vile streak of racial obscenities at her.

"Stop this shit right now!" Max yelled as he fought to break Veena away from Stacia.

"Get that fuckin' coon off of me!" Stacia spat.

"Bitch, you're just as much of a coon as me!"

"Fuck you, you fuckin' nigger! Fuck you!"

"Stacia, stoppit," Max roared as he struggled to restrain the wild woman.

"Let go of me!" Stacia screamed while trying to free herself.

"Peter wants to talk to you!" Max huffed and puffed.

At that instant, Stacia's insane tirade gradually began to dissipate. Without even straitening her shirt, the woman walked herself to Peter's office, with Max right behind her.

The second she walked through the door, there stood Peter right next to his desk with an appalled look on his blushing face.

"What do you want, now?" Stacia growled at the man.

"Have a seat!" He snapped.

"I'll stand, if it's all the same to you!"

Max closed the door behind him before taking his position next to Stacia in the middle of the floor.

"Do you mind telling me what that was down there?" Peter irately asked.

Pointing to herself as though she had no idea what was going on, Stacia replied, "You mean to tell me that you didn't see Veena put her hands on me first?"

"I saw not only you slap Veena in the face, but I also saw you swagger in here nearly forty minutes late, as usual!"

"As usual," Stacia furiously questioned. "I've been working here for the past seventeen years, and in those seventeen years can you name one day I've been late?"

"I can name almost fifteen days since last month!"

Stacia's rant came to a screeching halt at that moment. Just hearing Peter tell the truth out loud seemed to inflict a heavy weight upon her breathing.

"You know all that I've been going through these past few weeks! I can't help it that—

"That's just it, Stacia, you're a nonstop wrecking ball! We've been patient with you simply because we do understand your situation! But lately you've been falling apart at the seams! And now this," Peter shouted.

"I told you what happened down there!"

"Stacia, please," Max pleaded.

Stacia then turned to Max and said, "What, you're actually gonna stand there and keep quiet? I thought we were friends! Oh, that's right, we were friends seventeen years ago when I sucked your dick behind the shelves! That was when you stuck up for me!"

"That was a long time ago!"

"Look," Peter cut in, "this can't go on anymore! I'm fed up with the excuses and the behavior! I've tried to be patient, and this is how it turns out! You even missed last week's deadline because you were absent, again!"

"So, what are you saying?"

"That's it, we can't afford you anymore. You're terminated." He plainly stated.

It was if someone had shut down the entire building and cut off the lights all at once. The office in which the three were gathered remained eerily hushed for at least seven seconds before Stacia put her hands on her hips.

"I see." She soberly uttered. "I guess that's why Hitler killed himself."

"I beg your pardon?" Peter frowned.

"The damn gas bill your tribe gave him was too high. But then again, you're here, so I guess his mission was a complete failure after all."

"Get out!" Peter barked while pointing at the door.

"Fuck you, you fucking kike motherfucker!" Stacia yelled back before storming out of the office and into the work area. "You white folks had better wake up and look around you, because you're damn country is being taken over by the Africans and Mexicans! The Jews already have you enslaved; next thing you know you'll be serving Mexicans their food in their mansions while the Africans will be holding down all the jobs!"

Stacia continued to rage on and on while two security guards relived her of her I.D. badge and eventually escorted her out of the building altogether.

"Fuck all of you!" She hollered with fury while standing in the middle of the parking lot. "I hope this fuckin' place burns to the ground!"

Two Somali women, both with decorative scarves wrapped around their heads, meekly crossed by Stacia on their way into building.

"Look at this shit," Stacia pointed at the women, "they love comin' to this fuckin' country and using up all the welfare, but their fuckin' asses can't even respect us enough to speak the language or at least wear the kind of clothes we do! Look at that shit on their heads!"

Stacia grumbled and stomped all the way to her car. Once she was inside, she grabbed her aching head and held it strong and tight in her hands. It felt like someone had taken her skull and placed it underneath the wheels of a semi-truck.

She just couldn't stop the throbbing. Knowing that she had just lost her job of seventeen years was about as distant from her thoughts as the supper she had from the night before.

CHAPTER 42

D ee sat Indian style on the hotel room bed with a heavy book in between her legs. Her study was methodical if not subtly excruciating. For hours leading up to her bedtime the young lady had read either books or countless webpages to the point where her own eyesight was growing faint.

From one paragraph to the next she scanned with scrupulous attention before flipping page after with page with lighting speed. In just ninety minutes she finished a three hundred some odd page book before picking up another that was lying next to her and laying into it with the same disciplined devotion she had given to her earlier readings.

Old and new photographs of people under spells, hypnosis or demonic possession filled both the pages and Dee's eyes. The young lady read the causes and supposed ways to eradicate such occurrences.

She couldn't get the Taylors out of her head to save her life. Every picture she viewed looked just like Stacia. Every evil stare that the individuals handed the camera that flashed the photos gave Dee the impression that the tortured people would possibly jump right out of the book and into bed alongside her. After a while, Dee shut the book she was reading and dropped her head into her hands.

Patrick came out of the adjacent bathroom clothed in only a pair of boxers, a sleeveless undershirt and a stretched out, cavalier grin that he brought with him all the way to the bed next to Dee.

For a moment or two there sat a stale silence between the two before Patrick glared strangely over at Dee and asked, "You mean to tell me that you're not gonna say anything?"

Awakening suddenly from her lonely stupor, Dee glanced over at the man and grunted, "Huh?"

Holding on to his dangerous smile, Patrick pointed to the bathroom and said, "No comment? No smart-aleck remark about the epic smell?"

Dee took a whiff and shrugged her shoulders before hopelessly shaking her head and smirking as to say she wasn't all too amused with her fiancée's antics.

"What's the matter? You've been dead all day today."

Sighing heavily, Dee opened her book once again and hummed, "I don't know, I just had a lot of stuff on my mind."

Patrick lifted the book's cover before saying, "You haven't read this book since our freshman year. What gives?"

Dee wanted to dither on her response for as long as she possibly could, or at least until Patrick gave up and blundered off to sleep.

"I know you don't wanna talk about it, but…I was worried about the Taylors."

Twisting his lips in disgust, Patrick folded his burly arms and replied, "You're right, I don't want to talk about it."

Dee looked over at the man and asked, "Aren't you in the least bit concerned why they behaved the way they did?"

"It's not rocket science, Dee; all three of them are going insane inside that house. We warned them the best we could and Stacia still would not budge. What else can anyone do," Patrick tossed up his hands.

"It just amazes me that they would act that way out of the blue. And did you hear how Devon sounded that day, too? He didn't even sound like himself."

"So, you think they're possessed?" Patrick snickered. "C'mon, Dee, that's a little far-fetched, don't you think?"

"Far-fetched," Dee's eyes popped open. "How can you be skeptical after all that we've experienced?"

Placing his hand on her knee, Patrick said, "Honey, you do this all the time, you wear your heart on your sleeve and you end up getting hurt. What's going on with those three is a common case of cabin fever. They're cracking up inside that place."

"But what about what we saw on the tape? And in the hotel room," Dee persisted.

"I'm sure it was a paranormal occurrence, but once again, there's nothing we can do about it. What, do you wanna call the cops and have them pull the Taylors out of their own house?"

Dropping her already glum face, Dee ordered, "Don't make fun of me."

"I'm not making fun of you, but when someone attacks the woman I love, I fight back!" Patrick raised his voice. "I don't care what's happening inside that madhouse, they had no right to say all those things. Stacia's just another bullheaded black woman. No wonder I don't date any of them anymore."

"But what about the kids," Dee implored.

"Fuck her kids! The sooner we get back to Columbus the better!" Patrick yelled.

Dee's face took on a more shocked appearance before she looked over at Patrick. "Fuck the kids?" Her tone plunged. "This is coming from the same man that wants kids of his own one day."

Dee shut the book and climbed both herself and it out of the bed, leaving a vindictive Patrick all to himself for the evening.

CHAPTER 43

Day 31
11:27 p.m.

Much like a lonely zombie, Stacia blundered about the pitch black upstairs hallway, poking her head in each and every bedroom before coming to a complete stop at the stairs.

Her feet wanted to step onto the first stair that they made contact with, but the rest of Stacia's body was seemingly immobile, too skittish to move any further along.

She stood there at the top of the stairs with the most blank and puzzled look on her face, like she had forgotten what planet she was on. Her head was underwater, suffocating every rational thought that she imagined she could conjure; in fact, inside her brain was nothing but cloudy chaos, Stacia was physically present, and that was all that was left.

One slothful foot went before the other, and just like that, Stacia was slowly walking down the steps. The instant she rounded the corner that led into the living room, she immediately caught sight of a blue light that settled snugly inside the darkness.

Much like it had been doing for the past few days, the television was playing loudly to a half dead Sidney and Devon. The girl was laid out on the floor with lethargic, motionless eyes watching *Apollo Creed* get the final beating of his life from the likes of *Ivan Drago,* while the boy sat on the couch steadily picking away at his left arm with a dull butter knife.

Stacia only observed them for a moment or so before dragging her comatose body into the dining room. The entire house reeked of feces and urine. Littered all over the floors were newspapers, dishes and clothing, making the home appear as though a tornado had ripped right through.

Stacia came into the kitchen to find it, as well, completely black. Wandering around as though it were the first time she had ever set foot inside the room, Stacia passed by all of the drawers before eventually coming to a complete stop at one in particular.

She pulled open the wooden shelf and took out a sharp butcher knife. Her desolate eyes stared on at the blade before her lips began moving. "I should've killed that fuckin' bitch. I should've killed that fuckin' bitch."

Stacia repeated the hateful words at least ten more times before taking the knife and angrily plunging its sharp end into the counter's frame.

"Next time…I'll kill my mama." Her tongue dragged. "I'll cut her up and throw her parts in the river."

As soon as she was done talking to herself, the basement door slowly creaked itself wide open. Like she was being pulled, Stacia plodded towards and down the basement steps.

Even before she could set foot on the floor, Stacia right away saw Judy sitting Indian style in a corner all to herself. Without giving any thought to the old woman's mysterious presence in the basement, Stacia simply carried herself towards the woman and sat down on the floor, opposite Judy, in the Indian position.

Much like in the dream Stacia had a month earlier, Judy had the same fiendish, white eyes that beamed ever so pleasantly at her.

"Why here?" Stacia muttered at Judy.

"Because, he needed someone to be with him," Judy said in a gentle tone. "But…I see now that I made a very cruel mistake. You've no business being here."

"I don't wanna be here anymore."

"He doesn't want you all here. He's gonna kill you three."

"I don't wanna be here anymore."

"I died last night, Stacia; you all will die as well.

Right behind Stacia was the sound of something scaling across the floor. The woman gradually turned around to find a frame lying beside her. Stacia picked it up and stared hard in the blackness before ultimately seeing Dixon's picture within the frame.

Stacia lifted her head only to find Judy completely gone. When she was done gawking at the naked corner in front of her, Stacia returned her attention back to Dixon's image inside the frame.

With her hands gripping the picture as hard and tight as they could, the glass shattered, causing Stacia's hands to bleed profusely as she sat downstairs in the basement for the remainder of the evening.

CHAPTER 44

Day 32

"Yes, honey, I remembered the chicken wings." Detective Paulson reassured her daughter over the phone while rooting around her cluttered desk for something lost.

"Mom, you said that on last year's birthday, and you forgot to bring them."

"That's only because I was wrapped up in a case. You tend to forget, I work for a living, at a police station, nonetheless." Paulson smiled.

"Mom, do you even know how old I'll be tomorrow?"

"Lacey, I gave birth to you sixteen years ago. How can you even ask me a question like that?"

"Because, mom, you know how bad dad wants to throw you missing my birthday last year down your throat."

Paulson swallowed before rolling her eyes and saying, "Yeah, and I also remember your dad bringing his drunk fiancée with him to your birthday party as well. So I guess your parents were made for each other after all."

"Mom, don't blame yourself, you're nothing like him. Besides, he hates chicken wings." Lacey giggled.

Paulson turned her head slightly as so no one else walking past could hear her. "You have to be the only white girl I know that loves chicken wings." She chuckled.

Lacey laughed out loud and said, *"C'mon, mom, can you blame me? I mean, do you know any other white girl that can inhale wings like I do and still wear a size three?"*

"You play tennis, you have to be a size three, showoff." Paulson replied in a condescending voice.

"Oh, by the way, what presents did you get me for my birthday?" Lacey excitedly asked.

"Nice try, kiddo," Paulson twisted her lips while amusingly shaking her head from side to side. "Better luck next year."

"Just thought I'd slip that one in there," Lacey snickered.

"I see." Paulson humbly remarked. "Well, I have to get back to work. I'll see you this evening, seven sharp."

"You promise, seven sharp?"

"I promise, seven sharp. Love you."

"Love you, too, mom."

Paulson clicked the 'off' button on her cellphone before placing the contraption down onto her messy desk and allowing her conversation to melt inside of her.

As soon as the sentiment withdrew, she immediately went back to the laborious detail of searching through the collection of papers that were strewn all over her desk. From incident reports to mug shots, the woman persisted in her hunt before another call buzzed on her phone.

Paulson restlessly rooted around her desk until the buzzing became louder. Before long, she eventually found the thing. "This is Detective Paulson. How can I help you?"

Paulson listened intently to the somber voice over the phone before her memory suddenly kicked in. "Ms. Taylor, it's been a long time." She remarked with restrained surprise.

Paulson heard Stacia's gravelly voice and wondered if it was really her she was speaking with or someone else entirely. "Ms. Taylor, are you feeling alright."

Paulson accepted Stacia's quick response before the odd woman went on a long rant that seemed to perk up Paulson's suspicious attention at once. "Oh really," Paulson inhaled. "Tell me, Ms. Taylor, just how long have you known about this?"

While keeping her cellphone pressed securely against her ear, Paulson tore through her desk in search of a pen. The very instant she found it, she began scribbling a message on a piece of paper in front of her.

"Ms. Taylor, when was the last time you saw this person?"

Once Paulson was done writing, she went straight for her computer that sat right in front of her and started to punch away at lightning speed.

"Ms. Taylor, no matter what, do not engage this man, we already know how dangerous he is."

On her computer screen appeared a menagerie of mug shots that Paulson scrolled through with painstaking detail. "You don't know just how much you've helped us, Ms. Taylor. And by the way—

But before Paulson could even say another word, the person on the other end hung up the phone, which really didn't surprise or upset Paulson in the least bit, she had other matters to press out.

Within her database, Paulson was able to weed out whatever perpetrator she wanted to find. After nearly five minutes, the face that she was looking for instantly appeared.

Totally ignoring the daily rants and ravings of the police station around her, Paulson gazed on and on at the record of the sought after individual.

"Henderson!" Paulson called out to a fellow, plain clothes officer.

The middle-aged black man stopped just short of Paulson's desk before turning around and smirking, "Almost made it out."

Not taking her eyes off the screen, Paulson commented, "Sorry, I know breakfast is your favorite meal, but I got something else that may make you happy."

"What's up?"

"Do you recall a Dixon Crenshaw?"

The man stood and scratched at his mustache before replying, "No, doesn't ring a bell."

"He's the same Crenshaw out of Brooklyn, New York."

"Wait a second, do you mean the same Sergeant Crenshaw out of New York?"

"That's him."

"That guy served in Desert Storm. What's he up to now?"

"I just got a call from Stacia Taylor, and she tells me that not only have they been dating for the past year and a half, but that he confessed to a whole string of robberies, including the invasion of her own home. This is the guy we've been looking for all this time."

"Do you think she's credible?"

"It's hard to say; she sounded real strange over the phone. I just hope she doesn't do anything stupid like confront the guy If he's slime enough to rob her and her grandkids, then who knows what else he's capable of doing?"

"Do you want me to get an arrest warrant?"

Gathering her phone, sidearm and jacket, Paulson got up from her desk and said, "Yeah…and would you also get in touch with my daughter and tell her that I…I won't be home this evening."

CHAPTER 45

10:09 a.m.

Stacia laid in her bed with no pants or panties on and her legs spread eagle while she slid her dildo in and out of her snatch.

She wasn't exactly imagining anyone in particular on top of her, it was the just the feeling she needed that kept her coming over and over in rapid succession.

As soon as the knocking door downstairs interrupted her "alone time", Stacia tossed the dildo down to the floor and flung herself off the bed in an enraged heap. From there she gathered a pair of grey sweatpants, a pair of socks and her tennis shoes before tearing down the steps like a charging elephant.

The second she threw open the door, she saw none other than Dee standing outside on the porch with her hands stuffed inside her jacket pocket. The young lady had a meek look on her face, like she wanted to turn and run away at any second.

With an arrogant frown, Stacia stood at the door and asked, "Well, look what *The Amazing Chan Clan* brought back."

Dee dropped her head for a second before looking back up and saying, "Stacia, I—

"Ms. Taylor, to you," Stacia snapped.

"Ms. Taylor," Dee inhaled, "I wanted to keep my distance for a while before I came back again. Can I come inside, please?"

"You're fine right where you are. I don't want my house smelling like dead cat and noodles all over again."

"Stacia...Ms. Taylor, I don't know exactly what's happening here, but I think I may have an explanation of sorts."

"Tell me something, what sort of chink are you anyways?" Stacia pointed. "Chinese, Japanese?"

"I'm Vietnamese, Ms. Taylor." Dee bitterly responded.

"Well, call it what you like, you all still look the same to me, no matter what country you come from."

Dee cut her eyes momentarily before saying, "Ms. Taylor, Patrick and Scott don't want anything more to do with you, but I can't live with myself knowing that something is terribly wrong here."

"I told you people that this fucking house is not haunted anymore! What other proof do you want?"

"I have reason to believe that your behavior may be paranormal. This type of haunting isn't common, Ms. Taylor." Dee adamantly explained.

Stacia stood perfectly still while staring solid at Dee. Something inside the woman unexpectedly clicked. "Do you mean...possessed?"

Dee squirmed in place and remarked, "I think possessed is too...ridged, of a word. Anymore, someone hears the word possessed, and the first thing that comes to mind is spinning heads and green vomit. That's obviously not the case here. Rather, I believe that you and the kids may be under the influence of McFord's aura."

Still, Stacia would not budge from where she was standing. There was something inside of her brain that wanted to scream out, but that something was stifled.

"Ms. Taylor, I can't tell you to move out, but I can warn you. You can hate me forever, but as long as you three live here in this house, it may only get worse. And judging by the way you look right now, the worse is on its way."

"Tell you what," Stacia stepped forward, "you take your little self back to where you came from…and don't ever come back here again."

With that, Stacia slammed the door right in Dee's face and dragged herself over to the mirror that hung above the fireplace. What she saw wasn't her, at least not the "her" she was used to seeing. Her image was replaced with a thin, wild-haired, pale figure that resembled someone who had just crawled out of bed after an entire month. And yet, after staring at herself for what seemed like countless minutes, Stacia couldn't bring herself to the realization that something was wrong. She knew that it was right there on the very tip of her tongue, but pulling out the truth was a feat she was too weak to undertake.

Stacia dropped her lazy head only to lift it right back up and listen as the thumping of loud music outside caused the woman to turn away from the mirror and venture back to the front door.

She stood, waited and listened as the vehicle's door outside closed. Then the scatter of footsteps drew closer and closer to the door. Without allowing the individual to knock, Stacia opened the door to see Dixon with his right hand in the air, ready to pound at the door.

The man gave Stacia a revolting grimace before asking, "Damn, girl, what the hell happened to you?"

Stacia stepped aside to allow the man in. Once he was inside, she closed the door and went ahead of him for the kitchen.

Coming into the kitchen to join her, Dixon, with his frown still attached to his face, stopped short of the threshold. "What the hell happened in here? What, did you all shit and piss all over the floor or something?"

Stacia stood over the sink and poured herself a glass of water before gulping it down in one serving. She then slammed the cup down onto the counter and stared on at Dixon from afar.

Dixon slowly meandered his way over to Stacia with his hands out in a consoling manner. "I was kind of surprised when you called me this morning. I didn't think you wanted to see me again." He softly uttered.

Stacia's head hung down to the filthy linoleum. "What would make you think that?"

Dixon bobbed his head from side to side before muttering, "After what me and the boys did to you. You gotta understand, baby girl, you were so passed out from the night before that leaving you in your car was all we could think of doing. We was all so afraid...we just went by instinct."

Still, Stacia would not raise her head. Every word that Dixon was saying went in through one ear and out the other. Just listening to his voice sent a shrill rip down into her stomach.

"I'm sorry." He held out his arms "I'm sorry from the bottom of my heart, baby girl. I never meant to treat you like that. We were all high that night. Hell, I was both high and drunk all at once. You know how I get when I'm around my nephews."

"Yeah...I know." Stacia mumbled.

Dixon stood and looked down at Stacia with a strange face. "What's the matter, girl? Do you wanna tell me what's been going on inside this house? Why do you look like this?"

Stacia's eyes rolled up for a second or two in a devious manner before she turned away from Dixon and pointed her head to the stove.

"Stacia, I'm talking to you!" Dixon said aloud. "What's the matter?"

"Tell me something, what poor child did you steal from in order to give my children all they wanted?" Stacia questioned in a low, methodical tone.

Dixon stepped back an inch and asked," What did you say?"

Stacia then pointed her red eyes at the man and said, "You heard me."

Chuckling away his embarrassment, Dixon waved his arms in the air and said, "I don't know what you're talking about, girl. I think you've been in this house too long."

"All those people you stole from. Even…us," Stacia pointed to herself.

"What the fuck are you talkin' about?" Dixon yelled into Stacia's face.

"Why us, Dixon," Stacia questioned the man straight in his face. "How easy was it to point a gun in my grandkids faces? They had nightmares for weeks. How easy was it for you to beat me like a dog and point a gun at me?"

"You've done gone and lost your mind!"

"That night, you treated me like a piece of shit. Just like you and your nephews did just a few nights back. That's why you stayed away. That's why you didn't call or text, you were too ashamed. Were you ashamed to rob us, Dixon?"

Dixon began roaming around the kitchen like a dog chasing after its own tail. "Man, my nephews must have given you some potent shit that night, because you're thinkin' up some crazy stuff!"

"Do you wanna know what really gets me? That whole night, during that robbery, you yelled and screamed at me like a dog, but never once did I think it was Dixon Crenshaw. Of course, why on earth would I ever think it was the man I and my grandkids loved so much? I never once recognized your voice. I never once recognized your fuckin' voice!" Stacia hollered while pounding on the sink.

Suddenly, and without warning, Dixon lunged forward and wrapped his huge hands around Stacia's neck. "You think you're so damn good with your skeezer ass!"

Stacia took Dixon's hands and began to separate them from her neck. Dixon actually looked shocked to see such strength come from the feeble woman. But before Stacia could step back, Dixon backhanded her, sending Stacia crashing to the floor.

"I already called the police, motherfucker." Stacia wiped the blood from off her bottom lip. "They're coming to get your punk ass now as we speak."

Without uttering another word, Dixon irately reached down and proceeded to wrap his hands around Stacia's neck once more, only to have the woman fight back with the kind of ferocity that had she been in the right frame of mind would have surprised even her.

She kicked and clawed at the big man before Dixon hurled her into the stove. Above her head slid open one of the drawers, from out of the drawer fell a sharp knife that landed right next to Stacia, the woman picked up the utensil and pointed it straight at Dixon, but the man was too quick as he snatched the knife from out of her hand and tossed it behind him. He then picked her up and slapped her across the face so hard that blood flew from out of Stacia's nose.

Stacia fell back into the stove, but before Dixon could make another strike, seated directly behind her was a coffee pot. Stacia immediately grabbed the pot and cracked Dixon across the face with it. She then raced for the counter and grabbed a rolling pin before standing behind the man and placing the pin against his neck.

Stacia pulled back as hard as she could while Dixon struggled to free himself, but no matter how hard he fought, Stacia's grip was entirely too strong to withstand. The woman pulled back with so much might and fury that it caused her to foam at the mouth, much like Dixon himself was doing there on his hands and knees on the kitchen floor.

Stacia could sense that he was losing his breath by the second, which in turn caused her to only strengthen her pull all the more. She heard Dixon gasp and wheeze while watching his hands slowly drop back down to the floor.

Stacia's red eyes were void of any emotion or strain, but inside her head was Devon and Sidney. Just like that, her grip on the rolling pin loosened, sending Dixon falling flat on his face to the linoleum.

The man coughed, gagged and cursed while trying to get to his feet. "Fuck you…bitch." He gasped for air. "Fuck you and…your kids. After all I've done for you…motherfuckers!"

Stacia collapsed her body up against one of the bottom cabinets and watched with dead eyes as Dixon hobbled his way out of the kitchen.

Sweat drooled down her face while her body shook uncontrollably. Her mouth hung wide open as she struggled to regain her breath.

"Ride your ass home, bitch." Stacia panted like she needed a drink of water ever so badly.

Lifting her feeble body up, Stacia heaved herself out of the kitchen and through the living room. Out the front door she went before going to her car and pulling away, dinging Dixon's prized truck along the way as he struggled to climb his battered body inside.

CHAPTER 46

<hr>

Addington, Ohio: Population-756
4:15 p.m.

Addington was a small, rural town to the furthest most west point of the state of Ohio. Its wooded landscape sat all alone at the edge of a mammoth creek that stretched from the Ohio River and intersected at Lake Erie.

At its town square was assembled nearly the entire town's populace, give or take about three hundred or so, along with various old and fairly new cars, motorcycles and pickup trucks of all makes, models and colors, most of which had American and Rebel flags posted on the roofs.

The throngs of white people, both young and old, stood huddled amongst each other that cool, autumn-like afternoon watching and listening to the middle-aged white man way up front who was dressed in a red, silk outfit and a pointy, red hood that wasn't covering his entire bearded face.

The man was surrounded by four other white sheeted, fully hooded men, two on both sides while the oversized Swastika flag behind them waved gently in the brisk breeze.

With his megaphone pressed against his lips, the red clad individual stepped forward and began to speak. "I'd like to thank everyone for coming out today! The day of the white race," he loudly proclaimed.

At once, those in the crowd cheered, whistled, clapped and chanted "white power" in gleeful chorus.

"God in heaven has given us this day for a purpose, and that purpose is solely for us to come together for each other and ourselves, as one! You see, when the mud people gather, riots break out, but when the white race, the pure white race, gathers, we gather in solidarity! As one, and for each other!"

Once more, the mob exploded into a reprise of applause at the speaker's opening motivational stanza.

"We honor great people like Nathan Bedford Forrest, Margaret Sanger, Heinrich Himmler and Father Adolph Hitler! For had it not been for these great patriots of freedom, the entire white race as we know it would be extinct!"

The multitude broke out again in cheers that lasted nearly two whole minutes before they settled back down.

"Mother Sanger once said, and I quote," 'Birth control must lead ultimately to a cleaner race,' "It was those same words that ring true to this very day! America is overrun with all kinds of dark ones, wetbacks and Arabs! The same people who have sought the destruction of this once mighty nation! Which leads me to another quote of Mother Sanger's," 'They are human weeds, reckless breeders, spawning. Human beings who never should have been born.' "The white race has to be willing to stand up against such debauchery and proudly proclaim that we and we only are the pure race! White power!"

At once, the mass exploded into a one minute chant of "white power." Some pumped their fists, while others raised a Nazi salute in the air.

"The great Heinrich Himmler once said," 'We have only one task, to stand firm and carry on the racial struggle without mercy,' "Those words couldn't be anymore solid! I'm sick and tired of seeing my white people kowtow to the likes of affirmative action, like we should be ashamed of being white!

I'm proud of my whiteness, and every white person in America should be equally proud!"

Various chants of "Amen" and "Right on, brother," carried on throughout the crowd, making it appear as though they were all robot controlled drones of sorts.

"When I think of the worst of the worst, the Jews, the first thought that comes to mind is extermination! What began in Europe should be continued by us! These people are the epitome of all evil! Crucifying our Lord and Savior Christ Jesus, controlling all the money in the world and making sure that the white race is docile and out of the way! Heinrich Himmler said that Anti-Semitism is exactly the same as delousing. Getting rid of lice is not a question of ideology, it is a matter of cleanliness. In just this same way, Anti-Semitism for us has not been a question of ideology, but a matter of purity! When the white man gets a spine and stands up to this evil, we will purge this darkness out of our great nation once and for all! The Jews, the niggers, the wetbacks, Arabs, and the fags! Any and every evil piece of filth that has invaded our land for far too long! White power!"

The gathering, in harmony, chanted along with their respected leader as the men beside him raised their right arms in Nazi salutation.

"The Muslim sympathizing, communist loving, half breed mutt in the White House has been talking about hope and change ever since before he came into power! I tell my white brothers and sisters this, first, interracial relationships are a sin from Satan himself, and it must stop right now! The white person has no business cross breeding with anyone outside their own race! The white person who commits such a sin should be disowned from the white race! Second, we, too, believe in hope and change! We hope that all races die, and with their deaths, will come a change to America, a change that sees the greatest nation on earth go back to the values that made this country great to begin with!"

The speaker then put down his megaphone and turned to bring out a young, scraggly, chunky white man who was clothed in a white sheet of his own, but without his hood.

"Father Adolph made this quote!" 'He alone, who owns the youth, gains the future!' "That couldn't be more right than at this moment! I present to you, my nephew, Jamie!"

Seated in her bright red Ford pickup truck that was parked near the rear of the multitude was Lois, a white woman with brown hair and the looks of a female in her mid-sixties who was cracking a blushing smile while holding her cellphone to her ear.

"Uh, oh, now L.J.'s got Jamie up there." Lois snickered.

"Is he shaking like a leaf?" The woman on the other end of the phone asked.

"No, he's got this real serious look on his face, like it's the most important day of his life. Poor rascal," Lois belly laughed.

"Well, to him, it is an important day. He's been waiting for this all his life."

Lois momentarily pulled the phone away from her ear and dropped her head as not to stare at her son who appeared so different in her eyes all of the sudden.

"Hello?" The woman on the other end spoke.

Lifting her head back up, Lois replied, "Yeah…I'm here. It just amazes me at how many people showed up today. Jimmie had me take off from the bowling alley today because no one hardly bothered to show up."

"Shit, according to your brothers, this rally is the single most important thing since the Last Supper." The woman giggled.

"Yeah, tell me about it. If I hear one more time about how significant, or—

Before Lois could even utter another word, out of the corner of her left eye appeared a sight that she never imagined or ever wanted to see. The sight was that of a wild-haired black woman who was just aimlessly blundering into the sea of white people like she herself could just blend in without notice.

"Hello, hello, Lois!"

Trying to catch her breath, Lois blinked her eyes and muttered into the phone, "Oh…my…God."

"What is it?" The woman on the other end frantically shouted.

"Let me talk to you later." Lois stammered as she tossed her cellphone down onto the passenger's seat and got out of her truck.

Lois could see that the deeper the odd woman sank into the crowd, the more the people began to take notice and grumble amongst themselves.

Lois desperately barged her way through the masses in an effort to take hold of the crazed woman before it was too late. But it seemed that the more the gathering griped and murmured, that was all the more everyone on stage seemed to become alerted to the stranger in their midst, much to Lois' strong dismay.

At once, the speaker stopped talking, and with his right finger extended, he shouted into the megaphone, "We don't need any reporter from CBS, NBC or CNN here spying on us! This is white man's country! You've no business being here!"

Like a mass of angry bees, the entire crowd began shouting racial slurs at the black woman while shoving her from side to side like she was a pinball. Lois, however, fought on and on through the unruly throngs until she at long last caught up with the woman.

Lois grabbed the woman by the shoulder and swung her around to see the woman's sullen eyes and half grin stare back at her like all the mayhem she was surrounded amongst was a simple delight.

The very instant Lois saw beer bottles flying in the air, she shielded the woman with her jacket while escorting her back through the insane crowd and to her waiting truck.

Lois stuffed the uncanny lady inside before getting in herself and starting the engine. "Who the hell are you?" Lois screamed out in hysterical frustration.

Soon, the crowd began gathering around her truck to the where seeing her way out was virtually impossible. Lois did the only thing that came to mind first, she reeved the truck's engine as loud as she could, which in turn caused the masses to disperse and back away.

Lois was somewhat able to put her truck in reverse and take off, while having beer bottles tossed at her rear window along the way.

Flooring the gas, Lois, breathing in and out like she had ran a marathon, gazed over at the still grinning woman. "Do you know where you are? Who are you?" She yelled.

But the woman would not reply, she just sat in her seat and stared endlessly at Lois like she was in the thralls of falling in love with the woman.

"Can you even understand what I'm saying to you?" Lois continued to holler at the lady.

By that point, Lois got the sense that she wasn't dealing with just any ordinary half-wit. What sat beside her in her truck that afternoon was something that she wasn't prepared to cope with, but had no choice but to.

Lois couldn't have driven any faster that afternoon.

CHAPTER 47

L ois pulled her truck onto a piece of land that led down a wooded path. After about fifteen seconds, ahead in the clearing appeared a one floor, white and red house that looked as if it hadn't made its way out of the nineteenth century.

Lois veered the truck right in front of the house before getting out and aiding the offbeat character towards the home.

Without using a key, Lois barged her way through the front door and called out, "Where is everyone?"

Before Lois could even sit the woman down onto the recliner that sat next to fireplace, an older white woman hobbling in from the kitchen with one crutch, asked, "What's going on? I got half the town ringing my phone off the hook."

Out of breath, Lois knelt before the black lady and gazed deep into her lovelorn eyes. She could tell that the lady had lost something between where she came from and where she ended up.

With a surprised grimace on her face, the crippled woman stood behind Lois and asked with a gasp, "Who is this?"

Without turning away from the crazed women in the chair, Lois huffed, "I don't have a clue."

"Well…where did she come from?" The cripple stammered.

Lois continued to stare on at the lady before commenting, "I was down there listening to L.J., when out of nowhere, she shows up."

"She just showed up?" The cripple panted. "Showed up from where?"

"I don't have a damn clue."

"Does she have a name?"

"She won't speak. She just sits and stares like she's lost her mind."

"She looks like she's high on something."

"Either she's high as a kite, or, judging by the bruises on her face, she was in a heavy duty scrap and got her brains scrambled."

"Well…why did you bring her ass here?"

Lois glanced back at the woman and said, "Because, this town is already hanging on by a thread. The last thing we need is to have some black lady getting the shit kicked out of her in Addington of all places."

"Well, you'd better hurry up and get her out of here before all hell breaks loose."

"Hell already broke loose; I didn't think we'd make it out of that crowd alive."

"What the hell is goin' on here," Jamie all of the sudden burst through the front door in a bluster. "Who is she, ma?"

Lois rolled her eyes and said, "Don't worry about it, just go and make sure your uncles don't come here all fired up!"

Ripping off his white sheets, the young man stomped his way towards his mother and screamed, "This was supposed to be my fuckin' day, and this nigger shows up and ruins it all!"

"Jamie, your mom had nothing to do with this." The cripple stepped in.

"Bullshit! I'm gonna kick her black ass and—

Pointing her finger at the enraged boy, Lois spun around and yelled, "No you're not! I'm not spending another Christmas day visiting your sorry ass behind bars! Now, step back and shut the fuck up!"

"But she ain't got no business bein' here! This is our town; now the coons are taking over!"

"I said shut the fuck up!"

Without another word, Jamie grumbled his way out of the living room and back out of the house. "You're the only Klansman in the world who hates blacks, but loves listening to Lil' Wayne!" The crippled lady quipped out loud.

Returning her attention back to the woman before her, Lois once more peered deep into her eyes. "Now, I need for you to listen and listen very closely." Lois slowly articulated. "You look like you're drugged out, but this ain't the place for the likes of you to be drugged out. Do you know where you are?"

Still, the woman would not respond. She continued to sit in the chair with her bizarre expression that made Lois not only nervous but angry at the same time.

"Listen to me!" Lois loudly clapped her hands in front of the woman's face. "Do you know where you are?" What's your name? My name is Lois, and this here is my cousin—

"She doesn't need to know my name." Lois' cousin bitterly turned away.

"In about a few minutes or so, your life is about to get a lot more difficult, and I don't know if I'll be able to help you any further."

"You sound just like your mama." The black lady smiled ever so endearingly.

Both Lois and her cousin paused for what seemed like minutes before Lois reached into the woman's pants pocket and pulled out her wallet.

"Honey, my mama has been dead since 1981."

Lois rooted through the wallet, glancing at pictures, a library card and a *Victoria's Secret* gift card before coming to a driver's license. Lois read over the name, but when she came to the address her heart nearly stopped beating. With her mouth dry and hanging wide open, Lois handed her cousin the card and stuttered, "Read…read this woman's address out loud to me."

Lois' cousin took the license and said, "833 Husk Drive, Lane, Ohio, 47823. So what," she shrugged.

With her dangling jaw, Lois turned around. "Don't you recognize that address?" She softly uttered. "That's exactly where my father was murdered years ago."

Lois' cousin put the card closer to her face before her eyes bulged out of their sockets. "Holy shit," she gulped. "What the hell is she doin' all the way here?"

"What the hell is goin' on out here?" A short, bald, old white man with a walker cried out as he came shuffling into the living room from the hallway."

"Go back to bed, Uncle Harry, it's nothing!" Lois' cousin said.

The very second Uncle Harry caught sight of the woman seated in the chair the old man immediately began pointing. "What the hell is that damn pickaninny doin' in my house?" He screamed.

"Dear God." Lois closed her eyes in weary dread. "Uncle Harry, it's nothing! Just go back to bed; we'll take care of it." Lois firmly, but respectfully chided the man.

"Get her the hell outta here before J. Edgar comes by and throws us all in the hoosegow!"

Before Lois could even stand back up, outside, the roars of pickup trucks and motorcycles entering the yard came into full bloom. Lois' entire body began to tremble while she looked down at the lady in the chair who didn't once appear to care that her life was is mortal danger.

"Get her out of here!" Lois' cousin urgently pleaded.

But rather than do as she was told, Lois defiantly stood in front of the black lady with a balled up right fist and waited as four of the brutes made their way inside the house.

"Do you wanna tell us just what in the blue hell she's doin' here?" L.J. hollered as he advanced towards Lois enraged.

"L.J., just hold on," Lois held out her arms. "She's not in her right mind!"

"We ain't got to hold on for nothin'!" A skinny white man shouted.

Without allowing another wasted second to pass, Lois handed L.J. the driver's license. "Look at the address!"

L.J. snatched the card from out of Lois' hand and read. "So what," the man threw up his hands.

"L.J., that's where daddy was killed years ago!"

L.J. studied the card again before a sour scowl struck across his face. "She knows who killed daddy?" he grunted with a blank stare.

"L.J., don't stand there and pretend you wanna avenge daddy after all these years!"

"Boy, you still have your mother's sea blue eyes." The black woman grinned at the man.

It was Lois, her cousin, Uncle Harry and the four other white men that all stood perfectly still and hushed in the middle of the floor, appearing as if something or someone had sucked the very life out of each and every soul.

"What did you say about my mama, gal?" L.J. advanced towards the woman in an irate manner.

"Stoppit, L.J.!" Lois stood in front of the man. "There's something wrong with her!"

"What the hell are you, a double agent?" Another one of the men yelled.

For at least five minutes, Lois and the four other men argued back and forth about what to do with the woman before heavy whimpering began making itself known behind Lois.

Lois spun around to see the lady with her hand covering her mouth and her eyes protruding from out of her head crying ever so subtly, as though she had come to realize just what sort of situation she was in all of the sudden.

"Get her out of here now, Lois." Lois' cousin firmly commanded.

Helping the woman up out of the chair, Lois escorted both the lady and herself past the men on her way out the door and to her truck.

There were others outside the house watching the entire scene with blazing eyes of repugnance pointed at the two ladies. Lois, however, fully realized that no matter what, all that she had once known as a normal life had all but been erased in the span of one hour.

Skating onto the main road, Lois glanced over at the woman who was not only still crying, but cowering in her seat like a frightened little girl.

"Try and calm down." Lois said. "Do you know where you are?"

The woman shook her head no and continued to whimper uncontrollably. Truth be told, Lois was just as afraid as she was, if not more.

"Your driver's license said that your name was Stasha."

"Stacia," the woman blurted out. "My name is…Stacia Taylor. Where am I?"

"You're in Addington. That's a far cry from Lane."

Stacia turned her bugged out eyes to Lois and looked at the woman forever before turning back to the window and asking, "How did I get here?"

Chuckling, Lois replied, "I was kinda hoping you could tell me that. What do you last remember?"

Stacia grabbed her head and said, "I dunno. The last thing that even sounds familiar was an Asian girl. After that, I must've blacked out."

A few seconds of silence sat inside the truck before Lois said, "I saw in your license that you live at 833 Husk Drive. I once knew some folks that lived there."

Stacia glared hard at Lois and asked, "What folks are you talking about?"

"I once had an aunt that lived there years ago. She actually died just two days ago to be exact."

Stacia stared on some more before questioning, "Who else lived there?"

Lois glanced over at Stacia before returning her eyes back to the road again. "Look, something tells me that you're not in the right frame of mind. It looked to us like you were high."

"I'm not high! I don't do that anymore!" Stacia fired back with an attitude.

"Alright, you don't have to get snippy with me. I'm just letting you know the score."

"I wanna know who else once lived there." Stacia adamantly remarked.

Lois continued to drive on, not one time taking her eyes off of the winding, wooded road that seemingly spiraled on forever.

"My father was murdered there years ago. Is that what you wanna hear?"

Stacia sat absolutely still in her seat while gawking all around the truck in a baffled and agitated manner.

"What was all that Klan bullshit about back there?"

Lois sighed and said, "Those four guys you saw back at the house were my brothers."

"Did they…did they do anything to me?" Stacia shuddered.

"No, no, nothing happened to you while you were there. Now, whatever happened before you got to Addington is obviously still a mystery. But I gotta tell you, you sure scared the hell out of us when you mentioned my brother's eyes. Only our father referred to our mother's eyes as sea blue. You even said that I looked like my mother."

Stacia said nothing while keeping a suspect eye locked on Lois. Lois in return only glanced at Stacia and cracked a whimsical grin before saying, "Don't worry, if we wanted you gone, you would be. We McFord's once had a knack for making certain people…vanish."

Still, Stacia sat in her seat looking on as though she could make a jump and run at a moment's notice. Lois on the other hand paid the woman's apprehensive demeanor no mind, she was almost back at the town's square, and that was all that mattered to her.

"Oh my God," Stacia all of the sudden shouted out in agony.

"What's the matter?"

"My grandkids, they're at home!"

"You have grandkids?" Lois frowned strangely.

"I need to use your phone, please!"

Lois took her cellphone from out of her pocket and handed it to Stacia. Every so often she would peek over at the hysterical woman who appeared even more distressed than she was just minutes earlier.

"No answer?" Lois asked.

With tears streaming down her face, Stacia said, "I…I can't get a hold of them. Where's my car?"

"We're heading back downtown. Hopefully you left it there."

Stacia wept incessantly to the point where she appeared as if she could hardly even breathe. Lois wanted to say something encouraging, or at least hand the woman a sympathetic "it'll be okay," but she held back; even her own motherly instincts wouldn't allow her to hand Stacia the comfort that she possibly required to overcome the situation that she was buried underneath.

***

After about twenty minutes or so, Lois pulled the truck down the empty road known as the town square. Gone were the motorcycles and pickup trucks. Even the stage and the beer cans and bottles that once littered the ground were all but a memory. It was as if the prior event that had taken place earlier never happened.

Parked sideways next to a barber shop was a Saturn Aura. The instant Stacia spotted the vehicle, like an anxious child she wrestled with the doorknob to get out.

"Can you at least wait until I stop the truck?" Lois beseeched.

As soon as Lois came to a complete stop, Stacia jumped out and ran over to her car. Lois climbed out as well and stood next to Stacia's vehicle.

"It's getting dark out, and believe me, you, of all people, don't wanna be riding around here at night." Lois said.

Fiddling with her car keys, Stacia asked, "How do I get out of this town?"

Pointing south, Lois explained, "You'll wanna head down this way about thirty miles. Then hang a left at a sign that'll say *Norman's Cross*. From there, you'll go another ten miles before you hit the highway back to Lane. You sure you're gonna be okay?"

Without looking at her, Stacia shoved the keys into the ignition and veered away from Lois as fast as she could.

Lois stood there on the sidewalk and looked on at the Saturn that vanished quicker than she expected.

To her right was an old white man who was standing in the window of the barber shop with a hateful look on his face. Lois watched as the man yanked down the blind that covered the window before she tucked her hands into her jacket pockets and carried on quietly back to her truck.

CHAPTER 48

Day 33: The Final Day
12:19 a.m.

To say that Stacia got lost on her way home would be an understatement. Lois' directions were precise, however, once Stacia managed to get on the freeway her entire sense of direction became utterly disoriented due to the fact that she was a hysterical mess from worrying about the kids, and not having any recollection of her time in Addington; she honestly couldn't even recall hopping in her car and driving to the horrid little town to begin with.

But as befuddled as she was, Stacia would not allow any of her recent brain lapses to interfere with what was most important. Stacia roared her car around the corner that led to Husk Drive and rammed the vehicle up onto the curb before jumping out and racing towards the dark house.

Like a human battering ram Stacia barged through the front door before clicking on the living room lights and screaming, "Kids, where are you?"

The sound of running water upstairs immediately gave the Stacia the impression that the children weren't too far. She ran up the steps, nearly tripping along the way. The water was coming from the bathroom straight ahead. Without allowing another second to drift by, Stacia bolted down the hallway and into the bathroom to find the tub overflowing with hot water, so hot in fact that it was steaming up the entire bathroom.

Before she could even turn and run back, Stacia slipped on the hot wet floor and fell beside the toilet. While trying to regain her footing, Stacia felt the back of her head being forced into the tub.

Before she knew it, she was underwater, suffocating in the blistering liquid. As hard as she tried to pull herself back up the force that had her from behind would not relinquish its grip.

Stacia was not only losing what little oxygen she had left inside her lungs, she was also feeling the effects of the harsh water that was beginning to cause the skin on her face to burn.

But no matter what, Stacia would not relent. She was as obstinate as her captor. With all of her strength she hoisted her head out of the water and dropped her entire body down onto the hot, wet floor. Steam flowed from off of her face while she tried to get back to her feet.

Ignoring the relenting, burning pain, the very second Stacia was able to gain a stable footing, she ran out of the bathroom and back downstairs to find the television flipping off and on, as well as the pictures that were hanging on the walls dropping to the floor.

"Sid, Devon!" Stacia cried out in pain. "Where are you?"

Stacia then ran through the dining room and into the kitchen to find it brightly lit from corner to corner. Stacia stood in the middle of the floor and called out the kids' names over and over. When her eyes connected with the basement door, she knew immediately just what needed to be done.

Putting one foot in front of the other, Stacia made a direct course for the door, only to be stopped by the growling's of a grey and white wolf that stumbled its way into the kitchen.

Stacia stood perfectly still, not wanting to make any sudden moves before the creature. She didn't know where the animal came from, and she really couldn't have cared all the less. The entire house was falling apart in haunted dread; it was her children that mattered the most.

Making careful eye contact with the basement, Stacia ever so slowly crept her way over while the wolf continued to snarl its angry fangs at her.

Not wanting too much time to pass, Stacia boldly ran for the door, only to have the beast chase after her.

With her hand on the knob, the wolf managed to grab Stacia's right ankle with its teeth. Stacia kicked at the ravenous animal while trying ever so desperately to open the door.

After so much fighting, Stacia was at last able to unlock the door. She made sure to open it to a sliver as she slid through. She then shut the door as quickly as possible behind her, leaving the animal on the other end to bark and growl like the mad beast that it was.

Breathing so heavy that she could hardly even stand, Stacia limped her way down the steps. The vigorous stench of gas hung ever so thick in the air, it was so pungent that it caused Stacia to lose her balance. It smelled like someone had left a pilot light on for days.

The instant she reached the floor, Stacia cut on the light switch to her right. Lying on the floor in a corner was Sidney. Stacia, bloody ankle and all, limped over as fast as she could and scooped the child up in her arms.

"Sid, baby," Stacia loudly wept. "Sid, wake up!"

Stacia yelled at the girl and slapped her across the face just to get her to wake up, but no matter what, Sidney would not open her eyes. Stacia checked the child's pulse to find it nearly non-existent.

"Dear God...please help me!" Stacia wailed to the ceiling. "Please, baby, wake the fuck up!"

Soon, a scraping racket arose from behind Stacia. The woman spun around to see Devon, with a sharp knife in his left hand and a dull, entranced glare in his eyes.

Still holding onto Sidney, Stacia held out her hand and slowly panted, "Son…please put that down."

But it was as if the boy hadn't heard a single word his grandmother had said. Devon continued on with his knife.

At that point, with one child slowly dying in her arms and another preparing to end her life, Stacia realized the harsh truth that all she had worked for had all but slipped away.

She couldn't recall all that had taken place over the course of the past few days, and she really didn't want to. Stacia dropped all of her defenses and allowed her body to relax there on the floor. Suddenly, all that had taken place in her life, from her childhood, to her son, all the way to buying the house seemed absolutely insignificant. She wanted it all to end right there in the basement; whether it be from gas poisoning or being stabbed by her beloved grandson.

Stacia Taylor hadn't a care in the world at that moment. She felt alone and abandoned. Everyone she had loved so dearly was taken away, and to think that her life was going to end inside a haunted house of all places made her existence seem all the more useless.

Right before Devon could even take one more step towards her, Stacia all of the sudden heard clumping footsteps above in the kitchen. The wolf that was growling was nowhere to be heard. The footsteps, however, marched about in a back and forth fashion across the floor.

Now, she was mad. Devon was within arm's reach. With the quickness of a cat, Stacia snatched the knife from out of the boy's hand before grabbing him and holding his little body in her arms.

The child wrestled and struggled about in his grandmother's hold, but no matter what, Stacia would not let him go. She held him down as tight as she could before looking at Sidney.

"Wake up, Sid! We have to go!" She slapped the child across the face again and again.

Gradually, the little girl opened her eyes and began muttering. With Devon still fighting, Stacia then slapped him across the face as hard as she could before standing up and shaking the life out of the boy.

"Look at me, Devon!" She screamed into his face. "Look at me!"

At first, Devon's sullen eyes wouldn't connect with Stacia's, but after two more smacks across the face, the boy soon regained consciousness.

Gathering both children together, Stacia looked up at the stairs and yelled out as loud as she could, "Lucas…we're coming up!"

With both Sidney and Devon dragging their lethargic feet, Stacia pulled them along across the floor and up the steps until they reached the door. Once Stacia opened the basement door, she could spot no sign of the wolf. Only two feet to her immediate left was the backdoor.

With her arm stretched out, Stacia reached for the door's knob, only to be shoved backwards into the stove by a powerful force. The children as well were pushed back into her arms.

Soon, dishes, spoons, forks and knives came hurtling at the terrified three on the floor at lightning speed. Shattered plates came crashing down onto their heads while the kitchen table scooted across the floor at them. Stacia, with as much adrenaline as she could muster, yanked herself and the children out of the way.

The entire kitchen was alive with the uproars of an unbridled, paranormal rampage that was hell-bent on destroying anyone in its path. All Stacia could do was shield the children in her arms as the onslaught persisted to the point where even the cabinet doors were flying wide open. It was all a shred of madness that even a nightmare could not contain. It was as if the kitchen were caught in the midst of a whirlwind.

Just as it seemed as if the attack was over, one of the kitchen table chairs was lifted high in the air before being carried over and held above the Taylors' heads.

"Lucas…wait!" Stacia screamed with an outstretched right hand.

The woman could hardly breathe. Sweat was oozing down her face to where she could barely even see, but no matter what, Stacia would not take her eyes off of the chair that hung over her and her grandchildren in a threatening matter.

"Now…you listen to me." She stammered harshly. "You kill us…and we'll never let you go. The three of us will be with you forever."

Still, the chair levitated in the air, waiting for the right moment to lay waste to its victims. All Stacia could do was watch the chair as closely as possible.

Still shaking incessantly, Stacia continued, "If you think you hate us now…just wait. We will hunt you until eternity dies."

She honestly had no clue as to what she was saying, and realizing that she was face to face with a poltergeist of all things didn't seem to bear down upon her as much as it once did.

After about a full minute, two red eyes appeared before the Taylors. Soon, the chair that was floating in the air simply dropped down to the floor. Right before her face Stacia could smell what resembled moth balls breathe into her nostrils.

"Get…your… black… asses… out… of… here." A sinister voice hissed directly into her face.

The voice was cold as it spoke, cold like a hard winter. Stacia could actually feel the hatred emanate off the apparition's tone.

Before Long, the lock on the backdoor unhinged itself before the door flung wide open. Stacia, with her treasures in her arms, crawled across the linoleum and out the door onto the back porch.

The backdoor slammed shut right before the kitchen light went off. There were the Taylors, lying on the porch holding each other and shaking as though it were ten below outside.

All Stacia could do was look up at the stars in the clear, black sky and wonder, wonder when or if she was ever going to wake up again.

CHAPTER 49

Well, you did it again, Stacia. You fucked up once more. First you lose your son, then your house. Soon enough, your mind will follow. How much more can you possibly take?

Look at you; you're a broken down mess. You can't even raise your own grandchildren the right way. Everyone you loved is all gone now. Even your own house doesn't want you anymore. How fucked up is that?

I don't know, maybe it could have all worked out had things been different. But we all know that it can never be different for you, Stacia. All your life it's been one disaster after another. I mean, who actually believes in ghosts, let alone, a haunted house, for God's sake? But leave it to you to wind up in one.

But I'll hand it to you, you did try. You gave it that old Taylor toughness. I guess maybe next time you're just going to have to punch a little harder.

Who knows, perhaps your mother will let you back into her life again. Hell, if there's such a thing as ghosts, then anything is possible. Right?

Some days later:

Seated inside her car, Stacia snapped back to life. The words that she was hearing inside her head were still fresh and new, and they were still spitting all over her face like rain.

Gripped ever so tight in her right hand was her picture of her son, in the other hand was her cellphone. With glassy eyes, Stacia stared at the child that she loved ever so much while musing over his childhood and how hard they struggled to move up.

Stacia's hand began to tremble at that point, so much to where she could hardly even hold the frame any longer.

With a jittery jaw, Stacia fought to open her mouth while holding back powerful tears. "One day, baby. One day…we'll make it."

"Ma'am," a young, white man knocked at her window.

Once more, Stacia jumped out of her seat before spinning around and rolling down her window to see the man holding an object in his hand.

"Ma'am, we found this upstairs in one of the bedrooms."

Stacia viewed Dixon's picture only for a few seconds before she turned her face and spitefully muttered, "It's trash."

Without a word, the young man turned and went back into the fray of moving men that were steadily carrying loads of furniture and boxes from out of 833.

With apprehensive eyes, Stacia looked on at the home that she hadn't the nerve to step back in since the "final showdown" nights earlier. Everything from not only that evening, but from the very beginning lay upon her like a cold, wet blanket.

Somehow, she could sense Lucas lurking about inside amongst all the moving men. She could tell that he was staring at her from a window within, delighted with his handiwork. Stacia didn't care about his backstory, no more than he probably cared about hers. They were both rid of each other.

With her cellphone in her left hand, Stacia placed the frame of her son down onto the passenger seat before clicking on the phone and reading a days old text message.

Max: This is Max. Look, I don't know for sure what the hell happened, but I do know that no matter what, you're still my friend, and I'd like to remember you that way. Kohler is still pissed, so are a lot of the other folks in the warehouse. To say that none of them want to ever see you again is an understatement. While I can never get your job back here, I can't just leave my friend hanging on a limb either. I have a buddy who lives in Harrisburg, P.A. I told him about you. How hard of a worker you are, and how long you've been working here at Crumbley. He says that he could use another body there. I know, it's in another state, but it's all I can offer. If you decide not to take it I understand. I hate to see us break up like this, you've been like a sister to me, but maybe a change of scenery would do you good. No matter where you end up, I'm going to miss you. Drop me a line whenever you feel like it.

Stacia pressed the 'off' button on the phone before looking up at the blue sky and sighing. Behind her pulled up a red, Ford truck. Right off the bat, Stacia knew exactly who was behind the wheel.

She glanced at Sidney and Devon who were both fast asleep in the backseat of her car before she got out and walked towards the pickup and Lois who also was climbing out of her vehicle.

The two ladies met face to face between each other's vehicle and stopped. Stacia realized that her face was scarred and bruised up, but after all that had taken place, the woman hadn't a single care in the world. She and her children were no longer inside the house.

With her hands stuffed inside her jacket pockets, Lois looked at the house and said, "I haven't been here since I was a little girl."

Stacia, too, glanced at the home before turning to Lois and saying, "I can't believe it's already April. For a while, the days were running all together."

"How are your grandchildren?"

"Tired," Stacia sighed. "I can't quite recall what took place in these final days, but whatever it was, it sure drained them both enough to where all they do is sleep."

Lois scanned the neighborhood before turning back to Stacia. "When I last saw you, you were about half out of your head. For a moment, I thought something happened to you inside that house."

Stacia dropped her head to the ground before rising back up. "Like I said...I can't recall much."

"Or maybe you don't want to recall."

Stacia leaned her body back onto her car's trunk and blurted out, "Your father—"

"My father was a beast of a man." Lois brazenly interjected. "He hated everyone, including his own family. But, as much as he hated blacks, he couldn't help but to fuck one of them. Her name was Millie Wilson. Imagine that, a Grand Wizard of the Ku Klux Klan messing around with a black girl. Well, as stomach turning as it may sound, Millie fell in love with my dad, but old Lucas, being who he was affiliated with, couldn't have that. So he ended up strangling poor Millie and dumping her body in the junkyard. He then ran here to Aunt Judy's house to lay low until the heat died down. However, Millie had four brothers, four brothers with baseball bats. They tracked Lucas here and...finished him. Soon after, that's when Aunt Judy started to lose her mind. We had to send her to an asylum because of what apparently went on inside this place. I reckon it all was too much for her to bear."

Stacia's breath wanted to escape her at that moment. Every word that Lois spoke shook her to where goose bumps erupted all over her body.

"What I'm curious about is, why did you stay in there as long as you did?"

Stacia stood and stared at Lois for a moment or two before exhaling. "I was a bratty little girl, full of mouth and attitude. I got pregnant when I was fourteen, and that gave my mom license to kick me out of the house. My son and I crashed here and there for years before I finally got a job down at this warehouse. Well, soon, my son had two kids of his own. I raised them both from birth."

"Your life sounds just like mine." Lois said. "I bet your grandkids mother must be real proud of him."

"They have diffcrent moms." Stacia stated in a demure manner. "I did my dirt when I was young. I had a son to feed. I did a lot of things I'm not too proud of till this day. By the time I straightened my life up, I managed to save up a half a million dollars. That money was to be Sidney and Devon's college fund. They were to be the ones who broke this curse. I figured I could save some of that money by moving in here, but…that wasn't in the plans I guess. I reckon that's why I spoiled those two so bad; I wanted to give them everything I wasn't able to give their father."

Stacia watched a whimsical frown come upon Lois' face that instant, like she fully comprehended everything that she just explained to a tee.

"Where to now," Lois asked.

Stacia grinned for a second before saying, "A dear friend offered me a job in Pennsylvania."

"Is it a dream job?"

"Not exactly…but it's something." Stacia pressed her lips.

"Is your son coming with you guys?"

Holding onto her grin, Stacia turned away. "That child goes everywhere with us."

"Ma'am, we got all the toys." An older white man announced as he handed Stacia a box full of wrestling figures.

"Let me guess, that belongs to Devon." Lois smiled.

Giggling, Stacia said, "That boy would die without his wrestling."

With her box tucked securely underneath his right armpit, Stacia extended her hand. Lois responded in kind. The two ladies shook before Stacia carried both herself and her box back to her car.

In front of her was a U-Haul truck, behind her was Lois, who was steadily staring at the house that she and her grandchildren were leaving behind.

Before even putting the car in drive, Stacia did the unthinkable. Her head twisted ever so slightly to the right, in the direction of the house. She sat ever so still in her seat while sullenly taking in the home's grimy exterior.

Stacia could feel the man's hands hover all over her body again. The creepy voice that told her and her children to 'get out' lingered about in her brain like a blowing leaf in the wind.

Deep down, she knew that there was no such thing as ghosts, but that didn't stop Stacia Taylor from watching the house before her like it were about to grow feet and chase after her. There was something else inside 833, a force that went beyond anything she had ever seen in a movie, TV show or was told to by others over the course of her tumultuous life. It was evil inside the house, and that was exactly how Stacia wanted to remember her time there. There was no ambiguity of any kind, nor was there any sort of lost and confused soul dwelling about. Stacia wanted to live the remainder of her years knowing that she had felt wickedness at its core; she would wear her experience as a war trophy.

Without even giving 833 one last glimpse, Stacia cut on the ignition and pulled away in behind the truck.

CHAPTER 50

Later that night:

L ois drove her truck down a quiet Husk Drive before parking in front of 833. Beside her in the passenger seat were about seven empty White Castle burger boxes, as well as two empty packs of cigarettes.

The street was still that evening. Only two young white men carried on down the sidewalk on their way to God knows where. Lois sat and watched the house that for years she and the rest of her family didn't have the nerve to even speak of. It, along with her father's infidelity and death, was a forbidden subject both amongst the family McFord and in the town of Addington.

No matter what, she just couldn't stop staring at the dark house. It actually looked like it wanted to up and walk away. Out of all the homes on Husk, 833 looked like something someone vomited out. It had the most disgusting appearance to it.

"You know…me, mama and your sons actually breathed a sigh of relief when you were killed." Lois softly said under her breath, not wanting to speak too loud. "What did you do those people, old man? What did you do to them?"

Lois sat inside her truck for at least an hour, staring off at the house in a doom gaze before she got out and walked around to back of the vehicle. From within the truck's bed she took out a gasoline can and brown paper bag before she marched towards the house.

Lois stood boldly in front and looked up at the upstairs windows. "I'm not coming inside, daddy."

From there, Lois went around to the side of the house and doused the ground with the gasoline. From the front to the back and back to the front she poured before taking out her cigarette lighter and igniting the trail.

Almost instantly, the outside became engulfed in flames before the blaze reached the front porch and exploded inside. Before long, the house was alive with the crackle of gasoline entrenched fire.

Lois stood there in the front yard and watched the inferno carry on from the bottom floor all the way to the top. In the front window the woman could see a figure moving around inside the burning home. The figure stood at the window just staring back out at Lois.

Sidestepping the fact that she had just set fire to a house, Lois' eyes popped wide open the second she caught a glimpse of the person behind the window.

The woman couldn't bear to look on any further. Without allowing another second to pass, Lois took out a bag of salt from within the paper bag she had, ripped open its plastic zipper and hurled it at the house as hard as she could.

There Lois McFord stood before her late father…for the final time.

CHAPTER 51

Summertime in Addington:

The lightly bearded, mid-thirtyish white man pulled his silver and blue smart car in front of the two chair barbershop and sat for a spell.

Before even climbing out of his microscopic vehicle, Bruce examined his partially quiet surroundings with a dull curiosity. Like the little town in which he was visiting was about as impressive to him as a hot dog stand.

Clear on the other side of the street were three, old white men who were just sitting in three separate chairs in front of a carryout with a Confederate flag hanging lazily behind them. Walking across the street was two, young white men who didn't seem to be all too concerned with the fact that a semi was closing in on their heels.

Driving down the road, about to stop at a red light was a light green 1979 Pinto. Just the sight of the aged vehicle caused Bruce's head to spin at least three times in rapid succession, as did the various pickup trucks that tooled along down the main road like a parade was in session.

It was an old, rugged town, the kind that Bruce either saw on television or read about in books. He fondly recalled his grandmother's Norman Rockwell drawings that she hid up in the attic of her house when he was a child. Bruce smirked a bit at the rural images that seemed to come to life right before his eyes.

Taking out his keys, Bruce got out of his car and took off his navy blue blazer before whipping it around his shoulder and carrying on towards the barber shop.

The very second he entered through the door, two tiny bells above his head shot a delightful ring.

"Good morning!" A middle-aged, balding white man said out loud as he got up from out of one of the styling chairs.

"Good morning." Bruce said back with an amused grin covering his face.

Bruce gawked all around the small barber shop in a sort of subtle admiration. He honestly couldn't believe where he was at. It was like he had jumped into a movie.

Sweeping the floor was an older white lady with a blue bandana covering her hair, while an old white man sat in the other styling chair with his wrinkled hands folded in a meticulous manner.

"Is that your car out there, young man?" The old man asked.

Coming out of his trance, Bruce spoke up, "Uh…yes, sir, it is."

"Looks like one of those old Hot Wheels cars." The elderly gentleman glared outside the window.

"I don't think I've ever seen one of those cars before." The sweeping lady said while shooing away a brown and white cat into a room that was concealed by a curtain. "At least not in real life."

"God forbid you get into an accident, there won't be anything left of you!" The old man laughed out loud.

The three all laughed on for at least an entire minute before the barber said, "We don't see any of those cars around here."

"I'm not surprised." Bruce smugly muttered underneath his breath.

"What can we do you for?" The barber asked.

"I was just looking to get a facial trim."

"Well, you've come to the right place. Have a seat."

Bruce sat down in the chair and relaxed his body while the barber wrapped his white sheet around his neck and upper body.

"So, are you lost or just passing through here?" The barber asked.

"Uh, actually I teach at OSU."

"Oh really," the sweeper chimed in. "What brings you all the way up here?"

"I'm doing some research. I'm a parapsychology professor."

"A what," the old man squinted.

With a haughty smile from ear to ear, Bruce replied, "I study and teach on the paranormal natures."

Still, the three stood by with baffled expressions on their individual faces as to say that Bruce's explanation was clear out of their range.

"I study ghosts." Bruce clarified in a stale tenor.

"Oh, now I see!" The cleaning lady spoke up.

"You mean you go all over and hunt down ghosts like they do on The Sci-Fi Channel and such?" The old man's face lit up.

Blushing, Bruce said, "Well, not exactly, sir. I study and lecture on the phenomenon. My students are the ones who do all the investigating."

"Well, look at what we have here, a real star!" The barber gaily exclaimed with a pair of scissors in hand.

"Well, you see, I'm not a star—

"Hey, my name is Marge, and your barber today is Phil. That old coot seated right there beside you is George." Marge dropped her broom and excitedly scampered next to Bruce.

Holding on to his amused smirk, Bruce modestly explained, "Well…it's good to meet you all, but I'm not a star by any means. And if you ask me, The Sci-Fi Channel is full of it. I've never seen so many people encounter nothing one season after another."

"Well, just knowing that someone from a big university is here is good enough for us." George grinned.

"Are you here to investigate our town?" Marge salivated.

"Not exactly," Bruce stated. "You see, I'm actually here to follow up on another investigation that was abandoned by several of my students."

"Were your students doing their investigating here in town?" Phil asked as he clipped away at Bruce's beard.

Sniggering, Bruce responded, "Not really. Let's just say that they won't set foot in this town."

"I darn sure don't blame them." Marge folded her arms.

"They were heading up an investigation in Lane before dropping it altogether for unspecified reasons. I came here to follow up. Hopefully get some info from some folks around here."

"Well, we'll sure try to help the best we can." Phil said.

"I was wondering if I could get some information on the McFord family. Namely, a Lucas McFord," Bruce inhaled.

At once, Phil, Marge and George all stopped talking, giggling and doing everything else at that moment. Marge twisted her lips before picking up her broom and sweeping all over again while George slouched down in his seat and sighed heavily.

An uneasy queasiness settled inside of Bruce's stomach at that instant. "Did I open up a can of worms here?" He mumbled.

"Don't mind them; they're just not McFord fans." Phil waved his hand.

"Neither are you, Phillip." Marge shot back.

"The McFords aren't exactly as well liked around these parts as they themselves would want to believe." Phil articulated.

"How do you mean?"

"Hell, they own the entire town." George bitterly uttered. "It's been that way since the early nineteen hundreds; around 1902 or so."

"Really," Bruce's eyes stretched.

"Yep, and that means they own just about everybody in town as well. But not me," Marge strongly stated.

"You see this town?" Phil pointed outside. "About ten years ago we had a chance to get a Wal-Mart put here. But the McFord's stopped that altogether." 'We don't want any niggers or spics working there and moving into town!' Phil mocked. "Let me tell you, I don't go to the store to meet people, I go to shop and take my ass home."

"Yep, they ran Wal-Mart out, Sears and the pig farm." George said. "You can thank that youngest boy of theirs for getting rid of the pigs. Dumb ass got drunk one night and let all of the damn pigs loose."

"Just ten years ago this town's population was around two thousand; now, we're nearing the six hundred mark." Marge explained. "The McFord's run out business and people all because they wanna keep the town 'pure'. They're the ones who keep all that Ku Klux Clan bullshit going!"

"Yep, they just had a rally a few months back. I think someone said that a Mexican lady showed up and they ended up doing something with her."

"I don't think it was a Mexican girl, Phil." George scratched his head. "I thought I heard Clara say it was a Chinese girl."

"Hell, everyone in town is afraid of them." Marge fired back. "But what they don't realize is that folks are leaving because of them. One of their own just up and left a few months ago. She just hopped in her truck and never looked back again."

"So what about Lucas," Bruce asked.

"Old George would be able to tell you more about him than me and Marge. The only thing I know about Luke McFord was that he was the Grand Dragon, and that he was murdered down in Lane."

Out of nowhere, a clashing racket from behind the closed, brown curtain to the rear of the shop paused everyone's talking at once. Like it was being chased, the cat ran out of the room before hiding itself underneath a table near the front door.

"Damn, Marge, what is that cat of yours doing back there, now?" Phil frowned.

"Beats me, looks like he probably saw his own shadow and it scared him half to death."

Ignoring the clamor, Bruce turned back to George. "George, can you tell me more about Lucas?"

Sighing, George sat up in his chair and said, "Well, Old Lucas wasn't a very nice man, and that's putting it mildly. The unfortunate thing about it is that his sons all took up after him. They, like their daddy, are no good whatsoever."

Once more, the boisterous noise from behind the curtain shattered the attention that Bruce was trying to hold on to. He turned to see the bottom portion of the curtain gently sway back and forth.

"I bet that old possum got back there again." Marge methodically rubbed her chin.

"Not unless he's gained about five hundred pounds." Phil said in an alarmed tone. "Sounds like it's back there jumping off the cabinets or something."

"As I was saying, Luke McFord wasn't—

Right before George could even complete a simple sentence, from behind the brown curtain appeared Judy McFord, who was outfitted in an all-white, sequined dress and white shoes. She wore a petite smile upon her wrinkled face as she stumbled out of the back room and into the parlor as though she were learning how to walk all over again.

Phil, Marge and George all stood perfectly still. Marge's mouth hung wide open as her beloved broom shook in her hands. George sat motionless in his chair as his eyes bugged out of their sockets while Phil, with scissors in hand, right next to Bruce's face, nonetheless, couldn't budge a single inch from the floor upon which he was planted.

Bruce sat up and watched as Judy hobbled closer and closer to him before she stopped and stood right in front of the man.

Bruce could smell what resembled rotting eggs stem from off the woman's body, but he was entirely too enthralled with the strange lady who just suddenly appeared out of nowhere to even take notice of her foul aroma.

"I can tell you all you need to know about Lucas McFord, Bruce." Judy politely uttered in a gurgling grunt.

Bruce gazed around at the others who looked as if they were paused in mid-frame. He should have been concerned about their sudden shock, but the man couldn't seem to take his drooling eyes off of Judy.

Coughing and grinning, Bruce said, "Well, uh…I'd surely appreciate as much information as you can give, Mrs.?"

Judy just stood before the man and politely smiled.

CHAPTER 52

Seven years later:

Her hair was a little greyer. Face, a little more wrinkled. Her steps were a bit less youthful, yet and still, Lois McFord kept not a frown, but a kindness on her aging face as she was being led, un-cuffed, from one end of the prison to the other.

Clothed in an orange jumpsuit, the lady walked down a cell-ladened corridor that housed female prisoners of varying races and sizes. Some said the usual "hello", or "hey girl", while others simply looked on or ignored her.

The instant Lois reached her lonely cell she right away saw a letter seated neatly on her bed. Looking back at the black, female guard, Lois cracked a smile, "When did this get here?"

Shrugging her shoulders, the guard replied, "Beats me, girl, I just started my shift."

Lois watched as the guard carried on down the hallway before she ripped open the envelope to find a note inside. The second she read the name at the top left hand corner of the envelope, Lois immediately found herself somewhat surprised, but not to the point where she felt lightheaded and wanted to faint.

The words on the letter were jotted so eloquently that she wondered if the writer was who they claimed to be. But rather than investigate any further, Lois put her right hand over her mouth to keep herself from crying before sitting down on her bed and reading to herself.

Hey, lady, this is Stacia. You're a real hard person to find these days. But I guess I can understand, given the circumstances. Hope all is well with you. So much has taken place since we last saw each other. It's been like a regular roller coaster ride.

So let me start this way. The kids are just fine. My granddaughter is 16. She's gotten into politics for some reason or another. She's captain of her debate team, and Penn State is already offering her a full ride political science scholarship. She says that she wants to run for the Pennsylvania Senate, and then off to Washington D.C. Now, if I can only keep the boys away from her then she'll do okay.

My grandson is 14, and yes, the boy still loves his wrestling. He loves it so much that he competes on his eighth grade wrestling team. Last semester he came in second in the All-State Trials. The child swears up and down that he's going straight to that ridiculous WWE when he graduates from high school. Over my dead body.

Then there's me. Well, as you can imagine, moving to Harrisburg wasn't exactly my dream idea, nor was working at another warehouse. For the first year I sank into a deep depression over the move, the job and 833. But then something happened. One day while I was working on the assembly line, the owner of the company needed someone to work the computers up front. Don't ask me why I stepped forward, but I did. This man was so impressed with my computer skills that he made me his secretary. That position soon changed into Vice President of Talent Relations. In other words, for the past six years, I've been working up in the front office doing all of the hiring and firing. I even get to wear all of those fancy clothes that were collecting dust in my closet all those years.

About three years ago I got a call from The Travel Channel. They wanted to do a story on our experience in that house. I politely declined. And I use the word politely loosely.

When I asked the kids what they remembered about the place, they look at me like I've lost my mind. I think they recall certain things here and there, but for the most part, it's a blur, and that's a wonderful thing I guess.

As for me, it's just one of those things where you hardly believe it actually happened.

When I heard what you did to the house I wasn't all that surprised. I figured that just like myself, you, too, needed a conclusion. I'm just sorry that your actions got you put where you are now.

I still think about the house from time to time. I still get the occasional nightmare. After all these years it's still hard for me to admit all that took place inside. I know it wasn't all in my head, but the fear still grips me to where I have a difficult time believing it all. I still have a hard time trying to remember how I got to Addington. For the most part, most of what I can recall is yelling at a teacher or principal, being nasty to a few friends and waking up in a house full of Klan members.

I feel that if I sit down and try to remember too much then I will definitely lose my damn mind forever, so I just let it be and enjoy the blessings that God gave us.

I'm not bitter anymore, as a matter of fact, I can't recall being so happy in my life. I know I'm bragging like a fool, but I can't help it.

No, not everything is 100% perfect, but at least I can at last move forward. I used to hate my life, but now, now I understand. Sometimes we have to get busted and *bloodied up in our lives in order to see the light at the end of the tunnel. And we pray that we never make the same mistakes all over again. That's life. It sucks, but we move on.*

I hope I can see you again someday. I have a feeling you and I have a lot of war stories to trade between us. Take care, Lois.

Love,
Stacia Taylor.

Lois wiped a few trickling tears away from her face before folding the letter up and sitting it to the side. The rowdy woman outside her cell that was being carted away by two female guards didn't seem to put a damper on the woman's blissful mood as she reached over to a nearby desk and took a notepad and pen.

Hey, right back at you.

It's ironic that you write to me at this time, just two days before my release date, but it's the fact that you wrote at all that makes me smile.

Well, where can I begin? First off, dear old Uncle Harry finally croaked at the age of 103. My son is back in prison again, this time for prostituting his own girlfriend. And all four of my brothers are on the run from the FBI for bombing a mosque and killing two Muslims inside. So, needless to say, not much has ever really changed with my family.

Who knew that burning down a house would finally get me out of Addington once and for all? And when I say once and for all, I mean it. I'm never going back to that that dead man's town again.

Since I've been in here I've been meeting everyday with some ladies who run a bible study group. They dropped my name to some folks at a church about twenty miles away from this prison. Once I get out, they're going to not only provide me with a job, but also a place to live. So I guess just like you, I'm getting a brand new start as well.

Now, when it comes to that house, I think deep down I have somewhat of a clue as to what went down there, but much like you, it's a subject that some folks are just too skittish to discuss out loud. I can see now why Aunt Judy lost her mind in there.

I'm writing this for the very first time to someone who will definitely understand. The night I set fire to the house, I saw my daddy inside. I was so stunned that all I could do was watch until the cops came to pick me up.

That night, as I was being taken downtown, I prayed for my father for the very first time in my life. Perhaps that's what he needed all along, someone to actually pray his hateful soul into peace.

I can't even begin to imagine what you three went through inside that place, but I can tell that it somehow transformed you all. I believe that's why you and I are kindred spirits. We both have been haunted all of our lives in some form or another, and now, that light at the end of the tunnel only seems to be getting brighter.

Listen to me, I sound like a Lifetime Movie. Anyways, it really hasn't been all that bad in here these past few years. At least I didn't have to worry about paying bills or buying groceries.

I like to think that meeting you that day in Addington was a God send of sorts. You changed my life for the better, Stacia. I guess I was always looking for a way out, and there you were.

But, the more I think about it, the more I allow my mind to wander on the subject, I just can't help but to wonder, just how many haunted houses are in this state.

One of the inmates here gave me a quote four years ago right before she herself died. For the life of me I can't get it out of my head.

For deaths sake, this I utter,

there be never an end, never a finality, never a peace.

I know it sounds depressing, but I think it explains a few things here and there. It certainly puts my life into perspective. I guess all we can do is hope and pray we never end up in the same situation as old Lucas…or any other disembodied soul that's lingering around out there.

Love, Lois McFord.

Printed in the United States
By Bookmasters